D0443947

HOW
TO
BE
LUMINOUS

Also by Harriet Reuter Hapgood

The Square Root of Summer

HOW TO BE LUMINOUS

Harriet Reuter Hapgood

ROARING BROOK PRESS · NEW YORK

Library of Congress Control Number: 2018955863

ISBN: 978-1-62672-375-7

Our books may be purchased in bulk for promotional, educational, or business use. Please contact your local bookseller or the Macmillan Corporate and Premium Sales Department at (800) 221-7945 ext. 5442 or by email at MacmillanSpecialMarkets@macmillan.com.

First edition, 2019
Book design by Elizabeth H. Clark
Printed in the United States of America

1 3 5 7 9 10 8 6 4 2

There's no such thing as true black.

This is one of the very first art lessons. Squeezing black ready-made from a tube makes a painting look artificial, so instead, you mix the three primary hues: red, yellow, and blue. Because even the darkest shadow or deepest sorrow has a glimmer of color at its heart.

But I know there's another kind of black.

I see it when I close my eyes, and become a paint palette. This black is a bottomless ocean of dark. I dip my fingers in it, smear it across a canvas. Use a paintbrush and flick my finger over the bristles, splattering tiny constellations onto the paper. Each small, lonely speck the color of sadness.

PART ONE

The Dictionary of Color

CHAPTER 1
Life in Monochrome

The last color vanishes with an audible pop, as if it's been sucked through a straw.

And now everything I see is in black and white. Including this pillow fort. At seventeen, I'm too old to be hiding in one, but I can't bring myself to move. I'm a frozen tableau of *WTF?*, staring out through the duvet at my colorless bedroom.

In front of me, my window frames our back garden like an old photograph. It's the last day of August, and white sunshine is cascading over the monochrome flower beds. Roses and clematis and honeysuckle, all rewritten in gray.

There are more than ten million colors in the world, and I can no longer see a single one.

Literally.

The colors began fading ten weeks ago, the day after my mother disappeared.

The last time I saw her was the final day of school before the summer holidays. I was eating breakfast; she was leaving for work. Wearing her usual glaze-spattered smock, cigarette clamped in fuchsia-lipsticked mouth, she waved me madly goodbye. It reminded me of a tulip in a tornado.

After school, I went to her ceramics studio, expecting to find her absorbed in her latest piece. Instead, she had left the kind of note that inspires the police to search the rocks beneath Beachy Head—a cliff with incredible views of the sea, and England's most notorious suicide spot.

But as no body was found—and her long, rambling letter wasn't enough proof—she's not considered dead. She's missing. Vanished into thin air.

Ever since then, the world without her has looked a little chalkier. Like a drop of bleach has been added to the sky. When this first started, it made total sense to me: My disco ball of a mother was gone, of course I was seeing things a little askew.

But then the colors kept fading. With each minute, hour, and day that she didn't come bursting back through the front door . . . or send one of her habitually exuberant ALL-CAPITALS texts . . . or kick off her shoes and dance through the garden . . . the saturation drained from my sight. Until all that was left was the palest gossamer pastels. A last whisper of hope.

And now today. All morning, even these barely there colors

have been disappearing. It's the last day of summer; my baby sister's fifteenth birthday. By not coming home for Emmy-Kate, Mum is really, truly gone.

As I peep from my duvet through the window, the birthday girl herself comes cartwheeling across the lawn. Emmy-Kate is in black and white too. But I bet the dress she's wearing is pink. (The underwear she's flashing as she turns head over heels is *definitely* days-of-the-week.)

My sister concludes her acrobatics and springs upright, her gaze landing on my open window. She narrows her eyes, squinting up.

I turtle beneath the duvet, disturbing the world's stupidest house rabbit: Salvador Dalí.

"Shhh," I warn, putting a finger to my lips. Too late. His ears fly backward, listening as the back door slams, then two sets of footsteps come clattering up the stairs to my attic bedroom. Emmy-Kate's pony-princess prance, followed by Niko's steady clomp-clomp-clomp. No pillow fort in the world is safe from my sisters.

Emmy-Kate arrives first, spinning in her new froufrou frock.

"Minnie! Isn't this dress a Degas? It's *Dancers in Pink*," she says in her bubblegum voice.

With a famous artist mother, we're all walking art encyclopedias—Emmy-Kate, though, actually thinks and talks in paintings, using artwork as an indication of mood. *Dancers in Pink* is an impressionist piece, a blur of lighter-than-air ballet dancers. It might seem strange, given the circumstances, that she chooses a happy painting. But she's turning fifteen: too young to be told about a letter, a possible suicide, a cliff. As far as Emmy-Kate knows, Mum is merely AWOL, and innocent optimism is the order of the day.

I emerge from the duvet and croak, "Happy birthday."

Emmy-Kate tilts her head, setting off a cascade of what should be strawberry-blond hair. It's gray. Gray eyes. Shiny gray pout. My stomach lurches. Black-and-white vision would be a problem for anyone, but for an artist—even me, a total wannabe—it's an effing catastrophe. Before I can throw up from all this weird, Niko comes stomping into the room.

She snorts at the mess. Then at me, still in my duvet nest. Despite her glam-grunge appearance—think dungarees and flip-flops worn with pinup girl hairdos and perfect eyeliner— the oldest Sloe sister acts more like ninety than nineteen.

"Minnie—you're not still in bed?" she signs, rhetorically. Niko is Deaf, and the movement of her hands as she signs is exacerbated by the bandages on her fingertips. She's a bona fide art student, specializing in cutouts: Think paper snowflakes, only ten times as complicated. Injury is an occupational hazard.

I examine my pajamas, my location on the mattress, and sign back, "No, I'm on the moon."

"Humor. You must be feeling okay." Niko rolls her eyes. "Good. You can help me make the pancakes."

Note: *the* pancakes. It's our birthday ritual: a breakfast feast of pancakes and Nutella. Usually made by Mum—from a box.

8

This is the house that convenience foods built. But she has the fairy-dust ability to turn even the ordinary, even ready-mixed pancakes, into magic.

The three of us freeze as we consider this: the first tradition without her.

A newly subdued Emmy-Kate trudges to the door. "Minnie?" she prompts, with a single fingerspelled *M*. When it's only the three of us, we don't speak: we sign.

I clamber from my fort, as does Salvador Dalí. Niko leads us in a parade down the stairs: sister after sister after rabbit after sister. As we leave the sanctity of my bedroom, I glance out of the landing window. This view stretches across south London's skyline.

Despite distant tower blocks and terraced streets, I've never considered this city to be gray. It has too many trees and parks, lampposts and graffiti and fried-chicken shops; the concrete has too many variations. Smoky hues and soot and shadows and bricks and sidewalks.

But now it looks flat. As if it wasn't enough for my mother to walk out of the world. She had to take all the colors with her too.

Pale Pink
(An Ongoing List of Every Color I Have Lost)

Fairy roses scattering petals across the grass.
Strawberry slices atop heart-shaped pancakes. When
I was little, my unpainted nail beds beneath
Mum's shiny red ones as she held my hands,
teaching me how to sign to Niko. And blood, if it's
diluted with enough water. Like if you're in the
bath when you die, or a river, or the sea.

CHAPTER 2
The Color of Limestone

In early September, the morning before school starts, I wake predawn to find my heart attempting a jailbreak through my ribs. I sneak from the house, racing myself down leaf-lined streets, trying to outrun the black and white. Can't. Her disappearance follows me, an unshakable shadow. Double-decker buses blast by in pale gray instead of red, near-invisible against the asphalt.

Since I'm not exactly sporty, the fear and I run out of steam at the same time. I slow down and look around. Somehow I've ended up on the far side of Meadow Park. A huge, hilly wilderness that borders my neighborhood, Poets Corner, it contains everything from an outdoor pool to community greenhouses and a wildflower meadow. It's like a piece of countryside got spliced into the city by mistake. In summer, it throngs with people, but since it's early, only birds and joggers and grieving girls are awake. I step through the gates for the first time since the disappearance.

There's a library hush as I climb to the top of the hill, my destination the walled garden. Home to my mother's first-ever art installation: the *Rainbow Series I*. The work that made her famous—superstarrily so, like Rembrandt or Frida Kahlo.

I hold my breath as I walk inside, hoping for a siren, strobe lights, Mum's sudden reappearance in full color. Nothing happens. The *Rainbow Series I* is minus one rainbow—but it still takes my breath away.

Huge clay spheres as big as racehorses rest on transparent Plexiglas stands. They appear to float among the garden's flamboyant rosebushes. Tinier rounds, the size of marbles or peaches or beach balls, are embedded in the paths and suspended from pagodas. All are glazed in shiny nail polish colors—Mum's signature style. Ordinarily, they make the flowers look muted. Ordinarily, it's like God himself leaned down from heaven and began blowing bubbles.

If anything could restore my vision to a full spectrum, it would be this.

I take another step toward the spheres, then stop, noticing the visitors' plaque. This tells tourists and art pilgrims alike that Rachael Sloe won the UK's biggest art award, the Turner Prize, with this—her debut.

Underneath the sign, an impromptu memorial has sprung up. A gargantuan pile of cellophane-wrapped flowers, sympathy cards, half-burnt candles, and cutesy teddy bears. It's tatty from weeks of summer rain; the flowers at the bottom of the heap rotten and mushy. The whole thing is gross. Makes me think of morgues, reminds me that my mum's disappearance is headline news.

I give the memorial a wide berth, shuddering as I catch a whiff of the flowers. My skin prickles. I'm being watched . . . Actually, I wouldn't put it past my exhibitionist mother to teleport into existence right here in the middle of this garden. I spin round, certain she's here—

Emmy-Kate is watching me, peeking out from behind the biggest bubble like a mischievous Glinda the Good Witch of the North. Automatically, I stiffen. All I can think about is this enormous secret I'm keeping from her. Suicide. An ugly word, and one I worry will spill from my lips whenever we talk. It's been almost three months since we've had a real conversation.

Guilt manifests as annoyance, and I snap, "Stalk much?"

Emmy-Kate lifts her chin, defiant, and struts over to me. She's fresh from her Sunday morning swim; a damp towel drapes over her shoulder, and her long hair falls in wet curtains, dripping between our feet.

"Hardly," she says, wringing out a rope of hair. "I saw you from the pool and followed you here."

I shake my head, try to be nice. "Em, that's the dictionary definition of stalking."

Emmy-Kate smiles a tiny bit at this, as a breeze sweeps through the empty garden. She shivers, wrapping her arms around herself, eyes landing on the memorial. For a second, her face empties, like a squeezed-out tube of paint. I wonder how much she actually suspects about Mum being missing, but all she says, in a syrup-soaked voice, is: "Wow, that's grim. Seriously, *Whistler's Mother* depressing. Let's get out of here."

We walk side by side. Emmy-Kate's hands flit as she starts painting the air—she's a girl who treats the sky as her own personal canvas—and compensating for my silence with a lilting monologue on boys, breakfast, school tomorrow . . .

She's about to start sophomore year; I'm about to graduate. There's two years between us, and another two between me and Niko. Next year, I'll leave Emmy-Kate behind and join Niko at the Silver College of Art and Design. SCAD. The local art-school mecca and Mum's alma mater.

From this vantage point on the hill, the villagey neighborhoods of south London are laid out like a patchwork below. The streets of Poets Corner, the wide avenue of Full Moon Lane cutting through them like Broadway in New York City or the Champs-Élysées in Paris, and as vast. And a few miles in the distance sit the squat toads of SCAD's brutalist modern buildings.

Even though SCAD is close to my mother's studio, I've never actually set foot on the campus. Visiting before I'm actually accepted seems like I would jinx it. But years ago I did look up the website, copying the ethos onto a piece of paper that I pinned to my wall:

We believe art and design can change minds and move worlds. Immersive, imaginative, and hands-on—because theory without practice is like learning to swim without water. Let's get messy.

Back then, I totally bought into this concept. Now, I think: It doesn't get messier than a missing mother.

The thought guts me. It's instant wipeout. Mum abandons me on a daily basis. A hollow flies from the hole in my chest, expanding to empty the park and everything in it, me a tiny speck in the middle of all this nothing.

Because even if she comes back, there will never be a moment where she didn't leave me.

I stumble to a halt at the bottom of the hill, near the pool where my fearless little sister swims even in winter. Emmy-Kate takes a couple of steps without me, still babbling, before seeing I've stopped. She turns around, reading the hurt on my face.

Instantly, her eyes mimic mine. What Sloe sisters have in common—despite three different fathers, temperaments, and shades of red hair—is tissue paper–white skin, and eyes that play our thoughts like cinema screens.

"What?" she asks, worry crisping the edges of her voice.

I force myself to swallow away the emotional hurricane, since beyond Emmy-Kate, bumbling along in a tracksuit, is the Professor.

Aka Professor Rajesh Gupta. Bachelor, next-door neighbor, and, by some bizarre twist of fate, Mum's best friend. Think oil and water, chalk and cheese. My madcap mother and this buttoned-up theology professor, who looks and acts as though he was blown from the dust on a leather-bound book, have been thick as thieves my entire life. He was the first to show up at our door after the disappearance, bearing a casserole dish full of biryani. Unfortunately, his cooking is desert-dry, nothing like the fragrant, jeweled curries you can get in east London.

"Run away," whispers Emmy-Kate, only half joking.

"Shhhh," I tell her as he spots us and changes course, ambling over.

"Ah! Girls," he says, his forehead crinkling in sympathy. "Good, er, hmm." He jogs on the spot, coughs into his fist, then bends over and straightens up again. This is the entire sentence. The Professor brings his own personal tumbleweed to every conversation.

After he clears his throat for the ten thousandth time, Emmy-Kate bursts and says, "Okay, we were going home." She grabs my elbow, starts dragging me away. "Bye!"

"Good, good." The Professor checks his watch, bending and stretching again. "Well. Perhaps I'll accompany you, see how your, er—sister is. Lead, ahem, the way."

He jogs on the spot, leaving Emmy-Kate and me no choice but to walk on. When I glance back, I can't see the walled garden, or the *Rainbow Series I*, or the sky. I can't see anything.

Sky Blue
(An Ongoing List of Every Color I Have Lost)

*Sky, obviously. But not the stormy June
afternoon my mother chose not to come home.
The dress she's wearing in her SCAD graduation
photo. Forget-me-nots. Her pastel eyes.*

CHAPTER 3
Everything's White

As soon as the Professor follows Emmy-Kate through the front door, I duck away and go through the side gate, into the back garden. I can breathe more easily out here, among the overflowing foxgloves and roses. Our miniature Midsummer Night's Dream garden is tucked away like a secret between the house and the railway. And I'm a flower freak.

Something Mum and I have in common. The blooms flourish through her sheer force of will. She shapes all her surroundings to fit her particular aesthetic, from our chartreuse front door to this overgrown bouquet—and three redheaded daughters, despite being a natural blonde.

I close my eyes, bury my face in a humongous rose. Inhaling the myrrh scent almost makes up for not being able to see the color. I can imagine it, though. Apricot. A vivid pink-gold shade that's inherently Mum and brings her back to the garden like a hologram—striding past me with that shocking-pink-lipsticked smile, mermaid hair knotted atop her head, bone-thin beneath her artist's smock. She's holding a cigarette in one hand and a mug of coffee in the other: charisma fuel. Mum captivated everyone: us, the Professor, journalists, SCAD students.

She worked there for a while, after Emmy-Kate was born. She'd made the *Rainbow Series I* while still a student, and pregnant with Niko, and stepped straight into the professional art world after graduation. But then in quick succession I arrived, then Emmy-Kate, and she ended up having to return to SCAD as a lecturer. What her biographies call "the wilderness years" and we call "our lives."

Then, when I was twelve, she resigned from SCAD and made her headline-grabbing return to the pottery wheel, reinvigorated. Bigger, better, bolder, more famous.

That's the mother who's zooming around my imagination. Not Mum but her artist self, the one who makes Emmy-Kate look like a wallflower, sucks every inch of oxygen from a room.

It's so good to see her. I breathe in the rose, desperately, hoping to enhance this vision. Rachael Sloe, Artist, turns to me and says . . .

. . . and says . . .

I can't remember her voice.

The memory falters, flickers, fades.

My eyes fly open. The garden is desolately gray, and it's all too much: her absence. The uncertainty. The monochrome. And how have I already forgotten her voice? It's only been one summer.

I go slumping into the kitchen, where I find the Professor perched politely in his usual spot at the table, opposite Emmy-Kate. Silence and the Sunday newspapers are spread between them. Seeing me, Em makes a *grrr* of annoyance and zips from the room, hurling her damp towel onto the floor by the washing machine as she leaves. The Professor stands up—I know from experience he won't sit down again until I do. He's a nightmare at neighborhood parties.

"Hi," I mumble, attempting to skirt around him. He dithers, blocking my path.

"Well, now, er—Minnie," he harrumphs—but kindly.

Mum appears clearly again, now at the table, wheezing with hysteria.

What's wrong with me? I haven't so much as dreamed about her in eleven weeks, and now I'm visualizing her twice in one day. In full color, too. But perhaps the Professor sees her as well, since his face is broadcasting distress signals. Sloe-sister theory: He's madly in unrequited love with Mum. And has been for the past twenty years.

"How are you?" he asks, formal as a tuxedo.

"Fine." I tuck my thumbs into my cardigan sleeves, squirming. Ordinarily I don't mind the Professor, despite his aura of tweediness—he's a familiar mainstay, like a comfortable old sofa—but since I've become more or less tongue-tied, every conversation between us is stilted.

"Er, ah, er—Minnie," he huffs. "As I was explaining to er—Emmy-Kate, I have some good news. The university has granted me a sabbatical this year. I plan to write another book." He clasps his hands, like a bell ringer. "Which leaves me very much at your disposal for the, er. Until, um. For the *forthcoming*," he finishes.

Translation: The Professor is going to be working from home, right next door, for a whole year. Which means he'll be "popping in" practically every day. All summer long he's been checking up on us, bringing with him hours of awkward silences and inedible pakoras. Even though the social workers grudgingly approved Niko as our guardian—they side-eyed her Greenpeace T-shirts and general dungareed demeanor—the Professor has appointed himself our responsible adult. What with the lack of godparents, distant relatives, or even deadbeat dads.

All we know of our absent fathers is that there are three. Every time we ask for more details, Mum changes the story: They're cowboys, astronauts, rock stars, explorers, renegades; lifelong love affairs or holiday romances or one-night stands. She spins tales like clay on the wheel.

She keeps secrets.

Me too. There's one in her studio.

If I unlocked the door, I could trace my hands over her last movements: the swivel stool adjusted to her height, her finger marks fossilized in the bags of clay, a coffee cup with a lipstick tattoo on the rim. And four kilns, squatting in the corner like a family of Daleks. The largest is locked, on a cooling cycle from a glaze firing. I'm the only one who knows this: that inside the kiln is Rachael Sloe's last-ever piece of art.

The doorbell pulls me from my thoughts, the chime accompanied by flashing lights for Niko's benefit. When I escape the Professor and throw open the front door, Ash is standing on the doorstep, a guitar strapped to his back. With his skinny jeans, calligraphy swoop of dark hair, and mouth permanently curled into a half smile, he looks for all the world like Indian Elvis.

"Hey, Miniature," he says, opening his arms.

Surprise roots me to the spot, as though he's a total stranger and not my boyfriend of almost a year. (Not to mention, the Professor's nephew.) Ash goes to university in London but spends the summer holidays at home in Manchester, aka a million miles away. We've spoken on the phone, but this is the first time we've seen each other in person since . . . since everything.

"Hi," I say, focusing on the bull's-eye dimple at the center of his chin, strangely shy. "You're back."

"Came straight over," he says, his northern accent warm and worried. When I look up, he offers me a dialed-down version of his usual phosphorescent smile. My lip wobbles. Seeing my boyfriend in black and white—it's too weird.

"Ah, Min," he says, misreading my face. "It's all going to be okay."

He probably believes it. Ash is an optimist. He's happy-go-lucky and silver linings, a boy for whom toast always lands butter side up. My sisters and I all met him at the same time, one rain-drenched autumn afternoon two years ago.

We were dodging the weather at the National Gallery, sprawled with our sketchbooks in front of the blue-saturated *Bathers* by Cézanne, as if we were having the same picnic as the people in the painting. Emmy-Kate was making an abstract mess with oil pastels, Niko drew neatly with graphite pencils, and I was using every shade of blue felt-tip—cobalt, navy, azure, sapphire—to try out a new pointillism technique.

We'd been there an hour when a drop of water splashed on my sketch pad. Emmy-Kate nudged Niko, who poked my arm with her sharp pencil, and I sent a scribble of teal across the damp page. I looked to my right: This impossibly cute boy in a ridiculous puffer coat was shaking off the rain and sitting on the floor next to us. Headphones clamped over a flop of black hair, huge sneakers tapping to the invisible beat, he tilted his head at the painting.

Oh, effing wow, I thought, then looked back at my sisters.

"Holy Michelangelo!" Emmy-Kate signed. My tomato-cheeked sister had turned thirteen two weeks before and promptly been blessed with boobs and an unprecedented interest in boys.

"I know," I replied silently, noticing with alarm that Niko was blushing too. We were a triptych of pink.

Here was something we'd never encountered before, in all our years of inseparable hive mind and slavish devotion to the same favorite artists: a boy we all liked.

I peeped back at the boy to see if he was drawing *Bathers* too. He wasn't. He was looking at me. Well, at my sketch pad. Although sometimes, especially lately, that felt like it might amount to the same thing.

"Shit," he said as he pushed his headphones down and pointed to the rain-besplashed page. "That was me, wasn't it? Soaking your drawing? Sorry."

"Oh," I said, out loud. The three of us had been signing without speaking all morning—the grammar of British Sign Language was totally different to spoken English, and it was easier that way—and the word emerged from my unused mouth with a rasp. I rubbed at the splotches with my thumb, smudging the blues, wishing I could splash them across my beetroot face to cool it down. Emmy-Kate simultaneously interpreted for Niko as I said, "Yeah. But it's okay—I mean, now it's a watercolor."

I wasn't trying to be funny, but the boy laughed, a looping giggle that landed in iridescent pieces all over me. He kept grinning, amused, and I found myself smiling right back at him.

"Let me guess," he said, pointing to each of us in turn. "Minnie. Niko. Emmy-Kate."

This sunbeam boy turned out not to be psychic but,

somewhat unbelievably, the Professor's nephew. He was new to the city for his first year of university and Mum had sent him to find us, along with lurid and lyrical descriptions of who was whom. Another instance of her transforming the ordinary into the amazing: If the Professor himself had introduced us to Ash, perhaps we wouldn't have all fallen in love with him the way we did.

I'm so deep in this rainy-day memory of him it seems almost impossible that I'm actually standing on the porch, staring up at real-life Ash.

"C'mere, you," he says, pulling me into his arms. I sink against his soft T-shirt, his chest a place as familiar to me as the Tube map. My lungs fill with his warm, lemony scent, calming the unease I've been feeling all morning.

"Missed you, Miniature," he murmurs into my giant ginger cloud of hair.

Guilt tugs at me: Though I'm glad he's here now, for all the texts we exchanged this summer, I wouldn't exactly characterize myself as missing him. I don't get a chance to examine this thought, because—

"Ash!" We spring apart as Emmy-Kate comes bouncing down the stairs, barreling toward us.

She's ditched her swimming clothes for tiny shorts and a cutoff T-shirt; in places, the inches of bare skin are zebra-striped with paint. Em's always finger painted, but this looks like she's been rolling around the canvas naked. I wouldn't put it past her. She's the sister who inherited Mum's joie de vivre. For years, she's been vacillating between personalities—swimming nerd versus passionate painter—finally metamorphosing days after the disappearance into this junior femme fatale.

She pushes me aside and goes running into Ash's arms.

"Oof." He staggers, unbalanced by his guitar, and hugs her hello. Then they launch into their standard playground handclap/dance/greeting. For all his dreamy Disney-prince eyes, Ash is a goofball, and momentarily he transforms Emmy-Kate back into my little sister. Laughing, he takes in her paint-covered appearance and says, "Check you out, Junior Picasso. Happy belated birthday."

"Since you're here, we can have pancakes again," Emmy-Kate convinces herself, skipping into the kitchen.

I move to follow her, but Ash puts his hand on my arm, tugging me back. "How are you all doing, Min, really?" he asks, his voice low. "Em seems good. But are you all right?"

I love his Manchester twang, the way he slurs *all right* into one word: *aight*. But it's not a question I can answer. Am I all right? Okay, answers on a postcard, please . . .

I can't see color
and it makes me want to scream
or set fire to something
become a statue
delete my dreams
smash up whole planets with my fists
. . . all of the above?

I scribble out all of these ludicrous options and go for: "School starts tomorrow."

Ash tugs on his earlobe. "Yeah. One more year, then SCAD."

I make a face like broken glass, and he raises his eyebrows, surprised.

"Never mind," I say, and lead him into the kitchen, where the Professor has made himself at home by pouring tea. Ash tackles him with a hug, saying, "Uncle Raj, you're in the wrong house, mate!" Then he ruffles Salvador Dalí's fur and falls into a chair with his guitar, glancing at me for permission. When I nod, he bends over the instrument, spine curved. Ash has less than zero interest in art; he's all about the music.

Niko marches briskly in and taps Emmy-Kate on the arm, signing an order: "Put a cardigan on." As ever, she's dressed as a hippie-feminist-vegetarian: headscarf, dungarees, clogs, slogan T-shirt with this week's cause on it. Whales, trees, tigers—my sister's heart bleeds for everything.

The whole room sucks in a breath, watching her take charge. She huffs at Emmy-Kate's wet towel on the floor and removes the pancake mix from her hand; sweeps the newspapers from the table; hacks a loaf of bread into slices and shoves them into the toaster with a clang. Niko's always been the sensible Sloe sister, but lately she's gone into efficiency overdrive.

After all this, she greets the Professor, far more enthusiastically than I would. He signs-says his reply in the same ponderous fashion he speaks. Niko nods semi-patiently, then turns to Ash, who's still bent over his guitar. For a moment, she watches him strum, her own hands mimicking his as he shapes the chords. He looks up and smiles at her, saying a carefully clear *hello*, and slowing his playing. She smiles back. For a moment, it's as if the mechanics of the music are sign language.

When she spots me spying on them, she snaps out of it and asks me without speaking, "Is Ash staying for breakfast?"

I shrug, switching into silent Sloe-sister signing mode. "Probably, why?"

"Because then we'll have to invite the Professor too . . ." She doesn't look unpleased at this idea, but peers around the kitchen. "He didn't bring food, did he?"

We're signing too quickly for the Professor to follow. I confirm we're safe and Niko clatters down cereal, bowls, jam, and a rack of charred toast, then knocks on the table for our attention. When she has it, everyone obeys her command to sit. Except Ash, who hovers by our mother's empty chair.

"Aren't we waiting for Rachae—ahh." He breaks off, eyes widening in mortification. Emmy-Kate is interpreting for Niko and her hands freeze in mid-air. "Sorry," Ash mutters, sliding into Mum's seat. Under his breath: "Shit."

I crunch Coco Pops, my heart stuttering. I've had eleven weeks to absorb Mum's absence, fill the gap, get accustomed. But with Ash here, acting as if the hole she left is brand-new, it reopens the wound. Conversation falters.

After breakfast, Ash and I retreat to the back garden,

flopping down on the grass. It's a gorgeous morning: toffee-scented sunshine, September spreading itself out like a quilt.

I yank up a daisy, start tearing out its petals one by one. This could be the exact same plant with which Mum taught me the trick when I was little. Picking off the petals with her slim, quick fingers and reciting, "Loves me, loves me not."

I remember her handing me a daisy to try it, and laughing when my chubby toddler fists tore it in two. "Okay, not daisies," she said. She dug around on the lawn and handed me a spherical cloud on a stem. A dandelion puff. "Try this. Close your eyes and make a wish. Then take in a big breath and blow all the seeds off."

Before she became an artist again, the garden was her element. Somewhere in this jungle there are raspberry canes from a jam-making era, the hole where we made a hippo mud bath for baby Emmy-Kate, pint-glass slug traps dug into the soil. The last daisy petal is *not*, and I drop the bent stem by my side, wishing myself into the flower bed.

"I have to tell you something," I say, staring up at the flat gray sky. "About Mum."

"'Course." Ash slides his warm fingers into my hand, shuffling toward me through the grass.

"She left us a letter," I explain. This is something I couldn't bear to tell him by text. "Before she . . ."

Before she left sounds as though she went on holiday or to one of the artist residencies she's been going to in the past couple of years, leaving Niko in charge for two or three months at a time. But *before she died* isn't truthful, either. Without a body, there's no end to this.

She left her credit cards. She took her passport and her studio key, as if she planned to come back. She left herself as a question, unanswered.

I can't use the words *suicide note*: those syllables aren't discordant enough for what they mean. Anyway, it's open to interpretation. Her letter was too uncertain for the police to call it definitively: rambling, unhappy, incomprehensible, but not specific. And there's still the kiln. Her last work, waiting for her.

"She left a letter, anyway," I say, trying again as clouds begin to move faster overhead, the Earth spinning inexorably onward. "A goodbye letter. I'm the one who found it."

Ash sucks in a breath, squeezing my fingers. "Shit," he says. "I know, Min. I mean, Uncle Raj let me know about the letter. But I didn't know that *you* . . ." His voice cracks. "That you were the one."

I drag my hand from Ash's and make fists, coiling my body, shaking my head, a disbelieving ball. I'm about to be dragged under. Like Virginia Woolf, a writer who filled her pockets with rocks and walked into the river to drown. I've got whole mountains in my pockets. I've got an entire effing continent.

"Don't say anything to Emmy-Kate, okay?" I manage. "Niko knows, but Em doesn't."

"'Course. Hey, you. C'mere." I'm still balled up, but Ash circles his arms around me, bundling me to his chest. And gradually, in this comforting place, I relax. Rest my head on his shoulder, trail my fingers over his chest.

As we lie here, limbs tangled, the sun warms my skin. I let myself melt into it. Let Ash's sure and steady presence slowly envelop me. Breathe him in. His smell is more than lemons—it's warmth and clover and coconut oil in his hair. He smells like kindness. Memories of last year's kisses begin to echo through my heart. Ash has come home. Having him here feels like slipping on a favorite old T-shirt, thin and soft from years of wear.

I sigh contentedly. Then jolt awake, stiffen in his arms. This is not okay. It's not okay to let my guard down while she's—

dead gone missing a body

I scramble from his embrace and stand up, loathing myself for allowing this small moment of joy. Ash follows suit, lumbering upright. He doesn't bat an eye at my sudden movement, but brushes the grass from his jeans, then pokes at my toe with his ginormous sneaker—he wears blinged-out ones the size of canoes.

"Hey, Miniature," he says. "All right? I've got to go, but chin up."

I peek at him. He's giving me an over-the-top Looney Tunes smile, designed to make me laugh. All I can give him in return is a watery one. Ash reaches out his hand to my cheek, softly tilting my face up. He leans in, possibly to press a kiss on me, but I'm turning my head and we crash into each other, an awkward hug. A brief flurry of lemon-scented confusion, then he's gone.

Bright Yellow
(An Ongoing List of Every Color I Have Lost)

*Daffodils. The Post-it notes Mum left
scattered everywhere, scribbled with ideas for
new sculptures, research, love notes to us,
art we HAVE TO SEE! Ash's kiss.*

Cherry Red
(An Ongoing List of Every
Color I Have Lost)

*Flashing red lights on the police car. A lipstick
called Flirt Alert that Emmy-Kate took to wearing
the autumn we met Ash. The pattern of veins
when the optician shines a light into my eyes at my
contact lens checkup. I had one the week after the
disappearance, passing with flying colors (ha),
even though I couldn't discern red from green
on the chart.*

*That's how I know it's not an eyesight problem,
but a Minnie one.*

CHAPTER 4
The Color of Paper Cutouts

The moment I step inside the wide-windowed art space of Poets Corner High on Monday, the back-to-school clamor in the room fades. Even in this behemoth London school, silence and stares have followed me all day: Everyone knows.

I shift uneasily in the doorway, feeling the weight of my classmates' whispers. For the first time in my humdrum life, I'm hot gossip. Half the room gives me sympathetic smiles; the other half won't meet my eye. Including a new boy, huddled in a corner seat, beanie-clad head bent over his sketch pad. He alone is immune to the hubbub that greets my arrival.

I'm starting to sweat from the stares and mutterings when finally Ritika Okonedo takes pity. She breaks free from a clump of friends and jogs across the room, looking like she's going to scoop me into a hug. At the last minute, she skitters to a halt, bops me awkwardly in the shoulder.

"Hey, Minnie. Good summer?" she asks. Then promptly slaps her forehead, shaking her box braids. "Damn. Not, obviously. Sorry about . . ." Ritika twists her earring, fidgeting. "You know. Your mum."

I nod and she smiles, already retreating, as though what's happened to me is contagious. And I go back to lurking alone. Here's where a best friend would come in handy. I'm friendly with everyone but don't have a group to belong to—I've always preferred the company of Sloe sisters. At lunch and breaks, Emmy-Kate would hold court with her swimming friends, while Niko would shake off the communication support worker who accompanied her to lessons and hang out with her BSL-speaking, save-the-world girl gang. And I drifted between the two groups.

I can't sit with Emmy-Kate this year, not when I know the truth about Mum and she doesn't. I'm making a mental note to hide behind the bike sheds at lunchtime, when a piercing taxi whistle rings out. Ms. Goldenblatt—the closest a teacher can get to Wonder Woman—strides into the classroom, cowboy boots clicking. Everyone scurries to sit.

Ms. Goldenblatt takes attendance, then jangles her bracelets, gazing round the room. Her eyes linger on me for a full minute before moving on. "Welcome back, people," she bellows. "One year left. Shall we make it count? We'll start the curriculum next lesson—zhoozhing portfolios, prepping for exams. Today, I want to go back to basics. Your tool kit." This is how she starts every term. With the tooooooool kit. "I want a *perfectly* toned color wheel from everyone."

As per tradition, there are boos at this basic assignment—and a paper airplane from Ritika. Ms. Goldenblatt bats it away as it whizzes past her dark waves, adding, "Think about it. A musician practices scales. You need the building blocks. Oh, and we have a newbie among us. Everybody! Please welcome Felix Waters. Now get to it."

The room erupts as chairs are scraped back and people jostle for paintbrushes and palettes, jars of water, and rags. With the spotlight finally off me, I can breathe again. I inhale the whole room: paint and fresh turpentine, familiarity.

"Minnie." Ms. Goldenblatt clunks over, dropping into a squat next to my stool. "Got a minute?"

She flicks her enormous earrings out of the way and clasps her hands underneath her chin, looking up with the same wide-eyed pity as the social workers and the police family liaison and the Missing People charity worker and the journalists who tracked down our address and rang the doorbell for days. This is what happens when someone you love disappears: They're replaced by hundreds of strangers.

"Oh, Minnie," says Ms. Goldenblatt in her throaty way. "I was so hugely sorry to hear about your mother. You poor girls."

My eyeballs swim. This is how it's been all morning, in homeroom and every class. Teachers determined to have their sympathy moment. I know Ms. Goldenblatt means it, though, so I give her a meek "Thank you."

We're following the script for a bereavement, but it's not right. Missing is a new planet. One where the trees are hollow and there are no oceans, a place without a sky. Suicide is in another effing galaxy.

Ms. Goldenblatt's hands, fingers laden with plastic rings, move from her chin to her chest, where she presses them against her heart. "Let me know if there's anything at all you need?"

I nod and she stands up, half sitting against the table, as if we're at the bus stop. "And on another topic entirely—let's talk portfolios . . ." She beams encouragingly. Ms. Goldenblatt has cheeseball tendencies. She attends all the school plays, standing up and dancing during musical numbers. "Let me guess, all pottery, all the time? I couldn't tear you away from clay last year."

Oh, yeah. Soon after Mum returned to professional art, she invited me—and only me—to come to her studio. The first time she taught me how to throw, she stood at my shoulder at the wheel, her hands over mine, her hair tickling my neck. Afterward we stood side by side at the sink, washing the dried-up clay from our fingers.

"Want to know a secret?" she asked, bumping me with her hip. "Dry your hands and hold them out."

I looked up, meeting her eye in the mirror. She winked, squeezing a tiny dab of something from a tube into my palm. I lifted my hand to my face, and took a deep breath. Glycerin.

"Um . . . So what's the secret?"

"Neutrogena Concentrated Norwegian Formula," she replied.

"You sound like a commercial." I sniffed again, then rubbed the cream between my palms. "Mum, I'm not sure a hand cream you can buy everywhere counts as a secret."

"No, the secret is that ceramicists have the best skin. See?" She vogued her hands around her face in the mirror, posing, her nails painted a lurid neon yellow. When I went to bed that night, I was wrapped in a haze of her smell, only now I knew the secret ingredient, and my sisters didn't. I hugged the knowledge to myself.

"Earth to Minnie." Ms. Goldenblatt clicks her fingers in front of my face. "Clay, yes?"

I know exactly what my teacher is talking about. Where Mum threw her clay into enormous bubbles with fat, round curves, I got into the idea of clean lines. In fact, I got obsessed. Last year I made tiles, hundreds of them. The plan was to spend this summer glazing them, then splice them into a kind of ceramic patchwork quilt. Not that I've ever completed a finished piece of art—it's the ideas I'm into, the potential. And I haven't touched clay—or paint, paper, pens, ink, anything—since the last day of junior year. Since visiting Mum's studio after school and finding the letter. There's no way I can finish the project.

"Actually," I improvise wildly, "I thought I'd try a few other things out. Experiment."

Ms. Goldenblatt's eyebrows fly up so fast I think they're

going to shoot right through her hair. "Amazing," she enthuses, though I think she feels so sorry for me, she'd pretend anything I suggested was brilliant. "Whatever you finish," she adds, stressing the word lightly, "SCAD is going to love it, I'm sure."

She clasps my shoulder, apparently the go-to sympathy spot, and moves on to hassle Ritika, bellowing as she strides across the room: "Paper airplanes, huh?"

I blob a set of paints onto my palette, then pull out my sketch pad. The vast blankness of the white paper pulsates in front of me, seasickness-style. For three months, Emmy-Kate has done little else but paint, and Niko spends all her time with SCAD friends, or sequestered in her room. The house is filling up with abstract paintings and trails of tiny paper scraps. How can I possibly keep up, when I can't see in color?

I grab a Sharpie and write down:

I CAN'T BEAR THIS

Minutes inch by. Ms. Goldenblatt circles the room, handing out fact sheets for the art-school application process. It's different from university: the aforementioned portfolio. You don't need to write a novel to study English, but you're not allowed to learn art until you've already made it. The Wonder Woman bracelets jangle again as she calls out, "Forty minutes, artistes."

Eff. I shove the fact sheet aside and stare at the blobs of gray paint on my palette. Art is going to be impossible. Everything comes down to color. I pick up the Sharpie again and start making a list:

1. *Tickled pink*
2. *Green with envy*
3. *Paint the town red*
4. *Out of the blue . . .*

OED. Definition of *out of the blue* in English:
out of the blue (also **out of a clear blue sky**)
PHRASE
informal Without warning; unexpectedly.

I'd say my mother walking off the top of a cliff meets the definition. Except it doesn't. Not my spontaneous, seesawing mother. It sounds exactly like something she'd do. That's sort of the problem. I believe it, and I don't want to.

My heart is starting to speed up; my palms are sweating. I close my eyes and take a couple of deep breaths. It doesn't help, because out of nowhere I can smell Neutrogena Concentrated Norwegian Formula. Glycerin. It's so distinct, Mum could be here in the room with me. The spasm of misery catches me so quickly, I fold in half. I'm origami Minnie.

I tear the top sheet from my sketch pad and crumple it in my fist, then stand up, knocking over my stool with a bang that draws every eye in the room.

"Minnie?" Ms. Goldenblatt asks, her voice coming at me from a distance.

But I'm already stumbling from the door, rushing down the stairs, bursting out into the open air and trying to quench my empty lungs. And as I run, my list of questions grows:

What about time heals?

What about this too shall pass?

What about all the things people say that are turning out not to be true?

How can you even start to heal when your mother chose to leave you?

Clay

(An Ongoing List of Every
Color I Have Lost)

Halfway between brown and gray, it fades and fades and fades to biscuit beige as the water evaporates. It can take hours to throw a piece. Weeks for it to dry. Days to heat the kiln and fire it once, days to cool it before glazing and firing it again. You have to be patient. You have to wait for her to come home.

CHAPTER 5
Not Fade Away

I spend the rest of the day hiding out with the Rainbow Series I, ignoring the parade of sad-eyed art pilgrims who periodically turn up with flowers and take photographs, as if this is another London tourist destination alongside Big Ben and St. Paul's Cathedral. And once school lets out, I ignore Niko's annoyed *where-are-you?* texts, only going home when it starts to rain. Even then, I linger in the back garden with Salvador Dalí, trying to subdue my pinwheel heart.

When I finally slip inside, the kitchen is empty and smells fusty, like an abandoned building. Which it technically is. Upstairs, both my sisters' doors are closed. From behind Emmy-Kate's comes thumping music, a squeal of her laughter—then a boy's low chuckle. She's bringing boys home now? For some reason this seems like the loneliest thing on the planet. Not to mention, she's fifteen!

I skitter around, not wanting to be the one to fix this, give her the birds-and-the-bees conversation. Where's Niko? She should be playing chaperone. I examine her door, biting my lip. Bedrooms are sacrosanct. It's a lifelong pact between us— one of many, actually. Not that there's ever anything to see in Niko's room. She's neat as a pin: books shelved, bed made, art materials organized in plastic storage boxes. It couldn't be more different from the explosion of stuff that populates the rest of the house.

I shrug off the pact, peep through her keyhole.

My older sister is at her desk. But she's not cutting up paper: She's writing frantically in a notebook—with her eyes closed. Kind of like she's in a trance. Surrounding her are hundreds of huge lit candles. The tall pillar kind you find on the altar in cathedrals. The flames flicker, sending occult shadows across her face.

Whoa. Oh . . . kay. I back away from the door. Emmy-Kate is sequestering herself with boys, and Niko is holding a séance. We're all losing it. And it's Mum's fault. At this, a fireball of rage swells in my chest. Instantaneous, red-hot. I want to take London apart with my bare hands until we find her. I want to hurl myself down the stairs.

Instead I text Ash to come over, lurking by the front door until he arrives and, hand in hand, we go upstairs to my attic bedroom. Aka the Chaos Cave.

The floor is layered with eight million floral frocks, dog-eared art books, rolled-up magazines, makeup, discarded shoes, empty chocolate wrappers, unfinished art projects, tufts of rabbit fur, old sketch pads, and boxes and boxes of broken pastels and half-used squares of watercolor.

My desk is as messy as the rest of the room, my portfolio right where I left it last summer. Next to it is a shoebox filled with dozens of unglazed tiles, yet to be fired. I swallow hard, and look away.

"As usual, I love what you've done with the place, Min," says Ash, turning toward me with a smile. Like yesterday, it's a subdued, toned-down version of his usual off-the-charts grin. "Busy summer, was it?"

We both freeze in place, realizing what he said. His eyes widen, and the half-smile wipes out.

"Crap. Sorry." Ash knocks on his forehead, sending his damp flop of hair wayward. He's brought the smell of the rain inside with him. "I'm an idiot. I meant . . . It was a joke, about the mess. No time to tidy, and all that. I . . ."

I take a deep breath and interrupt his stuttering: "It's fine. I know."

The three of us sit on the bed: me, Ash, and his guitar. Sometimes it feels as though I'm in a love triangle with my boyfriend and music. Today, I'm happy to let the music win out. It's not like I'm a barrel of conversation. While Ash plays, I gaze at the Chaos Cave: It's a cocoon, rain-dark, the view of the garden blanked out by the murky weather.

I point to the misty nothingness of the garden and say, "I feel like I'm in a plane."

"Yeah?" Ash beats on his guitar and starts playing a sixties song called "Leaving on a Jet Plane."

I lie back on the duvet and stare at the cobwebs on the ceiling, listening as he goes through his human jukebox routine, song snippet after song snippet. Eventually he runs out of plane songs, moves on to flying. Then birds.

"What's this one?" I ask as he sings something about broken wings and learning to fly.

"This?" Ash repeats the refrain. "'Blackbird,' by the Beatles. Wait, fuck. Sorry. Again. I'll play something else . . ."

I put my hand on his arm, say, "No, it's okay. I like it."

The Beatles are Mum's favorite band. Her only band. She listens to them all the time, won't allow any other music in the house, even though she was a teenager in the nineties, not the sixties. She says they're the ultimate boy band.

I'm thinking of her in the present tense. Is, not was. But what's wrong with that? People don't stop being themselves when they die or disappear. Death and disappearance don't undo heart-shaped pancakes for birthdays or the way she wore sequin party dresses to Emmy-Kate's swimming competitions.

Her perfume *is* Noix de Tubéreuse by Miller Harris; she *is* addicted to black coffee and hard peppermints and Italian cigarettes. I think of her breaking off halfway through conversations, clicking her fingers, before sprinting to the studio to succumb to some random notion.

46

She suffers from sinkholes.

That's what we call the days and weeks when her electricity blinks out. When she turns into a broken clock instead of a mother. The times her white-blond hair grows dirty with grease, she lies in bed all day, eats nothing—or nothing but toast, whole loaves of bread at a time, even though she looks like she's made of bones. But there hasn't been a sinkhole in five years.

Except . . . suicide is the ultimate sinkhole.

I'm desperate to stop thinking about this, so I say to Ash, my voice coming out in a too-loud clang: "Remind me which album this song is from?"

"*The White Album.*" He changes songs yet again, starts crooning along to "Hey Jude." Only, as usual, he sings "Hey Minnie" instead.

The words *The White Album* are snagging on my brain for some reason, ringing a distant bell, the world's faintest déjà vu. Didn't Mum have a piece called *The White Album*? It sounds vaguely familiar—not that I know her work off by heart. She was prolific. The stuff she made when we were little was mostly sold to private collectors; the *Rainbow Series I* is the only piece on permanent public display. I've probably only ever seen about half of her output.

Ash's song comes to an end and he places the guitar on the floor, then lies down next to me. We're face-to-face, body-to-body, ankles intertwined. "Hey Minnie," he sings again softly, cupping my cheek with his hand. Tentatively, he pushes back my mountains of hair and strokes his thumb along my earlobe. He kisses my forehead. I close my eyes and he kisses my eyelids, then my jawline, then my cheek. We're like a dance. Calm washes over me, the way it did yesterday in the garden.

This time, though, I try to ease into it, instead of jumping like a scalded cat. This is a good thing. Despite being apart for a summer, and my whole life turning upside down, he and I are slotting right back into how we were before. Picking up right where we left off. Which was . . . well, there was a lot of kissing. No sex, yet. But the way things had been going between us, it seemed inevitable, sooner or later. It was a hair beyond our fingertips, on the horizon.

Ash is smiling, eyes half-closed as his hand slides inside my cardigan, resting on the same spot on my rib cage it always does. The room turns quiet. Even the rain is silenced. All I can hear is our breathing, in sync, and the slow, uneasy panic of my heart.

Ash moves his mouth toward mine. "You okay?" he asks. I'm not, quite, but I give a tiny nod. Because perhaps this is how I can turn the clock backward. Restore things to how they were.

But as our lips meet for the first time in forever, this line from the goodbye letter runs through my head: *disappear into the sky.*

Dark Green
(An Ongoing List of Every
Color I Have Lost)

*Meadow Park in the rain. The bitter looks
Emmy-Kate and Niko gave me whenever I showed
off about going to Mum's studio—I was the only
Sloe sister to whom she'd given a key.*

CHAPTER 6

The White Album

Over the next couple of days I find myself drawn back to the Rainbow *Series I* after school. Despite Ash's return, I still feel like I have the flu: a constant headache, sandpaper throat, limbs made out of lead. Existing is exhausting.

I'm here again now, squished beneath one of the titanic bubbles, hidden from view. The earth is still damp from rain; drops cling to the heavy clay that hangs in the air, inches from my face. This is something I do a lot: hiding out. Overpopulated city, big school, terraced house, nosy neighbor, two sisters, and a larger-than-life mother—solitude is sometimes something of a necessity.

Now, this is where I feel closest to Mum's spirit, here with her more-alive-than-alive art. I press a hand to the curved sphere above me, feeling for the sculpture's heartbeat, and whisper, "Where are you?"

And bam, here she is, lying next to me. Wearing coral lipstick and jabbing a lit cigarette in the air like a demented firefly, saying, "Should we shake things up, Minnie? Get another rabbit?"

The relief of hearing her voice again fills me up.

"The first one is bad enough," I tell her, and she smiles lopsidedly. I smile back.

Music starts leaking from the air. "Here Comes the Sun" by the Beatles. Although actually, there's a veil of translucent cloud over the September sky, diffusing the light. For a moment, I think the song is coming from her. Then a buzzing begins and, duh, it's my phone. Mum fades.

The screen shows half a dozen texts and a missed FaceTime call, all from Niko. I ignore the messages, thinking of my ringtone. Another Beatles song. I never followed up on that brain snag from Monday, *The White Album*.

I google it and get a hundred thousand million Beatles results. Duh. But as soon as I add Mum's name—and scroll past dated articles about her missing status—a Wikipedia article pops up. It says *The White Album* was made the year Emmy-Kate was born, her last piece before she abruptly retired from art. There's a tiny picture. The caption underneath reads:

Rachael Sloe (b. 1978)
"THE WHITE ALBUM" (2004)
Mixed media—glazed stoneware and dry ice
A haunting installation piece. The only work of the artist's that lacks color.

I turn my phone sideways so the image fills the screen.

The White Album looks like broken eggshells—from one giant mother-effing goose—and feathered wings, suspended from the ceiling of a gallery. But the matte glaze means the pieces don't reflect any light. They recede, imperceptible and ghostly.

It reminds me of me: floating through this strange other-worldly dimension of nocolor. More than reminds me, actually. Looking at *The White Album* is like lifting off my skull, the way you would the top of a soft-boiled egg, and peering inside my own brain.

I shudder, shaking the worms below. Queasy claustrophobia slithers in, a new awareness of the heavy clay sphere above my head, how no one knows where I am.

Upping the creepiness quotient: footsteps. Heavy ones, shuffling through the garden. I roll over, peering out from underneath the bubble.

An emo art pilgrim in a beanie hat and Doc Martens boots is standing in the middle of the walled garden, wearing the same expression of slack-jawed awe that hits everyone who comes here. He's toting a sketch pad under one arm but looks a little too young to be a SCAD arthead—more my age than Niko's.

His shoulders are bowed, but even so, it's obvious he's skyscraper-tall. And unhappy. I can feel it clear as day from where I'm lying: He's the epicenter of his own personal earthquake, and his sadness shakes the ground. Ugh. *Join the effing club*, I think. I'm sick of people commandeering my mother's tragedy for themselves.

Speaking of which: This guy's gloomy gaze lands on the memorial, worn after the rain. I'm expecting him to move toward it, leave a drawing as some people have been doing, but he turns away, stepping farther into the garden. His eyes are on the ground, so as he strides past my bubble he sees me straightaway, but doesn't put it together for another few footsteps.

"Uhhh . . ." he says, doubling back and peering down at me.

I blink up. Beneath the beanie, he has loop-the-loop dark curls that fall in front of his eyes, which are shadowed from lack of sleep. Pale skin, almost as white as a Sloe's. His face is all angles, with the kind of cheekbones Emmy-Kate would kill for, and familiar too . . . I flash back to Monday, to the new boy in my art lesson with his head glued to his sketch pad. Same dour dude, I'm sure of it.

And here I am, hyperaware that I'm stuffed beneath a priceless, prizewinning artwork.

"Cool idea," he says, apparently unperturbed, as though he comes across horizontal girls every day. He cups a cigarette to his mouth, lights it, takes a long drag. "There's a few sculptures that make me want to do that. Get a different perspective on the work."

How pretentious. My face burns with annoyance and I start wriggling free, but he's slumping to the ground and sitting on the path, blocking my exit. His satchel falls open next to him. My inner snoop can't help peeking inside: pencils, charcoals, hard pastels, ink . . . Yup, definite arthead. No doubt he's SCAD-bound.

"So, I'm Felix," he offers, Eeyore-dreary, fiddling with his cigarette. His fingers are callused. "I think we're in the same art class? At Poets Corner High?"

"I'm Minnie." I pick at a run in my tights, letting a century go by before giving up and adding the unavoidable, which he'll find out anyway: "Sloe." I wave around at the *Rainbow Series I* to make it clear: Yes, uh-huh, *that* Sloe, go ahead and speculate.

This name is going to follow me my whole life. To SCAD, if I ever summon the courage to go. My professors will have automatic expectations, assumptions. And forget about trying to be an artist, as a career . . . Her disappearance has only made it worse, put the name Sloe in every newspaper in Britain. I might as well be called Minnie Monet or Minnie Matisse. Nothing I make will ever measure up.

"Yeah, okay, wow. I mean, I know." Felix shakes his head, setting off a roller coaster of curls. He peers through them at me: a frank, open examination that unpeels me down to my bones.

Obviously he knows exactly what's happened—men on the effing moon know what's happened. It was on the ten o'clock news, the front page of the *London Evening Standard*. The internet is filled with artheads sharing photos of her work, hashtagging them #RachaelSloe, #missing, #haveyouseenher.

It's more than that, though. Felix looks the exact same way

I feel. Like an atom bomb has gone off. But how dare he? How can his own grief compare to mine? He's mourning Rachael Sloe, Artist. Not the real her who dances with Salvador Dalí and can only cook fish sticks.

"I'm sorry about your mum," he says, fixing me with these rainstorm-sad eyes. Gross. Stop it. You don't even know.

My mouth pinches in sharp resentment. "Thanks."

"Yeah." He pauses, tapping his cigarette and spilling ash over the path. Some of it lands on one of the tiny spheres embedded in the concrete, but at least he wipes it off. "I'm actually a fan. I mean, I really liked her work."

I bob my head stiffly, wrapping my arms around my knees.

"This—" He touches the bubble next to us. Possessiveness consumes me: I resist the urge to smack his hand away. "It's, wow. Seeing it for real. It's more-*more* than I thought it would be, you know?"

"Uh-huh."

"So, anyway," says Felix, sounding cautious—like he finally senses he's unwelcome, "I heard Ms. Goldenblatt say you're this clay obsessive . . ."

Oh, no. Don't tell me he's a ceramics nut. Does he think we're going to bond because he likes her art, likes clay? Him and a thousand others. When Niko started at SCAD last year, she complained about this—that students would approach her wanting to talk about Mum, but wouldn't make the effort to learn a sign or two, or even fingerspell. This is what will happen to me next year: I'll be another Rachael Sloe clone. "Me too." Felix stubs out his cigarette on the sole of his boot. "Clay, I mean. In fact—"

He breaks off as a pair of tourists comes loudly into the garden, laughing and talking. They take out their phones, snapping photos not of the art but of the creepy memorial-cum-shrine, then each other in front of it. Suicide selfies.

I look away, catching my reflection in the bubble. My mirror image self is pale to the point of invisibility, with a frenzied fog of gray hair. She seems far away, and I don't know if it's because my vision is fading or I am.

The tourists come traipsing through the *Rainbow Series I*, close to where we're sitting, their voices still raised. They don't know it's a cemetery. "You okay?" Felix asks in a low voice.

I ignore him, sinking down to the ground and sliding back underneath my bubble. Who cares if this emo-doom-Byron boy thinks I'm weird? I put my hands over my eyes, thinking, *Go away. Everybody.*

When I open them again, he has. All that's left is a cigarette butt on the path, and a crushed-up chalk pastel, ground beneath a Doc Martens boot.

CHAPTER 7
A Whiter Shade of Pale

As we sit down to dinner on Saturday night, Emmy-Kate throws salt over her shoulder. Halfway through the gesture, her eyes widen and she goes statue-still, but it's too late: A snow flurry of grains pitter-patters against the window behind her.

"I just . . ." she croaks, hiding behind chlorine-scented hair.

But the imitation of Mum is too vivid. I can't shake the thought of her finally coming home. Standing out there in the garden, watching us from the dwindling twilight: the strange way we're starting to coalesce around her absence like an oyster around a pearl.

Ash is here too, and the Professor. Niko invited him after he "popped in" again this afternoon. I understand why she's insistent the three of us eat together at least once a week—she's paranoid about impressing the social workers. But why encourage him? He's got his own microwave, next door.

"Well, anyway. It *was* Friday the thirteenth yesterday," Emmy-Kate signs/says, in a teeny-tiny voice.

At this, even Niko eyeballs the salt. But before she can do something so uncharacteristic as to make a mess, the Professor swoops in and grabs it, shaking it over his food.

We're eating chips and sausages—vegetarian Quorn ones in deference to Niko, Ash, and the Professor, but otherwise our standard plate. Even before Mum disappeared, we had a revolving diet of pizza and microwave meals. We eat the way we do so she can focus on her work instead of what she calls "domestic drudgery." It hasn't occurred to any of us to learn how to cook.

"All the best food groups are frozen," Mum claimed years ago, during another dinner; this one without the Professor.

The four of us were gathered in the kitchen. We hadn't seen her properly in months, not since the day she'd unexpectedly announced she was going to her studio to start a new series, her first since Emmy-Kate was born. We'd never before in our lives glimpsed artist her, a mother who only had eyes for clay. She'd been making a series called *Girls in the Moon*, ceramics glazed bright purple. She'd finally completed it that morning and wanted to celebrate over frozen lasagna and too much wine.

Emmy-Kate cut into the lasagna, discovering that the charred outsides concealed a still-frozen center. She put the knife down, freeing her hands to announce, "Kind of like a Baked Alaska."

"Well, goes to show—Sloes are kitchen-incapable," Mum signed, then waved her hand to indicate this was a given. In doing so, she sloshed red wine over her dress. "Crap."

Laughing, she grabbed the salt and threw one handful on the stain, then another over her shoulder, onto the floor.

Niko groaned in mock despair. "Muuummm. The kitchen's messy enough as it is."

Mum threw another handful of salt around deliberately, then wagged a finger, giving her an electric smile. "Domesticity is the hobgoblin of little minds."

"That's consistency!" Niko pointed out, clearly trying not to laugh.

It was funny how quickly we slipped back into being ourselves, even after months of barely seeing her. She'd been eating at her studio a few neighborhoods away, practically sleeping there, or leaving the house in the middle of the night to adjust the temperature on the kilns—there's no automatic way to do it. But now that she was finally home for good, things snapped back to normal in an instant.

"Oh, same diff." Mum's hands paused as she gulped her wine, ignoring Niko's rapid-fire arguments.

We were all signing silently, a constant flurry of movement and laughter. Recently, we'd had to slow down and speak, too: While Mum had been at the studio, the Professor had played babysitter and we'd eaten with him each night, going at his signing speed and vocabulary, a hodgepodge of voices and signs and interpretation. But today Mum had suggested, "How about only my girls? It feels like an age since I saw you all."

"This means I don't have to tidy my room ever," Emmy-Kate decided. "Because of the hobgoblins."

"Exactly," Mum agreed. She pushed away her plate. "Minnie, let's phone for a pizza."

"Another one?" Niko asked.

"Hey, I'm teaching you girls how to be geniuses, here." Mum signed and swigged wine and smoked, all at once. "Skip the cooking and the cleaning and get creative. How do you think the great artists did it? Everyone raves about Picasso, but no one spares a thought for poor Mrs. Picasso doing all the vacuuming while her husband doodled."

Emmy-Kate burst into giggles; even Niko was snorting. I had to hang up on the pizza place, I was laughing so hard. I never expected her to quit SCAD altogether barely two weeks later, nor to start a new series that lasted almost a year.

The next time she took a break from the studio, we were warier with our hearts.

Now, forks scrape in silence against ceramic plates. The Professor periodically clears frogs from his throat. Niko is trying to engage Ash in conversation, signing slowly, her face pinkening in frustration when he asks her again and again to "Repeat?" Next to me, Emmy-Kate is shoveling in chips at demonic speed. As soon as she clears her plate, she signs-says, all in one breath, "I'm finished may I please leave the table I'm going upstairs to do homework thanks bye."

It's the beginning of a mass exodus. The Professor retreats next door. Niko looks from me to Ash to his guitar, biting her lip. When he doesn't make a move toward it, she tells me she's going out with some SCAD friends, glancing behind her as she leaves.

I'm stacking the dishwasher, wondering if doing so makes *me* a hobgoblin, when Ash comes up behind me. He wraps his arms around my waist, nuzzling his face into my neck. "Finally," he says. "Hello." This is the first time we've touched all evening—kissing in front of his uncle, my sisters, is too *Flowers in the Attic*.

"Hi." I'm turning to face him when I see something through the window.

A pair of high-heeled shoes, tumbling from the sky. They're followed fast by Emmy-Kate, climbing down the trellis from her bedroom. WTFasaurus? She jumps barefoot onto the grass in a tiny dress and raccoon mask of eyeliner, retrieves the shoes, then goes flitting from the garden—Cinderella in reverse.

I tell myself that this is definitely not my problem. In fact, Emmy-Kate has the right idea. What if, instead of hanging out with Ash, I followed her? Ran into the night and lost myself in London's vast streets, abandoned my whole life the way Mum has: the SCAD destiny. Monochromacy. Art. The Professor. Even the sweet way Ash is looking at me right now. Sex.

We end up on the sitting-room floor, Salvador Dalí stretched full-length on the sofa above our heads. Ash takes out his phone and starts scrolling through playlists.

"Uh-oh," I say. "Let me guess, you want to play me some noisy grime band that hasn't heard of melody?"

He laughs. "You'll love this one, I promise."

"You always say that," I point out, but my words get lost in the loud frenetic music beginning to blare from his phone. Ash wiggles his eyebrows and starts beatboxing ridiculously along. Affection for his idiocy surges.

But the thing is, even a song as fast as this sounds despondent. Everything does. All I want is for Mum to walk in the door, hear this awful not-music, and crack up laughing.

And it's not my artist mother I miss—the intense, semi-possessed one of the past six years. I miss the Mum of the wilderness years. That mother would be dragging me to my feet and doing a stupid dance to this terrible tune. Lifting the rabbit from the sofa and settling there with a book, the three of us competing to squish in with her. Little Emmy-Kate always won; Niko too, so they could sign one-handed, their spare hands wrapped around mugs of herbal tea. And my place was always the floor, leaning back against her legs as she poked her cold feet against me. The exact same spot I'm in now.

And maybe I'm not even missing *that* Mum, but *that* Minnie. Pre-teenage me.

A girl who'd never used a kiln or kissed a boy, who had all her colors and both of her sisters.

I stare at the sitting-room door until it flies open and she's standing in the doorway in a bright blue ballgown, soaked in seawater and holding an enormous pink conch shell. "Inspirational!" she shouts. "Minnie, twelve weeks underwater was what I needed—the new series will be ocean blue. I'll call it *The Beachy Head Adventure*."

It's as if she's standing beneath her own personal spotlight, the Milky Way. Mum didn't only have sinkholes. There were these other times when every aspect of her would hit fast-forward; she'd grow louder and happier and whirlier. We thought of it as being starlit.

The beat on the phone goes bass-line ballistic, rattling my ribs. The door slams shut.

"Oops," says Ash, jabbing at the volume before propping himself up on one elbow, looking down on me. "Everything all right in there?" he asks, pushing back my mound of hair and tapping my forehead. "You look a million miles away. What were you thinking about?"

I can't tell him I was picturing Mum, crawling out of the seabed after three months. I can't tell him that whenever I see her, she's in full, lurid color, but the world—including him—remains stubbornly black and white. I'd sound . . . crazy. Given my DNA, it's not a thought I want to pursue.

"I was thinking, are you *sure* you're good at music?" I say. "Because I think you might have cloth ears. I mean, that song was . . . Would you even call it a song?"

"All right, Grandma, that's it," threatens Ash. He rolls over, starts tickling me.

I yelp in protest and he laughs, a lock of hair falling in front of his eyes, making him look more Elvis-y than ever. "Name one band," he says, cocking his eyebrow, "that isn't the Beatles."

"I . . ." My brain draws a blank. "That proves nothing," I argue, "and anyway—"

He kisses me before I can finish, both of us laughing into each other's mouths. Briefly, I float above our entangled bodies, looking down at myself pretending to be normal.

Ash rearranges us as we kiss, draping himself lazily half on, half off me, his leg hooked over mine, one hand on my waist. We have things down to a fine routine. Gradually, his fingers slide up to my rib cage. There's usually a line, right beneath my boobs, where I stop him going any further. But this time, for some reason, I slide my own hands under Ash's shirt.

"Yeah?" he murmurs, his breath warm in my ear.

"Yeah."

It's like pushing a button marked WARP SPEED.

I don't know which of us is leading this, but my cardigan goes vamoose beneath his fingers—which are now everywhere. In my hair and underneath my dress and undoing my bra and sliding into my underwear, all at once. And I'm not thinking about how sad I am anymore. I'm thinking: wow, I'm so effing *alive*. I can feel Ash—his hard-on, I mean—pressing against my thigh. We roll over and over, tumbling into the sofa. Something goes crash.

Ash straightaway peels himself from my mouth. His face is flushed, eyes sleepy, lips puffy from kissing. "Whoa," he says, shaking himself like a dopey dog. "Wait, what was that?"

"Nothing." I shake my head, try to kiss him again. The moment we popped apart, all the other stuff came rushing back in. And I want to obscure it.

"Min, hang on a sec." Ash squeezes my hand and rolls off me, looking like an upturned beetle for a second. Then he sits up, looking around. "Oh, shit."

"What?" I push myself upright, smoothing down my dress and shoving my hair into something less *just-been-kissed*. Then I see what Ash sees, and gasp.

Mum's ashtray. A chunky ceramic, made by her. Usually it sits on a side table next to the sofa. Now it's in two sharp pieces on the floor. None of us, not even Niko, have been able to face clearing it out, and it's still full of cigarette butts. Or was. A pile of ashes besmirches the rug. Salvador Dalí gives me a disapproving look over his floppy ears. A riptide of regret swells.

Not only about the ashtray. But what happened—that crazy, out-of-control kiss. That's never happened before. And I know if I take Ash's hand and lead him up to the Chaos Cave, we'll land on my bed and continue it. Have sex. Or at least take another huge step toward it. Then another, and another.

I'm no longer sure if I want to.

It's not that I'm not curious—about boners and blowjobs and the mechanics of the whole thing. (I mean, I get the basic idea.) But I don't want to lose my virginity in monochrome.

And sex is like jumping off a cliff: a split-second decision that can't be undone. You don't get to take it back, even if your feelings later change. The same way I can't unbreak this ashtray.

I'm not sure if Mum understood how long forever really is.

. . . . .

After Ash says good night, I go upstairs to the Chaos Cave. My window is open, blowing in cool September sky. It's deepening in that strange city way where dark never truly arrives. You never see stars in London; only a dustbowl of silvery gray. There are too many lampposts, too many phones and happy houses, too many people. I want to turn out all the lights at once, plunge this huge metropolis into the same bottomless night I'm trapped in.

I miss my mother like I miss yellow.

Without Ash's kisses to hide in, my brain drifts toward the possibility of her sprawled, bloody, across wet rocks; or a body bloated and unrecognizable at sea. Grotesque images that have gone flash-flash-flash through my head all summer. Ever since the day I found her letter.

As soon as the last bell rang for the end of the school year, I headed straight to Mum's studio. There was a storm brewing: London crackled with heat as I walked down Full Moon Lane beneath a boiling mauve sky. When I reached the studio, underneath the overhead railway line, the door was locked.

Mum wasn't inside, but she'd left a fan blowing, so she was due back at any moment. I was propping open the door to try to cool the stuffy space when I heard the piano plink of the kilns.

Clay kilns don't roar with fire the way you'd imagine; they're not loud or mechanical. They give off the occasional soft, quiet ping, like a fork tapped lightly on a glass.

I hadn't known she had pieces ready to fire. She'd been working on a new series for weeks: *Schiaparelli*. Stoneware columns glazed in shocking pink. But every time the pots had dried enough to go in the kiln, she'd smashed each one down to dust. Intrigued, I checked the kilns' control panels. Three were covered in dust sheets, but the largest was cooling down from a pre-glaze cycle—meaning she must have put something in at least yesterday, or the day before.

I was thinking about sneaking a peek through the kiln's spyhole when the rain arrived—with joyous abandon. It smacked down on the asphalt, bouncing in through the open door, pooling in puddles on the floor. I turned around to watch, and that's when I spotted it—a piece of paper folded in three and propped up on her wheel. Her handwriting, oddly uneven on the back, addressed to me:

MINNIE

A shiver blew through the empty studio, along with the rain. Then, after I read the letter, white noise: time moving in stops and stutters along with my newly malfunctioning heart.

I don't remember calling the police or curling up and hiding under the worktable to wait, but I must have done because that's where I was when they arrived. Shivering on the cold concrete floor, watching the rain and the red light from the police car flash-flash-flash across the wet yard, the last true, pure color before they began to fade.

Someone made hot, sweet tea, and a blanket was put around my shoulders. I answered question after question—what was she wearing when had I last seen her had she done something like this before was she on any medication could we have a description a recent photograph where did I live who should they call where was my dad—

That one almost made me laugh. I'd never needed a dad, not when I had a mother whose presence was so enormous, she filled the father-shaped hole in my life the way night-scented jasmine engulfed the garden in summer. And now she was gone and it was too late to ask who else I came from.

Ever since that afternoon, the questions have blurred into my own, unanswered ones:

Will her body wash up one day, like Virginia Woolf's? Are any of the #RachaelSloe sightings on the internet real? Will this goodbye echo through my life or does it get better? What to do with all this hopeless hope if she never comes back? And how do I survive when THERE ARE NO COLORS LEFT?

Certainty thrums through me: Mum lost her colors too.

More than once. The first time would have been the year Emmy-Kate was born and Mum made *The White Album*—her only work without color. That's it, that's why she gave up making art. It had nothing to do with having three babies—she was waiting for the colors to come back. When they did, she went right back to work.

But then it happened again, I'm sure of it. That's why she kept smashing the *Schiaparelli* series instead of glazing it pink. Only this time, she gave up for good. She didn't survive without color a second time. So where does that leave me?

Plum
(An Ongoing List of Every
Color I Have Lost)

*Our moth-eaten rug, clawed to pieces by Salvador
Dalí and covered in cigarette burns. Emmy-Kate's
most notorious boy-grabbing bra. A bruised heart.
The frantic sky right before the storm.*

CHAPTER 8

Just Like a Dream

It's midnight and Emmy-Kate still isn't home. She must be a pumpkin by now.

I can't sleep. Salvador Dalí and I are curled up on my bed, where I've been since Ash left, replaying our kiss over and over. Now we've done *that*—hands under clothes, bra pushed aside, skin against skin and bodies writhing—there's no way to go back to fully dressed kisses. The only way is forward.

I stare out at the Chaos Cave. Lampposts cast artificial light across the room, illuminating everything from the SCAD mission statement to the corkboard above my desk. It's crammed with dog-eared exhibition postcards, copies of favorite paintings—the California swimming pool of David Hockney's *A Bigger Splash*, the precise watercolor of Eric Ravilious's *Cyclamen and Tomatoes*—and photos of Niko, Emmy-Kate, and me. There's a mini poster from Mum's Tate Modern comeback show; a cinema ticket from my first date with Ash. But something's missing. My studio key usually hangs from a ribbon in the top right corner. They're both gone.

I push Salvador Dalí aside—he gives an indignant snuffle—and slide out of bed, walking to my desk and scouring the messy surface. My eyes skate over the box of tiles, then back again. Aha. The key, its ribbon, and the pin that usually holds them in place have fallen inside. I reach in and scoop them out, my fingers brushing the loose preparatory sketches I made for the tile quilt.

After returning the key to its rightful place, reknotting the ribbon and pushing in the pin extra-hard, I sit down and review the sketches. Sheet after sheet of tessellated tiles. Ms. Goldenblatt's encouraging scrawl anoints the corner of one page: *love it!* But it seems to me as though a stranger drew these. They're not exactly inspiring me to start kneading clay. And another memory is beginning to bloom in my head, like a hothouse orchid.

I try to ignore it, open my portfolio. The spine creaks from lack of use. Page after page is filled with different techniques and styles, different mediums—watercolors, oils, acrylics, gouache, collages, pen-and-ink—photographs of abandoned sculptures and sketches of objects that I never got around to making, or never finished. Nothing is complete. Halfway across each page, the paint or ink or collage fades out, giving way to reveal the initial pencil lines of the idea. Like I gave up.

The memory is pushing at my mind now, clawing its way in. A day at the studio last winter, when Mum cranked the stereo to ear-splitting volume, booming out the Beatles and singing raucously as she began to slap huge handfuls of clay on the wheel. She covered herself and me and the walls and ceiling in her quest to find the shape it was going to become.

I shake it off, keep leafing through the portfolio. I'm trying to find me in here, and I can't. There's no signature style, nothing that unmistakably says: *Minnie Sloe made this.* Not the way Emmy-Kate's sparkle is evident in her abstract acrylics, how Niko is so committed to cutting up paper she cuts her fingers too; and Mum is a ceramicist through and through.

"What do you think, Salvador Dalí?" I ask out loud, to stop thinking about her.

I pick up an ordinary writing pencil and find a blank page, tentatively starting to draw. It's too late. The memory comes crashing in.

Mum hadn't moved from the wheel all day. She barely let it stop spinning in between slapping down a new piece of clay to make off-kilter stalagmites. But as each skyscraper reached its zenith, she smashed it down. Splat! She stopped only to suck on a cigarette or shake a fist at her own efforts. I watched from my own workbench, yawning.

At some point she yelled, "Come *on*," to the clay, but I took it as her exhorting me to move. For once, her effervescence wasn't totally infectious, but I dragged my fingers through a bag of clay anyway, dropped a fistful on the workbench, and listlessly started kneading.

There was a rhythm to it. Pushing down with the heels of my hands. Pulling up and pushing down again. Cutting the stiff clay in half with a wire and layering it, then kneading again. The Beatles and the trains overhead and Mum's frustrated, exhilarated shouts faded out, until there was nothing but me and the clay. Squishing it over and over and over.

"Min?" When Mum pressed a hand to my shoulder, I flew out of my skin.

"Sneak much?" I complained.

"Honey, I've been saying your name for hours."

She was peeling off her smock, her hands already washed and dried and anointed in glycerin. I glanced around. The sun had thickened into dusk, and Mum had finally finished a piece without splatting it. "Check it out," she crowed. "*Schiaparelli* begins at last."

She looked down at my own hunk of clay, which was so overworked it had crumbled into pieces. Her blue eyes flicked to me with a *kapow* flash of worry. It was only there for a split second before she stuffed her concern behind a mile-wide smile and rapid-fire words: "Ready to call it quits, honey? Want to hit Il Giardino, share a tiramisu? We can make Emmy-Kate love us by picking up pizza."

She kept babbling even as I nodded, sweeping the useless clay crumbles into the bin, not letting up until I more or less forgot that look on her face.

What did I see in her eyes that day? Worry, fear, unhappiness? Was it something to do with me, or was that the start of one of her sinkholes and I missed it?

The fact she's not here to answer a single one of my questions is unbearable. Yet somehow my body is bearing it. I think people should split in two when stuff like this happens.

I shiver, feeling the breeze from earlier race in through my open window. I go to shut it, then change my mind; stick my head out instead and yell, "Where *are* you?" Shout it over and over again, hammering my fists on the windowsill and hollering at the railway line.

This doesn't make me feel much better, so I howl it, werewolf-style: *Arooooooooooo!*

A shout of "Shut up!" drifts down the street, and I do. The last thing I want is to wake up the house next door. The Professor in his pajamas? Eek. I give one last, inaudible howl under my breath—but Mum doesn't show.

Emmy-Kate does, though, like night-blooming magic. She emerges from the shrubbery, shoes dangling from one hand, and peers up at me with wide eyes. For a second, she looks about twelve years old: her gawky, swimming nerd, tree-climbing self.

Then she turns and whistles softly. A boy in a baseball cap pushes open the back gate and arrives at her side, taking her hand. Whoa. I blink, and Emmy-Kate is back to looking like the current iteration of her: her inappropriate dress a bright, brittle carapace, accessorized with shiny lipstick and dozens of shaving scabs at her ankles.

She looks up and puts a finger to her lips, swinging onto the trellis. Even though she's tiny, it trembles beneath her weight, shaking the roses from their slumber.

"Good night, Minnie," she says from halfway, challenging me to withdraw. I do. Her voice is the last thing I hear before I fall asleep.

Shocking Pink
(An Ongoing List of Every Color I Have Lost)

*Mum's fuchsia mouth print on every
coffee mug until Niko bleached them.
The punk-rock hairstyles of SCAD students
streaming along Full Moon Lane to campus.
Heart emojis on texts from Ash. Schiaparelli,
her last, unfinished, series. The ineffable essence
of my mother's work—a tremor of YES that
ran through her soul and into her art, and
that I can't even come close to imitating.*

CHAPTER 9

When Clay Dries, That Color

I wake to a telltale creak.

Every Sunday for as long as I can remember, Emmy-Kate has climbed from her window at dawn to go swimming. I roll over, peering through the curtains at the pall of early autumn that surrounds the house, amazed she's awake after coming home so late last night. In the thin morning light, I see not Em but her baseball-capped Romeo making his clandestine escape. Roses incline their heads as he goes by. I can't believe he stayed the whole night!

I bury myself beneath the duvet, trying to delete this information so I don't have to deal with the pang of jealousy it provokes. Emmy-Kate is sneaking in contraband boys; throwing salt, and painting with her hands. She's walking through the world with a carefree heart.

Sometimes I suspect Mum split her genes between us three ways, the way white light refracts to reveal the primary colors. Red: Niko got the brains and the bossy boots, the commanding presence. Yellow: Emmy-Kate got the free-spirited beauty, the kind accompanied by orchestras. What if I got the other thing? Blue. The thread of melancholy that ran through her.

I wish I had Em's devil-may-care frivolity. But contemplating last night's kiss with Ash—let alone sex!—gives me the same sensation as when I think about returning to the ceramics studio. Dread.

By the time I stumble downstairs, Emmy-Kate is sitting pretty on the kitchen counter, wearing a swimsuit and sweatpants, spooning in cereal. Niko is at the table, scrawling what looks like a shopping list on a watercolor pad. She flips it shut when I come in. The kitchen is in the doldrums, as though a dirty rag has been wiped across the air.

Emmy-Kate puts down her bowl but doesn't quite meet my eye, starts signing a mile a minute about some new art-supply shop that's opened up on Full Moon Lane.

"It has this motto." Her hands cascade. "'Let's fill this town with artists.' Isn't that cool?"

I stop paying attention, instead examine the walls lined with her abstracts and Niko's cutouts, the shelves bowed beneath hundreds of Mum's plates. Whenever she started a new series, she'd practice her glaze colors on crockery.

"Actually, I think this town is already full enough of artists," I interrupt Emmy-Kate. She's still not looking me in the eye. As if she's afraid I would actually want to talk about her nocturnal visitor!

Niko has been watching our hands. She jumps in, signing, "I agree."

Whoa. We exchange fleeting, dumbfounded expressions. She and I on the same page about something? Emmy-Kate lifts her cereal bowl and tips it to her mouth, slurping. Milk sploshes to the floor.

Niko clears her throat as I sit down. Her hair is in pin curls beneath a headscarf. Today's slogan sweatshirt: REPEAL, from last year's Irish abortion referendum.

"Speaking of artists . . ." she begins. Then pauses as she takes a long sip of coffee. "I was thinking . . ." she continues, her hand movements stretchy and languid. "We should think about getting Mum's things organized. Clean her room, box up a few things."

"What! Why?" The questions fly from my fingers.

We can't get rid of her stuff. When someone goes missing, it's not the same as a death. You can't cancel bills or shut off phones or give away shoes. Every day, mail addressed to Ms. Rachael Sloe lands on the doormat and there's nothing we can do about it. Glittery gowns and stained smocks billow from her wardrobe, saturated in her smell. Tubes of her pink lipstick fall from the bathroom cabinet whenever I open it; the shower caddy holds a half-used bottle of purple shampoo to stop her hair going brassy.

The house is holding its breath for her return. If she walked in right now, she could pick up where she'd left off—take her handbag from the back of her door or throw herself onto the sofa and pick up the book she left there, turn to the page where she last folded down a corner.

If we pack these things into boxes, she won't be able to come back.

I ignore the voice that says, *But, Minnie—if she does walk in, this very second . . . isn't what she's done unforgivable?* I doubly ignore the voice that tells me this is irrational because she's not coming back anyway.

"What things?" asks Emmy-Kate, hyperalert.

Niko sits up straighter. "The house is a mess," she tells us, looking down her patrician nose. "I don't want the social workers to come round and see it a pigsty. There's stuff on the floor everywhere, I can't invite anyone over. Let's have a tidy up." She pauses, flipping open her watercolor pad again and jotting something. Then puts down her pen and adds, "At least we should wash her sheets, do her laundry, clean her room."

Although Emmy-Kate visibly sags with relief, I notice her eyes flit to Mum's mobile phone, which is plugged in on the counter, all of us waiting for the day it rings. "Whatever," she signs, hopping down and grabbing her swimming bag. "Mum's only going to mess the place up again anyway when she gets back."

She bangs the back door as she leaves for the pool, her last sentence staining the air.

I squirm in my seat, picturing Niko clearing up Mum from

around me. Rolling up this rag rug from beneath my toes, putting away the gardening flip-flops she kicked off by the back door, taking down her ceramic vases from the mantelpiece. Tidying this mess she left us into neat boxes.

"Perhaps we should burn down the garden," I tell her, "and stop drinking coffee."

"Don't be obnoxious, Minnie," Niko signs, then drums her fingers on the table, her eyes a nonchalant challenge.

Neither of us signs anything else. The room swells with a hundred things unsaid, unsigned. Things that, actually, have nothing to do with Mum. Our eyes are still locked when my phone starts playing "All You Need Is Love"—otherwise known as the ringtone I have set for Ash.

"Saved by the bell," I tell Niko, waving my phone. "It's Ash."

. . . . .

In the hallway, I look down at my phone. The photo I have set for Ash's calls is one I took last spring in Meadow Park: He's wearing sunglasses and eating soft serve, the ice cream daubing his nose. For some reason, my fingers hit the END CALL button. I'm freaked out after Niko's bombshell. After last night.

I go trudging up to the Chaos Cave and sit at my desk, feeling twitchy. Then, picking up yesterday's abandoned paper and pencil, I begin to draw.

At first, drawing feels rough and rusty, like I'm a bicycle that's been left too long in the shed. The pencil is as unfamiliar in my hand as a chopstick; I'm holding it too tightly. Then, little by little, I loosen up. The work starts to flow. Thinking of Ms. Goldenblatt and her *tooooool kit*, I draw circle after circle until my fingers relax and the pencil transfers fluidly to the paper.

Then I draw flowers. The cliff-bend curves of my favorite spring blooms: frilly bearded irises, frothy sweet peas, sweet-scented nemesia. I can't make the versions in my head come out right, so I move to my bed and look out of the window to draw from life. The garden is on the wane—hydrangeas and roses are all that's left of summer, but they'll do. My pencil versions blossom on the page, tight cups of petals and thorny vines, until I get hand cramp and have to stop.

I rub my hand, flexing my fingers. There's a thick gray pencil smudge on the side of my palm. The paper is covered with flowers, fine as porcelain, around which I've unconsciously doodled the words:

WHERE IS THE LOVE STORY FOR THE GIRL WHO IS BROKEN-HEARTED?

Not my line—Niko's. From her graduation art exhibition. A dark-goth-emo-poetry paper cutout she made the summer she left Poets Corner High. It hung like bunting across the gym. I'm trying to figure out how her words came out of me when I hear Ash's bright voice calling my name, his footsteps on the stairs.

My heart flies out of the window.

I don't know why, but I don't want to see him yet. I'm not ready to talk about last night, or roll around this bed doing more of the same, or listen while he plays guitar. This minute, I'm happy sitting here in silence, teaching myself how to draw again.

I flip my sketch pad shut and peer out of the window, wondering if I can pull off an Emmy-Kate and climb down the trellis.

My room is too high up. And in a fit of insanity the other night, I googled it—Beachy Head. The cliff is dinosaur-ancient (an era I happen to love), formed so long ago it sounds like a joke: a hundred million years. Five hundred and thirty-one feet high.

Three stories below me, the garden zooms in and out of focus.

My mother's body appears, lying broken on the grass, covered in seawater, then disappears.

The terror is incandescent. Every part of me lights up like a Christmas tree.

Bodies are so vulnerable. If I fell, I would break. The bus Niko takes to SCAD could easily crash. Emmy-Kate might be drowning in the pool right now; a psychopath could strangle Salvador Dalí.

I cringe away from the window, nauseous, as Ash's voice sounds from right outside the door. "Miniature? You decent?" A soft knock. "Can I come in?"

Pause, I think desperately. *Pause, pause, pause.*

I want to take the Earth in both hands and hold it still, Superman-style. Stop the spinning for a little while so I can breathe. I need a small bit of space.

Before I can overthink what I'm doing, I hide under the bed.

Barely in time. From my vantage point among the dust bunnies—also the real bunny, who turns out to be down here too—I watch as the door swings open, and Ash's giant sneaker-clad feet saunter into the room. The floorboards squeak, then fall silent.

Psycho Minnie psycho Minnie psycho Minnie. The words thunder in my ears, so loud they scare Salvador Dalí into hopping away from me, out into the bedroom. He starts sniffing Ash's ankles.

"Hello, you," says Ash, crouching down to the rabbit. I catch a glimpse of his longish hair and the familiar whorl of his ear. A guitar pick tumbles from his shirt pocket onto the floor. If he glances to his right to pick it up, he'll see me. I hold my breath as he stands up, out of sight.

A few seconds pass, then: "All You Need Is Love."

The ringtone blares out above me, my phone still on the bed. Ash taps his foot in time. When the music cuts out, he starts talking.

"Hey, Miniature, it's me." Pause. His shoes squeak, turning and picking their way back to the door. "I'm at your house, but you're not here, so . . . Okay, call me later?" Pause.

It sounds as though he wants to say something else, but he

doesn't. I hear the faint click as he closes the door, the heavy tread of his feet going down the stairs. And I let out the sneeze I hadn't known I was holding. Salvador Dali turns his head and regards me with solemn distaste.

Twelve weeks since my world ended, and here I am, totally effing unhinged.

CHAPTER 10

The Sun Is Bleaching
Everything in Sight

The next morning I trail Emmy-Kate to school, dawdling in the sun. I might not have color, but at least I still have light. It pours from the empty sky, all over my upturned face; pooling on the sidewalk, dripping from the railway line and the trees. Their leaves are beginning to curl at the edges like old sandwiches.

As I walk, I text back and forth with Ash.

Minnie: Hey . . . Sorry I missed you yesterday

Ash: S'all right! Where were you anyway?

Minnie: At the pool with Emmy-Kate

Ash: Nice. So . . .

Minnie: So?

Ash: So, when am I seeing you? :)

We're coming up to our one-year anniversary. Here he is, a troubadour with music in his fingertips, five-foot-ten-inches' worth of charm in skinny jeans and a flannel shirt. My boyfriend, who loves my sisters and Salvador Dalí and me, maybe. He's the only constant in my life. So how come I'm avoiding him instead of telling him about my whole monochromacy deal?

Three little dots appear on the screen as Ash types, so I quickly write—

Minnie: The weekend? Come over for dinner on Friday
Ash: Count me in ♥

Ten paces ahead, Emmy-Kate sashays in nonuniform satin platform shoes—stolen from Mum's wardrobe—hair damp from an early swim. Her skirt is rolled up, the shirt untucked to cover the lump of fabric. As she air-draws, it wafts from side to side like a duck's tail.

Usually she'd be bugging me all the way to school, but today we're not walking together. I suppose she's still avoiding me in the aftermath of the boy in her room. But she does occasionally glance not so surreptitiously over her shoulder to check I'm not going anywhere.

Every time she does, I stumble. Two conflicting desires are rising: to catch up to her and confess everything—that Mum isn't necessarily missing and that's why Niko's intent on boxing her up. That I've inherited the broken portion of her brain. That I think I know what a sinkhole looks like, and it's an artwork called *The White Album*.

But some part of me likes that Emmy-Kate doesn't know about the letter, doesn't know what a sinkhole really is. It makes me feel as though Mum belongs to me more. I'm in on her secrets.

"Earth to Minnie." Emmy-Kate bounds in front of me, sing-songing and yoo-hooing and wiggling her arms in my face. Pale gray, she's a spectral jellyfish.

I blink. I've sleep-followed her into the cafeteria. A place I didn't set foot in last week. With good reason—already, people are turning to stare. Open curiosity marks the faces that look up from early-morning homework and coffee. Whispers are exchanged behind hands held in front of mouths: *the Sloe girls. The redheads. Their mother is missing. You know, the famous one.*

I shrink. Unlike my queen bee of a sister, who's preening, air-drawing with artful self-consciousness. Here under the fluorescent lights, her dark bra is obvious beneath her white uniform shirt. Jealousy caterpillars through me the way it so often does when I'm confronted with Emmy-Kate's looks, her beauty presented as though she's handing the world a giant bunch of lilacs.

"Cup of tea?" She doesn't do the official BSL hand shape, but homesigning. Growing up, the whole family had weekly lessons, but inevitably we added our own signs to the mix:

89

secret passwords and shorthand. Not quite our own language, but unique.

My stomach is already doing the jitterbug; tea won't help. And it means sitting at a table with Emmy-Kate, who's peering at me with plaintive bug eyes and is possibly now ready to talk about her boyfriend. Or, more likely, Niko's plan for a tidiness blitz. Ugh. I shake my head.

"C'mon, Min." Emmy-Kate pigeons her toes, blinking heavily mascaraed lashes. When I don't answer, she signs "Fine!" and huffs away, a hum of chlorine in her wake.

I wonder if she would still swim if she knew our mother had potentially taken a swan dive into the English Channel. The second I think this, fragments of the conversations around me drift to the surface like seaweed:

I was so wasted I wanted to die.

Urgh, kill me now.

Mr. Wong's lessons are so boring I want to overdose.

Mate, if she doesn't text me back I'ma slit my wrists—

I'm shaking. The pale room begins to darken.

I glance up, expecting to see a blown bulb. The strip light is buzzing above me as per usual, but the room is turning soft black at the edges of my vision. I feel as though I'm sinking deep under the sea, unable to breathe. I open my mouth to speak, to call after Emmy-Kate and ask her if it's getting dark in here or is it me? and my lungs fill with salt water.

I choke on it. Thrash out my arms and touch nothing but

ocean, a cold that constricts my ribs and makes black blink in front of my eyes until that's all I can see.

Then there I am, drowning in the dark.

. . . . .

"Minnie?" Ms. Goldenblatt almost trips over me when she emerges from the art room. I'm crouched in a ball in the empty corridor outside. She ducks down, puts her hand on my shoulder. "Is everything all right?"

"Ah—" I gasp out this nothing of a reply, unable to answer through this mouth full of seaweed, or explain what's happening to me.

"Deep breaths," she says. "Breathe for me? In one-two-three, out one-two-three. Good." She takes her hand back, pushing her bracelets up her wrists. "Come on."

Ms. Goldenblatt leads me back through the classroom, which is filled with easels, then into her office, where I wash ashore. She hands me a glass of water.

"Want me to send you to the office, see if you can go home?"

I shake my head and she kicks her foot onto her opposite knee, leaning back in her chair and rattling her bracelets again as she fixes me with the pity eyes. I look away. Her desk is as cluttered as mine; there's a stack of portfolios on the floor, reference books everywhere. It's a little like the studio—organized chaos, the same smell of paint-turps-dust—but peaceful. Niko says Ms. Goldenblatt has a different aura from Mum.

"Are you seeing the school counselor?" she asks, owl-eyed.

"No, I, um—" I start coughing. The thought of talking about my monochromacy, about visions of my dead mother, makes my whole body constrict.

"You okay there?" Ms. Goldenblatt waits for me to finish coughing. "Look, Minnie. You're my next lesson. I'm happy for you to hide out in here for the hour if you think it'll help. Read a book. Curl up. Get started on the homework. But you know what I think might be good?" The bell rings and she waits it out, ponytailing her hair in her hand, then letting it fall. Then she smiles—it's one step away from jazz-hands. "Art! Like, art therapy. We're doing self-portraits. Tons of tonal color mixing, deep focus on the proportions; it could really soothe you." She's still raving like a kook as she stands up, encouraging me out of the door and back into the classroom. "You know, to think about something else. How is your portfolio coming along?"

I mumble something noncommittal.

The classroom is filling up, my classmates piling in and jostling each other and lunging for seats. Ritika waves hello from the melee as I plop into the nearest seat, which turns out to be next to, ugh, Felix Waters. Ms. Goldenblatt gives her signature whistle, clambering onto her desk, and everyone settles down. I glance at Felix. He's sitting underneath his own personal rain cloud. Our moods match: We're a couple of sad sacks, drooped behind easels. His eyes shift to mine, then away, grunting a wary hello.

"Before we begin," Ms. Goldenblatt announces, "you have homework! Find a partner, pick a gallery. Choose something—anything—to draw. A sculpture would be good, or other visitors, the staff. I want a series of speed sketches by next week: thirty seconds, a minute, five minutes, half an hour. Try a few of each. Everybody clear? All right. It's self-portrait time. Aprons on and show me what you're made of."

She winks at me and I turn to my easel, examining it through brain fog. Everything's hazy and distant, like I'm swimming through thick glass. A sheet of paper has been pre-taped to the board, alongside a tiny hand mirror. It's cracked; I can't see my reflection properly.

But it doesn't matter. I know how to paint a portrait of me: I'm the sound ice makes when it breaks. Wind rushing up through rotten floorboards, and short winter days when leaves kiss goodbye to dying trees. I am clay that cracks in the kiln.

I breathe in and out, one-two-three, and concentrate on laying out my palette like a clock: red at twelve o'clock, yellow at four o'clock, blue at eight o'clock. The color wheel. The tubes are labeled, so it doesn't matter that all I see is gray, gray, and gray. I can paint by numbers.

"So . . . we're working together, I guess." Felix's dark voice breaks into my thoughts.

He's tilting back in his chair, balancing it on two legs, shoving both hands through his curly hair. Classic tortured-artist pose. I stare at him blankly and he adds, "On this homework thing?"

I rewind to Ms. Goldenblatt's words—find a partner—look around the room in alarm. Everyone else is already paired up: Ritika and her best friend, Bolu; David Christie with Jim Parkinson; Isabelle O'Carroll and Alex Fong; and so on round the room, like Noah's ark.

"We could meet after school," says Felix, as though our partnership is a done deal.

I dip my brush in what I think is yellow. Say quietly, "That's okay, we don't have to go together."

Felix tips his chair forward, scuffing his boots on the floor. "Look. I don't know London," he says. "I can google a gallery, but you'll know where the good stuff's at. All I know is your mum's sculptures in the park."

Ugh. I recall his super-mourning at the walled garden. There's no way I'm drawing the *Rainbow Series I* with Felix. He'd probably invite himself to Mum's studio for a behind-the-scenes tour.

"I don't—"

"You don't what?" Felix interrupts. His face is a thunderstorm. Then he shakes his head, looking away and ducking to peer into his mirror. "Never mind."

He grinds his jaw as he starts sketching gridlines on his paper. I catch myself examining his profile in detail, as if I'm trying to work out how to draw him instead of myself. The coal-dust curls he mostly keeps stuffed in a beanie. His face is all angles, perfect for a sculpture: straight nose and forehead, high cheekbones and narrow chin, downturned mouth.

He glances at me and I look away abruptly, grabbing a brush and daubing on a color at random.

"Can you choose a place," he mutters, "and we'll go and get this over with?"

"Fine." I remind myself of Emmy-Kate at her most mutinous.

"Fine," Felix mimics.

We're both bristling.

Then it's as if he teleports somewhere else. Blink, and he's in the art zone—prepping his palette, plopping down the paints in a messy cacophony that's in total contrast to his dour demeanor. He doesn't bother with an apron. His clothes are already bespattered. He leans close to his easel, the brush caressing the paper with a strange intimacy that makes me look away.

I stare past my painting to a day from a few years ago, when the three of us were hanging out in Meadow Park with Mum. This was before she returned to art, when she lectured at SCAD and had sinkholes but at least she was here.

It was cool and spring, daffodils popping up Whac-a-Mole all over the park. Despite the chill, we bought ice-cream cones from the pool café and ate them spread-eagled in the wildflower meadow, with its overarching sky and church-spire view. From the ponds, nesting ducks were quacking happily.

Niko was telling us about crop circles, and when Emmy-Kate finished her cone, she began making snow-angel movements in the long grass. Tendrils of her strawberry-blond hair, already growing lighter now that winter was behind us, caught on the stems.

"You look like a Frida Kahlo painting," Mum told her. She stretched, peeling off her sweater and balling it beneath her head for a pillow. Underneath, her floral tent dress looked like she'd parachuted to earth.

"What painting?" Niko asked.

We all shuffled a little closer to Mum. Winter had been sinkhole central, but mentioning art—and finishing her ice cream at a normal speed—suggested she was emerging.

"*Self-Portrait with Cropped Hair*," she told us, her hands moving in and out of the wildflowers like butterflies. "The one with the song lyrics painted on the canvas. They go like this." She started swaying: "'Look, if I loved you it was because of your hair. Now that you are without hair, I don't love you anymore.'"

"No way." Emmy-Kate cackled, sitting up and throwing her hair over her shoulders like a shampoo ad. "You'll *always* love me," she added, preternaturally confident.

Mum hooted with laughter, grabbing Em around the waist and tickling her to death.

I reached for my sketch pad and felt-tips; Niko too. Emmy-Kate wriggled free so she could sign, "I'm going to draw *Self-Portrait with Amazing Hair*."

Mum laughed softly again, resting her arm across her eyes. Gradually, she fell asleep and time lapsed into birdsong. And without any discussion, the three of us merged brains, all sketching the same thing. Her.

Later, we compared drawings. I still have mine, pinned to my corkboard. In it, Mum has her eyes closed and she's lying down. Her dress is purple, spread out like a tablecloth. And she's in the air, not the grass. Floating halfway up, caught between Poets Corner and the sky.

Back in Ms. Goldenblatt's classroom, the bell rings. I put down my brush.

"Meet you on the steps after school," Felix says, shouldering his satchel. He pauses, looking at the self-portrait on my easel and raising his eyebrows, dark eyes glinting. "That's . . . That's really cool."

Look, if I loved you . . .

I examine my work. It's a true self-portrait this time: me, not Mum. Only I'm out of focus. Because maybe it's impossible to see myself clearly, when all I think about is her.

Turquoise
(An Ongoing List of Every
Color I Have Lost)

*Plastic school aprons. The Victoria line and
the biggest bubble in the* Rainbow Series I. *The
sky the morning Mum disappeared, with no hint
of the storm to come.*

CHAPTER 11

Much Longer Without Color, Minnie Will Freeze

I'm on the bus with Felix Waters.

We're traveling a few neighborhoods south of Poets Corner, our silent journey enlivened only by the gathering clouds. By the time we reach our destination, the day has turned squally, rain spitting down in occasional sporadic drops. We get off the bus and my hair instantly frizzes.

"Another park," says Felix, jamming on his beanie and squinting from me to the gates in confusion. It lends him a shy look instead of his usual arrested-in-a-pool-hall expression. For someone who doesn't wear a leather jacket, he has the motorbike-gang vibe down. "Aren't we supposed to go to a gallery?"

"Trust me, this is better," I say, leading him through the gates. This space is even bigger than Meadow Park, but flatter and more tree-filled, sheltering us from unexpected flurries of rain. "Follow me."

Felix stuffs his hands in his back pockets as we walk, so his elbows stick out when he twists to talk to me. "Another of your mum's pieces?" he asks.

I don't answer. We walk between an avenue of trees, the asphalt path littered with the first of autumn's shiny chestnuts, and emerge in front of an artificial lake—filled with dinosaurs.

Seriously. Life-sized ones. Thirty hulking concrete giantosauruses prowling through the shallow water, rustling ferns and terrorizing the ducks. Twenty-foot-tall prehistoric beasts, deep in London suburbia.

"Holy shit," says Felix, faintly impressed. "Welcome to Jurassic Park. Okay, better than a gallery," he admits, glancing at me. "What is this place?"

"They're Victorian," I explain. "From the Great Exhibition. The very first dinosaur sculptures in the world. They're hollow inside, like houses." We lean against the railing, watch the beasts. "One time, people had a New Year's Eve party in the Iguanadon." I point across the lake to a colossal, fat crocodile-y thing with hundreds of teeth. "When I was little, I wanted to move inside it and make it my bedroom."

I'd forgotten about that until I said it. Mini-Minnie, tucked inside a dinosaur house, no Niko or Emmy-Kate allowed. The same way I hid under the bed when Ash came round yesterday, or how I frequently slide myself under the bubbles of the *Rainbow Series I*. Huh.

"Careful," says Felix. "I think that one might actually be alive."

"They had dinner in it," I tell him. "Mock turtle soup, hare, pigeon pie, orange jelly."

"Okay, now I know you're inventing things." Felix straightens up—and looms. It's like standing next to Godzilla. He blinks down at me, face beaded with rain, bobbing his head to a nearby bench. "Shall we get on with it?"

We get settled with our sketch pads, the wind sending ripples across the lake, blurring the Megalosaurus and Ichthyosaurus behind waving ferns.

Felix fiddles with his phone. "Setting a timer," he explains. "It should keep going off at intervals. New drawings whenever it beeps, I guess."

I shrug. "Okay."

Ten seconds pass with my hands frozen over the page while Felix whips thick marker-pen lines across his paper. His phone beeps. I take a deep breath, trying to recall how it felt to draw the flowers in my room yesterday, but the phone beeps before I can relax into it. I make tiny scratchy marks on the page, but—*beep*.

I give up and watch Felix instead. For once he's not scrunched up. He's looking at the dinosaur, not the paper, flicking his wrists in loose, light movements.

I drag my finger through old raindrops on the bench, writing sentences that dissolve the moment they're formed.

WHERE ARE YOU? WHERE ARE YOU? WHERE ARE YOU?

"Listen," says Felix without looking away from the dinosaurs, or ceasing his hands' endless roaming. His words come out one by one, between the distractions of the drawing. "But"—*pen swipe*—"Okay, so"—*crosshatch*—"here's the thing"—*new page*—"about your mum."

Ugh. I huddle inside my coat, wishing conversations had an ejector seat. I don't want to hear his condolences, how sad he thinks it is. The world lost such a great artist, robbed of her potential, blah blah effing blah.

"Mine too," Felix says in such a low voice I almost don't catch the words. "Last year. Drunk driver. I was in the car. She died. I get it."

Beep.

Felix stops drawing and looks at me.

I look back.

Beneath his beanie, Felix's curls are getting darker and thicker instead of frizzing out the way mine do in this damp air. It makes him look Greek or Italian, like he should be climbing out of a lake in baking sunshine. But his sorrowful expression matches mine so closely we might as well be identical twins. And, oh, I see: It wasn't my mother he was mourning at the *Rainbow Series I*. It was his own.

So he does get it. Grief is a language that Felix speaks. Here in this cold park, with this unhappy boy, I can sink into my sadness like it's a feather duvet. My whole body sighs in succor.

"Anyway." Felix shrugs. His phone doesn't beep, but his hands return to his sketchbook anyway, start moving so fast they're a blur. The drawing seems to emerge of its own accord on the page, as if it already existed and time is catching up. This makes sense: The one person who gets me is another arthead.

Let's fill this town with artists . . .

"Let's what now?" Felix flicks his eyes to me briefly, then back to the dinosaurs.

Apparently, I'm now thinking out loud. Along with seeing Mum everywhere I look, losing all my colors, and drowning in the school cafeteria. I think of *The White Album*. I think of sinkholes. I think of Virginia Woolf's suicide letter, which begins: *Dearest. I feel certain that I am going mad again.*

I'm not certain if this is madness or grief.

I tilt my head back, letting the occasional rain freckle my eyes and face and lips.

"You know, I had the same thing when my mum . . . Back then, anyway. Artist's block." Felix gestures to the pad on my lap. I look down, seeing the streak his pen leaves on the dampening paper.

The ink bleeds across the page. I watch it blob and leak and form a flower, then say, "You think I have artist's block?"

"Don't you?"

I can see why he thinks that—my artist mother disappears and I stop creating. But it's not true. Toward the end of last year, when I got super-obsessed with those stupid tiles, I was already having dreams of the kiln not firing, pots shattering, glazes turning to air in my hands. Every time Ms. Goldenblatt pushed me to apply to SCAD, I wanted to turn inside out. When I walked down Full Moon Lane to the studio, I'd keep my eyes averted from the campus.

How can you want something so much but be afraid of it at the same time?

Wind gusts, splashing the lake all over me, and the rain finally begins to fall for real. I feel like a chalk sidewalk drawing, that I'll be washed away by morning. I put my sketchbook down and rest my chin on my knees.

Next to me, Felix has forgotten my existence again. He moves his pen in bold slashes, like a sword fighter, not noticing the rain. It's as if he's scooping up handfuls of it and smearing and smudging them, reshaping the weather into art, not caring that it's staining his skin, his clothes, until it's impossible to tell Felix from ink from rain.

I'm not sure whether he's painting the world, or the world is painting him.

And suddenly I know that I want to do *that*.

I don't want to be the girl who plays second fiddle to her sisters; who hides beneath clay bubbles and has all these colors trapped inside her heart.

I want to be the girl who lives in full effing color.

Burnt Orange
(An Ongoing List of Every Color I Have Lost)

*Chestnuts, like giant marbles scattered on sidewalks
from Crystal Palace to Poets Corner. Leaves
preparing to tumble from trees. The way autumn
is crunching quickly through time, and there are
now so many days between her and us.*

CHAPTER 12

The Color of Alabaster

I'm going to unlock the colors.

After school on Wednesday I'm alone in the house, for once. Heart going full brass band, I slip inside Mum's bedroom for the first time since spring, and go in search of her secrets.

The room is a museum. A mausoleum. The air is wreathed in her perfume and stale cigarettes—another ashtray overflows on her nightstand, next to a stack of art books. Evidence of a final all-night inspiration session, probably research for the *Schiaparelli* series. There's a lipstick-marked wineglass, and her duvet is balled up, as though she recently leaped out of bed.

It's obvious that Niko hasn't yet embarked on her threatened clear-out. It might make sense to wash the bedclothes, tip away these ashes, but it's so final. I'd preserve the whole room in resin if I could.

Dust swirls as I creep across the room, floorboards creaking gently beneath my bare feet. An evening dress is discarded across her chair; a pair of high-heeled sandals toppled underneath.

Her dressing table is the worst part. There's a pot of moisturizer with its lid off, dust gathering on the surface that still holds her finger marks. I screw the lid back on, then, irrationally, take it off again. Strands of pale hair trail from her hairbrush. A thickly glazed ceramic bowl is filled with silver earrings; another holds lipsticks in every shade of pink. Fuchsia, coral, Mexican, French, Barbie, shocking, carnation . . . I lift up her bottle of Noix de Tubéreuse and inhale, instantly regretting it when I'm hit by amber-and-violet *her*.

I swipe a finger through the dust on the mirror and write:

I MISS YOU. COME BACK.

"What am I doing?" I ask my wide-eyed reflection. Mirror Minnie has no answer. We turn away from each other, scanning the room for big honking clues. Something more than a goodbye letter and a kiln I don't yet dare open; something to tell me that Mum and I share a brain. That I'm right: She lost her colors too.

I skirt around the bed, not yet willing to touch the place she last slept. And I know that there's nothing underneath it but a plain, unlabeled shoebox, probably swathed in dust. My sisters and I discovered it a few years ago—Mum's room has never been part of the no-snooping agreement—tucked down in the dark. The only item in the house that doesn't match up to the Rachael Sloe aesthetic.

It's also another Sloe sister pact, an unspoken one this time: None of us open the box. Ever.

Pulse thumping in my ears, I hurtle to the bookshelf in the corner, which is stacked two-deep with research notes, old magazines in which she was interviewed or featured, folders of press clippings, exhibition catalogs, auction listings . . . The library of a life, lived. Somewhere in all this will be the origins of *The White Album*.

Grabbing a stack of ring binders, I perch gingerly on the arm of her chair, trying not to disturb the dress. I don't want to undo the folds she left in the fabric.

I start with an exhibition catalog from last year's retrospective at the Museum of Modern Art in New York. I've never seriously studied her work before, all the pieces at once, but as I flip through the pages, holy supersized, Batman.

I'm blown away by the epic scale. Seeing her whole output—even on paper, even in black and white—there's no escaping how bold and bodacious her work is. Every piece is a ten-ton, Stonehenge behemoth, fired in industrial kilns or made in several separate pieces at the studio and assembled with cranes.

The biographical snippets in her press cuttings are equally larger than life. Mum was accepted at every art school in London. She made the *Rainbow Series I* in her final year at SCAD, won the Turner Prize six months after graduation—when she was six months pregnant. She was only four years older than I am now. My heart sinks a bit. I can't imagine myself winning prizes and making art in four years' time. I can't imagine myself in four years' time, period.

Mum lived at the speed of light, trying to cram in all her experiences at once, as if she knew her life wasn't going to last long. But how could she have known at seventeen, at twenty-one? Unless the sinkholes started when she was as young as I am now. Perhaps that's why she hurtled full-tilt toward art: She craved color. Her life depended on it.

Only one profile comes close to identifying the sinkholes. I come across the paragraph in an interview from a couple of years ago:

Sloe starts talking at a rapid clip—so fast the recorder barely catches it—alluding to her synesthesia as a living thing, the closest most modern artists come to the nineteenth-century concept of muses. "I call it the madness gene," she says, amid edgy laughter. "It's living with all your senses turned up. But if I lost it . . . I wouldn't survive." She blinks, those blazing blue eyes looking a little lost themselves, for a moment.

I know the exact expression the journalist is talking about. When she would blink, slowly, more and more; her batteries beginning to shut down.

I check the date of the interview. Two summers ago. Was she already lost, back then? I don't remember a hint of a sinkhole. She showered every day. Sang along to the radio when I visited the studio on Saturdays. If anything, her super-human consumption of coffee and cigarettes and wine increased. She filled the house with flowers. Drank too much each night and clutched the Professor's arm while shrieking with laughter so often, Emmy-Kate began to theorize that they would get married. That summer she was so starlit, she was celestial.

I do remember getting up for a glass of water one muggy night and noticing the lights were on downstairs. When I crept into the kitchen, she was surging back and forth across the room, chainsmoking, her clay-covered smock billowing behind her.

"Mum?" I said.

She jumped, turning around with her hand pressed to her chest. "Jesus, honey." She puffed out smoke, then air, sounding annoyed. "Don't creep up. You frightened the life out of me."

"Sorry." I scuttled to the sink and started running the tap. "What are you doing up?"

"I'm not, really." She shook her head, stubbing out her cigarette. The ashtray on the table was full, a medicine bottle beside it. When she noticed me noticing this, and swept it into her pocket, out of sight, relief flowed through me. "I got back from checking on the kilns, and I was still a little revved up. I'm going to bed soon."

"Okay." I stood there uncertainly, holding my water. "So . . . 'night."

I crept upstairs to the Chaos Cave, listening out. Minutes later, I heard the front door opening and closing. She was heading back to the studio. It was after midnight.

I turn back to the article, noticing a new, unfamiliar word. *Synesthesia.*

My mouth moves, trying out the sound. Then I pick up my phone and google it.

OED. Definition of *synesthesia* in English:

synesthesia

NOUN

psychology A sensory perceptual phenomenon. An impression of one sense relating to another; e.g., the color of music.

Letters have colors. The number seven might smell of chocolate, while three has a hibiscus scent. Green can make you hear music; pink can taste like nectarines.

Or sometimes, maybe, colors could vanish . . . ?

Is that it? Mum had synesthesia. Do I?

"Probably."

I jump. Mum is standing by the window, looking out at the waning light. This is the first time I've imagined her wearing sinkhole clothes: baggy jeans and a sloppy sweater, cobwebbed with holes and hanging off her bird body. When she turns around, I see she's lost weight. Her collarbone sticks out. She tucks greasy hair behind her ear, revealing shadowed eyes, and smiles in a funereal kind of way.

"I am so fucking tired, Min," she says, slumping on the bed, landing on top of the duvet and making a muffled moan into her hands. Every hair on my body stands to attention.

"Mum? Mummy?"

She sighs, emerging from her hands and giving the mattress a desultory pat. I crawl into the space next to her, upset at how cold her skin is.

She's translucent, less vivid than the other times I've seen her. Does this mean I'm forgetting her? I don't want to. I want to hold on tight. Because how am I supposed to get the colors back without her, know if I'm crazy without her? She would know what to do. The same way she taught me everything about clay, everything about alchemy.

"Mum . . . I need your help with something."

"Did you know *There's No Blue in the Bible*?" she answers, cryptically.

Her second work after her comeback six years ago, shown in London's Tate Modern Turbine Hall. Vast, rounded slabs of every blue, interspersed with mirrors, filled the cavernous warehouse space. Walking through it felt like tiptoeing through the sky.

"Yeah. I remember." I bite my lip. "I've been thinking. I might want to make something different. Something . . . not clay."

She smiles in a broken way that sends my heart careering round my body, and says, "Wouldn't we all?"

Goose bumps run up and down my arms. "What do you mean?"

"Nothing." Mum sighs, wiping a hand across her face. Her voice is ultrafaint, like she's transmitting these thoughts from space. "There isn't any blue in the Bible."

"Mum!" I'm close to tears. "Stop being enigmatic and tell me."

"I *am* telling you, Minnie. You're not listening." She rolls over to face me, her hand reaching out and hovering over my huge hair but not quite touching me. She gives me a tiny smile. "There's my orange girl. Did you know zebras can't see orange?"

"No." Frustration nags at me. "Tell me about *The White Album*."

She shakes her head. "You know the answer."

"But I don't. Mum . . . I lost all my colors."

"Ah, Min. There are more colors in the world than you'll ever know about."

The door flies open and Mum fades from view.

I suppress nausea as Emmy-Kate barges in, resplendent in a tiny dress and Mum's shoes. When she sees me, her eyes bug out a little, but she doesn't seem excessively shocked. I get the impression this isn't her first time sneaking in here.

"Who were you talking to?" she asks, wrinkling her perfect nose.

"Myself," I tell her. Which is close to the truth. I don't believe in ghosts. It's not Mum I'm talking to but her memories.

"Weird," says Emmy-Kate. "Are you helping Niko tidy up Mum's room?"

"No. Go away—you're breaking the pact."

"So are you," she points out.

I throw a pillow at her.

She dodges it and starts slinking slowly around, peeping at me as she opens the wardrobe with an eerie creak, trails her fingers through the dresses there. Fiddles with the scarves draped over the bed's footboard. Picks up and puts down books, flits her eyes beneath the bed, and generally agitates me.

Without a care, she lifts up the evening dress from the chair and holds it against herself, examining her reflection. My hands make fists, but it's too late. The dress is ruined. I think about telling Emmy-Kate Mum is maybe dead, watching her face fall.

Instead, I take out my phone and type dementedly, writing *help I can't see any colors and I think I might be going mad* into Google and hitting GO.

"Can I have these?" Emmy-Kate holds up a pair of hammered-silver earrings. They dangle from her fingers, catching the light and flashing like fish in a fast-moving stream.

"Yeah, I suppose."

She smiles, hooking the earrings through her lobes and tossing back her mane of silken hair—a movement so identical to the one Mum would do before setting out for some party or gallery opening or awards ceremony, it smashes me into ten thousand smithereens. I look down.

My phone is showing the results of that ridiculous search. Link after link telling me to seek help, call the Samaritans or NHS Direct, talk to my GP—all things I have no intention of doing. Like Ms. Goldenblatt telling me to see the school counselor. And say what? *Dearest, I feel certain that I am going mad again . . .*

Because if I *am* going crazy, like her—what then?

A few searches down, a link catches my eye:

EnChroma | Color for the Color Blind

Enchroma.com

"EnChroma glasses open up a world of color for people with color blindness."

It turns out that "seeing the world through rose-tinted glasses" isn't only a metaphor. It's a pair of hi-tech color-correction sunglasses all the way from America. A $430 miracle. I pounce on the link, adding a pair of sunglasses to the online basket at random.

"Who are you texting?" Emmy-Kate cocks her head at me. "Ash?"

"None of your business," I reply automatically.

"Min-nie, who are you—"

"Emmy-Kate, go away, will you? Climb out of your window. *God.*"

She rushes from the room, slamming the door behind her with a gust of angry wind that wafts Mum's silk dressing gown and knocks her handbag from its hook.

She left it behind. Her phone and wallet were inside, but she took her studio key with her to Beachy Head. As though she planned to come back and open the kiln.

The police have touched and cataloged everything inside, from the broken lipstick stub to her old receipts, so it doesn't matter that I'm lifting it from the floor, finding her wallet, prizing out her credit card. This is something that doesn't need to be preserved in resin.

With trembling fingers, I type the credit card numbers into the box on enchroma.com.

A button flashes up: TO COMPLETE YOUR PURCHASE, CLICK "BUY NOW"!

I click, squashing the voice in my head that sounds like Emmy-Kate saying, *Minnie, what are you dooooiiiiiing.* Then I cover my tracks, restoring the room the way I found it. Putting the press clippings back on the shelves, refluffing the duvet, trying to rearrange the folds in the dress.

Emmy-Kate has spilled face powder on the dressing table. I smear it up with my sleeve, not wanting anything to inspire Niko to start her cleanathon. She'll strip the bed, remove the wineglass, delete all evidence that Mum lived and breathed and slept and dreamed in this room. She'll put away the books from the nightstand, and we'll never know what Mum was researching.

I double back and look at the stack. The top one is a coffee-table book of Georgia O'Keeffe, one of my favorite painters;

then there's a biography of Yves Klein—this cool French dude famous for inventing a new shade of blue. Everything comes back to color.

I take the books to my bedroom, then go downstairs and join my sisters for another sorrowful frozen dinner.

CHAPTER 13
The Color of Newsprint

There's a lilting breeze as I dawdle home from school on Friday, lifting litter in soft circles around my ankles, wafting London smells through the constant hum of traffic. Exhaust fumes and kebabs and the faint rot from overflowing garbage bins. I think about *The White Album* as I walk, letting my feet navigate these streets by memory.

I know this neighborhood by heart. The overground trains that rattle across my pillow as I fall asleep; my favorite florist next to the fairy-tale children's bookshop on Full Moon Lane. Neon-lit fried chicken shops, the independent cinema, bus stops and Meadow Park and the pool and towering oak trees. But I don't think I know who *I* am anymore.

With one step into the empty sky, Mum has made me a stranger to myself.

When I turn the corner onto my road, I immediately see Ash a few yards ahead. I'd forgotten I invited him over and anyway, he's earlier than I would have expected. It gives me a brief flash of annoyance.

With headphones on, he's oblivious to my footsteps behind him: He struts along, a supersized silhouette in his puffer coat, guitar strapped to his back. We're so close I could call out his name or toss a paper airplane past his shoulder or reach out my hand to touch his shoulder.

For some reason, I don't do any of those things. And the longer I wait to catch up and say hello, the more difficult it becomes. So I end up playing Red Light, Green Light, creeping behind him all the way to my house. I linger at the gate, next to a heap of whipped-cream roses, as he rings the doorbell. Through the transom window, I see the lights flashing.

Ash turns slightly, sliding his guitar from its straps, and catches sight of me standing there. Time syrups to a stop. All the recent awkwardness crash-lands on the path between us: Saturday's kiss. Me hiding under the bed. Creeping up behind him.

"Min?" Ash smiles, befuddled, clearly trying to work out how I've appeared from thin air. He pushes back his headphones, runs a hand through his hair.

"Um, boo?" I say. "Surprise."

The way things used to be between us: Ash would have gone supernova with amusement. He would have lifted me into a bear hug and spun me around and around like a merry-go-round.

Now: He chews on his lip, watching me carefully. He leans his guitar against the wall, then jumps down from the porch, smiling and coming to stand cautiously in front of me—it reminds me of the way we approach Salvador Dalí when he needs to go to the vet.

"How long have you been standing there?" he asks.

"I turned the corner, and there you were," I say.

Ash's eyes roam my face, the same way he reads sheet music. After a moment, he reaches out and tucks a strand of my hair behind my ear, smiling. I tilt my face up, like a flower toward the sun. It might be easier to kiss than to explain; and there's only so far we can go on the doorstep.

We kiss politely, mouths closed. Soft against mine, Ash's lips are dry and ever-so-slightly chapped; as familiar to me as Poets Corner. He's lovely, and lemony . . . but when I think of last weekend's hot-blooded-rolling-around-on-the-rug-wild-boner-out-of-control-super-kiss, I want to die.

Immediately want to unthink that thought.

I pull away with a slurping-suckerfish-toilet-plunger sound that makes Ash chuckle. He scratches the back of his neck, dimpling with confused amusement. Behind him, the front door is wiiiiiide open. And Niko is standing on the porch, watching us.

Guilt wraps around me like ivy. I instantly start reliving Bonfire Night last year.

The night was freezing, the air icy-clear. A snap-crackle-and-pop firework soundtrack played as we Sloes left the house, the sky covered in faraway sparks. Mum rapped on the Professor's door as we went by, hollering through the mail slot for him to come out and join us. When he emerged, a vision in tweed and an incongruous pom-pom-topped hat, Ash was with him.

By then, we'd known Ash a year, each of us nursing a separate, distinct crush. Emmy-Kate had a kind of hero worship; me, I straightforward plain *liked* him. But he and Niko, both university students, shared this inexplicable understanding, even though Ash's attempts at signing were slow and clunky. As he stepped out of the Professor's house, Ash went through his handclap routine with Emmy-Kate, bestowed me with a dazzling smile, then spelled out, intently, "H-E-L-L-O, N-O-K-I." She flushed, happily.

The six of us traipsed up Meadow Park's hill. It reminded me of when we were little, when Mum would lead us hand in hand like the tail of a kite. Only tonight, she was walking with the Professor, and Emmy-Kate was charging ahead, bobbing up and down through the crowd. She was wearing a sheepskin-lined aviator hat that made her look like Amelia Earhart. Every now and then I lost sight of her, before she'd reappear, earflaps bouncing.

Niko touched her hand to Ash's arm, commanding him to walk with her. She angled herself slightly away from me, keeping her distance from me and Em because she was a

SCAAAAAD student now. That was how she signed it: stretching the word in her fingers like toffee. It made me want to glue her hands together. Since enrolling at SCAD she home-signed less and used BSL more.

Through the sparkling dark, I watched them tentatively talking: signing slowly, lipreading, gestures, miscommunications and laughter. A language of their own, a little like the Sloe sisters'. Ash was clearly trying to tell her something about music; Niko formed chords in the air and he nodded.

When we reached the bonfire, the Professor spotted a group of friends, and Mum took Emmy-Kate to buy cotton candy. I produced a pack of sparklers from my pocket as Ash asked, "How's it going, Min?" The first time he'd spoken to me all night.

"I've never seen you without your guitar," I said, lighting a sparkler.

He laughed and started air-guitaring, like a total idiot. "This better?"

My heart did this overflowing Coca-Cola fizz thing, the sparkler beginning to crackle. I waved it as I signed, catching Niko up on the conversation and adding, "Incredible, was that 'Yellow Submarine'?"

Niko plucked the sparkler from my hand, dropping it in a puddle and stomping it with her boot. "They're not allowed, Min," she signed-said, rolling her eyes conspiratorially at Ash.

I stared at the ground, reduced to a toddler tantrum next

to willowy-tall Niko. Her auburn hair was piled into a ballerina bun, and the wide-open eyes she was batting were flicked with eyeliner. And Emmy-Kate, who was returning with a mound of cotton candy, was, well, Emmy-Kate.

When the first firework surprised us with a *whizbang*, the crowd surged forward, sending me stumbling sideways into Ash. His gloved hand wrapped around my wrist as he helped me upright, mouthing *All right?* and flashing me a smile as bright as the fireworks.

Another rocket exploded in a shower of dots, smearing smoke across the sky. Ash tilted his head down, saying, "Min, all right?" over the noise, his breath fogging the cold air.

His hand was still on my wrist. I stood on tiptoes to reply, and it made our faces not so very far apart. It gave me that Coca-Cola sensation again, and I thought of Niko and SCAAAAAD and the sparkler, and I said "Yeah" before quickly daring myself to kiss him.

A tiny experimental peck.

When I stepped back, Ash looked dazed and cross-eyed— as if he'd been bonked on the head with a frying pan—before breaking into his most dazzling grin. Over his shoulder, I saw Niko, her face painted with green light from the fireworks. Shock splashed across her face, the perfect eyeliner trickling down her cheeks.

Now, as Niko turns away from us, into the house, I catch a glimpse of the same expression on her face. And even though we're only a few feet apart, we might as well be on different continents. The animosity between us dates way back, to before the disappearance. But without Mum, I don't know how to find my way back to my sister. Motherless-me is lost without a map.

Rust

(An Ongoing List of Every
Color I Have Lost)

*Iron oxide. Pinwheel fireworks. The urban foxes
who strut through Poets Corner after dark,
scavenging from garbage bins and not giving a
hoot who sees them. Niko's glossy hair the night
I kissed Ash right in front of her.*

CHAPTER 14
The Color of Marble

The next morning, Saturday, Felix Waters comes slouching up the front path.

One minute I'm staring mindlessly out of the landing window, watching the crisp shadows turn the street into one of Niko's paper-cutout scenes. The next I'm thinking, *Hmm, that tall boy pushing open our gate looks familiar.* Then I go flying down the stairs.

I hop from foot to foot in the hallway, Rumpelstiltskin-style, then wrench open the front door before Felix can ring the bell. He's slumped against the porch, his hair a mass of bedhead. No beanie today, I note, though the jeans are as paint-covered as ever.

Through a yawn, he mumbles, "Hey, Minnie."

"Um, hi?" Confused, I step out onto the porch, half closing

the door behind me. The tiles are cool beneath my bare feet, the sunshine pale and creamy.

"What are you doing here?" I ask.

Felix holds up a sketch pad in ink-stained fingertips. "You never finished the homework. Thought we could try again."

"Oh." I fold my arms over my thin dress. My sisters are both upstairs, Ash said he'd come by again this morning, and the Professor's net curtains are probably already twitching: I don't want to invite this glowering, towering arthead into our domestic disharmony. I'm about to tell him to go away when curiosity gets the better of me: "How did you even know where I live, anyway?"

Felix gives me a smile so dark, it's a frown.

In black and white, I'd forgotten that our house is something of a spectacle. With its Jordan almond paintwork, chartreuse front door, and shiny, bee-shaped brass knocker, it sits in the middle of the brick terrace like a gift bow. A couple of TV channels even showed it on the news when we did the Missing People appeal, before the Professor made a series of barking phone calls on our behalf.

"Head's up, Alice in Wonderland . . ." says Felix.

I follow his gaze to my toes. Salvador Dalí has nudged open the door and is hopping out of the house, between my feet. I sigh, scooping him up, and bob my head for Felix to follow me inside. As I frog-march him through the house to the back door, I can sense his head swiveling at the bohemian decor, drinking in the bobbly rag rugs, endless Emmy-Kate originals, bright walls, miniatures of my mum's sculptures.

In the back garden, I plonk Salvador Dalí on the dew-anointed grass. He hops off to chew on a hydrangea.

"This is . . . wow," says Felix, looking around. "I half expect to see another dinosaur."

"Huh?"

"This garden. It's beyond," he continues. "Out of this world. Much more likely home for a—what did you call it? The thing with all the teeth."

"Iguanodon," I say. Seeing my life through Felix's eyes makes it all brand-new, the way I'm hoping the EnChroma glasses will transform everything back into color. I'm re-remembering the bright exterior, the art-crammed house, this wild jungle of a garden. It strikes me that none of us chose to be artists—but growing up here, within this aesthetic, there simply wasn't room for us to be anything else.

Felix retrieves a packet of cigarettes from his satchel. "Mind if I . . . ?"

I shrug in acquiescence. Emmy-Kate will probably come climbing out of her window any moment, and I don't want her to be encouraged to smoke, so I nod to Felix to follow me beneath a willow tree. The long branches form a bell jar, hiding us from view.

When we're ensconced in willow, Felix drops his sketchbook and satchel and leans back against the trunk. The boy can't handle being vertical—he's all slouch-hunch-lean. He kicks one boot up as he lights his cigarette and takes a deep drag. It's weird: I never thought I'd miss Mum's smoking—the way it made everything in the house smell stale and gross—but I do. I gulp in the scent.

"I can't believe this is London." He takes a long drag, then blows smoke from the corner of his mouth. His eyes are ringed in sleeplessness, panda-style. "I haven't seen this much greenery since we moved here."

"Are you joking? London is nothing but greenery."

"In what universe?" Felix shakes his head. "Could be you have to grow up here. Because all I see is concrete."

"Then you're not looking properly," I argue.

"Is that so?" He gives me a shark smile, watching me intently. The conversation between us flows the same way it did on dinosaur day: Something about our shared hopelessness is helping me to breathe a little easier.

"So, listen . . ." He puts out the cigarette on the bottom of his boot, discarding the stub in the wet grass without asking. I bristle, a little, and then he says, "I don't know if you've noticed, but I'm kind of an art nut? And Ms. Goldenblatt told me you'd be the best person to work with."

"I'm not," I reply quickly, although I'm secretly touched that Ms. Goldenblatt said that.

"Well, I didn't think so either." The joke is so unexpected—I didn't know the Prince of Darkness had a sense of humor—it makes me gawk. Felix gives me the ghost of a wink and says,

"But why not hang out with me anyway? I hear London has all this greenery we could draw."

"Because—" I'm answering automatically, then stop. Am I really going to tell him this? Apparently, yes: I don't know why, but the words are bubbling up in my chest, long overdue. I look away—to the dappled sunlight dancing through the willow branches, making the world spin like a mirror ball—and admit, "Because I lost all my colors. When my mum left. They faded out. The way the red leaches out of the paint in old paintings or something. Only it wasn't only red. It was everything. She was gone and so were they. Everything I see is black and white."

A train rumbles by, somewhere above us. In the distance, there's traffic, a dog barking, BBC Radio 4 wafting through a neighbor's open window. The Professor's, probably. I peep at Felix to see how bananas he thinks I am.

"That makes sense," he says, nodding with understanding. "So how—"

"Hey, Minnie, what are you doing?" Emmy-Kate's disembodied head pokes through the branches. She's dressed for the pool. When she spies Felix, her eyes dart from me to him, and narrow in suspicion. She signs, "Who the Leonardo da Vinci is this?"

. . . . .

When we follow her into the kitchen, Emmy-Kate hops up onto her usual gargoyle perch on the counter and folds her arms. Niko is deep in slow, concentrated conversation with the Professor at the table, his hands steepling between each sign like errant pauses. He stands up when we come in. Everyone stares at Felix. At me with Felix. The way they're looking at us, it's as if we came in holding hands.

I can't be bothered to explain what we were doing in the garden together; I sign and say, "This is Felix Waters. He goes to Poets Corner High."

"We're in art together," Felix adds, while I translate. As if the paintbrush in his pocket and the mess on his clothes and the tousled hair didn't make this obvious. He looks like he walked here from beatnik Paris.

There's this hour-long pause where none of us know how to behave. We haven't had visitors in the house since those early weeks, when we were overrun with social workers and police; and they took charge of the conversations. It's only now occurring to me that we should have had visitors—where were Mum's friends from the art world? Old SCAD colleagues?

Emmy-Kate and Niko are both staring daggers at Felix for some reason. Finally the Professor bumbles into action, blustering across the room, holding out his hand. "Professor Rajesh Gupta." He actually says that, the professor part.

"I heard about . . . your . . . wife?" says Felix, questioning me with a glance as he accepts the Professor's hand. He notices how I'm signing everything that's spoken and looks around quizzically. "I'm sorry."

Something spills over the Professor; he folds into himself for a minute. Probably communicating with his home planet. Then he shakes it off, saying, "Ah, hmm, no. I'm the girls' neighbor." Felix nods, puzzled, as the Professor continues. "You might already know the er—Emmy-Kate and Niko."

Emmy-Kate says sulkily: "I'm the *er*—Emmy-Kate."

When Felix turns to her, Niko signs-says hello. She taps her ear with two fingers, the sign for Deaf. In case Felix doesn't get it, she does it twice, before shaking her head firmly, and signing meaningless mumbo-jumbo that has more in common with the hand jive than BSL. This is what she does to test people on first meeting, to see if they're the kind who stare.

Her fingertips are free from bandages and paper cuts. I haven't seen her with a knife or scissors in a little while, actually.

"Is Felix staying for breakfast?" Emmy-Kate asks. Then adds, in BSL only, "Perhaps he can sit next to Ash."

"What are you talking about?" I frown, as we switch into silent Sloe-sister conversation. Although, for some reason, I'm relieved that Ash isn't here yet. "Felix came over to do homework. He's an arthead, like us."

"Oh, really?" Emmy-Kate hops down and plants herself in front of Felix. "I paint. These are my paintings," she tells him, gesturing to me to interpret for Niko. Signing and speaking is like simultaneous translation—it's easier for me and Em to take turns interpreting. "The paper work is Niko's; Mum does the ceramics, obviously; Minnie too." Her eyes are blazing. "What do you do?"

"I'm into clay," he tells her, unfazed. "Porcelain, actually. Some charcoal. Pen-and-ink. A little bit of everything."

"Huh." She scoffs. "You need to focus. Monet didn't invent impressionism by *dabbling*."

"Well, what about Michelangelo?" Felix counters. Entering this impromptu art debate, he stops slouching, stands upright. Brooding Boy becomes the Energizer Bunny. And am I over-thinking this, or does he keep looking in my direction? "That dude sculpted in marble, painted the Sistine Chapel, wrote po-etry, he was an architect . . ."

"Pffffft, special case," says Emmy-Kate dismissively.

As they argue, swapping favorite artists back and forth, the kitchen recedes. Emmy-Kate marches Felix around the room, trying to intimidate him with a tour of her greatest hits. The Professor stands forgotten by the table. Niko watches me trans-late the debate, smirking. I lean against the counter, wonder-ing what Ash will think of all this when he arrives.

Mum sticks her head through the open back door. Unlike everything else in the room, she's neon: yellow hair and blue eyes and Barbie lipstick. She's got her gardening gloves on, and denim dungarees that match Niko's.

"Pssst, Minnie," she hisses. "Come on, let's go."

Even though it leaves Niko on the outskirts of the Emmy-Kate/Felix argument, I follow Mum outside, walking through the garden and out onto the street.

I wonder what Felix would say if I confessed this element

of my monochromacy, that I see my missing mother in color. Back away slowly, not meeting my eye, probably.

When we reach the main road, Mum throws herself onto a bench outside the Full Moon Inn. The hulking and Harry Potterish pub presides over Poets Corner, heralding the promise of Full Moon Lane's mile-long stretch of bakeries and bookshops. It's a building fit for Beauty *and* the Beast.

"Wow." Mum exhales, peeling off her gloves and throwing them into her lap, then turns to me with a wicked smile. "Oh, boy. Wow—again."

"Um, what wow?"

"That bee-yoo-tiful boy, Minnie. The one you couldn't take your eyes off in the kitchen, Felix. You know why he knocked on the door this morning, don't you?"

"Actually, he *didn't* knock . . ."

"Details." She waves her hand, dismissing me, a pearl ring on her finger the size of a gobstopper. "He reminds me of the boys at SCAD—you know, there's a reason I graduated pregnant . . ." She nudges me, laughing. "Here comes trouble . . ."

"I don't think so," I tell her. "I'm going out with Ash, remember?"

Mum raises an eyebrow. "Isn't Ash why you left the house?"

"I left the house because you showed up . . ."

"Hmm, and who's in charge of that?" She points to the road. "Here he comes."

"Ash?" I spin around, follow her gaze.

Ash is coming down the steps from Poets Corner station,

not noticing me as he turns away down the road that leads toward my house, taking a swaggering sidestep to avoid walking into Felix—who's heading straight for me. I hold my breath, instantly aware that I don't want them to meet. I don't know why: perhaps because of what Mum said, that Felix is *bee-yoo-tiful*. And trouble. And I told him about my monochromacy when I haven't yet told my boyfriend.

Luckily, it's London and they're strangers: they pass within a hair's breadth, ignoring each other, totally unaware of the person they have in common. Ash bounces from view and Felix arrives, all Doc Martens swagger and scowl. He sits down next to me, right where Mum was, but isn't now.

"Hey, again," he says.

I stare at his profile. There's a smudge of paint on his jaw that I didn't notice before, near his beauty marks. He has three—chin, cheekbone, and one beneath his left eye, like a comma.

"Are you stalking me?" I ask.

He cocks his head. "I live here."

"You *live* in the Full Moon Inn?"

"My dad's the new landlord." He says this in a *no trespassing* tone.

I nod and lift my feet onto the bench, circling my arms around my knees. Resting my chin on them, I watch the traffic queuing up to drive under the railway arch.

"So I had this idea," says Felix, as though everything is totally normal and I didn't walk out of my house barefoot in the middle of a conversation. "Your scary sister inspired me, actually—she's a force of nature. Anyway, I've worked out how to fix your whole monochrome deal. Close your eyes."

I shoot him a glance and he urges, "Trust me."

Feeling idiotic, I close my eyes. The sun plays patterns on my eyelids as Felix's low rumble of a voice washes over me: "Now tell me about your favorite piece."

"I feel like I'm being hypnotized."

"You are getting very sleepy . . . Come on."

"My favorite piece of art? It's a sculpture."

"Yeah? Is it in London? Could we go and see it? Keep your eyes closed."

"Yes. Well, no." I shake my head. "It's at Tate Britain. That's over the river from here, miles away. And it's not on display anyway. It's in the archives. You'd have to be a SCAD student or a historian to get permission to see it."

"So how do you know about it?" Felix asks. "What's so great about it, if it's hidden in a cupboard?"

"The original is still on display; that's where I saw it. In Paris . . ."

"La-di-da."

I smile, putting my arms behind me on the bench, stretching my legs out, basking in the sun. The day has warmed up. This is nice—bizarre, but nice—talking with my eyes closed. Without my weirdo vision, my other senses come alive. London's soft soundtrack. The faint smell of cigarettes from Felix, his spicy cologne. The sculpture I'm talking about grows more distinct.

I saw it when Mum took us with her on a research trip to Paris; a holiday where Emmy-Kate ate so many crepes, she threw up in the Louvre. I smile again at the memory.

"Why will this help me get my colors back?"

"Step one is thinking about the piece of art that speaks to you the most." *Felix has a great voice*, I find myself thinking. The kind that could do voiceovers for film trailers. "The thing you connect with. Step two is working out why you like it. Step three, you create something that makes you feel that same way. Step four is boom, your colors come back."

"You think it would work that easily?"

"Worth a try." He adds, gently mocking, "So, go on. Tell me about this fancy Parisian sculpture."

"Well, it's white," I say, "so it might not be much help. White marble. Two people. Rodin—the artist, Auguste Rodin—he found the glow inside the stone. This couple are kissing their way out of the stone, and it's practically giving off light." I smile one more time, remembering seeing it in the artist's house on the Left Bank, sun pouring in through the windows. The rose gardens outside reminded me of Meadow Park.

"You're talking about *The Kiss*," says Felix. My eyes fly open. He's giving me a look so intense it could be X-ray vision.

My fingers are tingling, pins and needles running up and down my arms. I'm surprised to find I want to plunge my hands into clay, or grab a hammer and chisel and attack a block of stone. I can feel the marble beneath my palms, cool and inviting.

"I would love," says Felix, "to see *The Kiss* in real life. It looks like a sculpture worth lying underneath."

He holds my gaze so wolfishly I wonder if I'm Little Red Riding Hood. And too late, I remember why there are multiple versions of this particular artwork. The French original tells the tale of adulterous lovers: It's famous for the couple almost falling over with lust, almost falling out of the stone in their passion. A near-identical edition was made for London, with one key addition: It was specifically commissioned to emphasize the man's arousal.

I rhapsodized to Felix Waters about A GIANT FRENCH HARD-ON.

"You could make something like that," he says in a voice so deep it could be a bottomless lake. "Harness the light that way. Have you ever made porcelain?"

Liquid clay. Completely different thing from Mum's heavy pots. Instead of shaping it on the wheel, you pour it into molds and tip out the excess, forming a shell as thin and delicate as a robin's egg. When fired, it turns white and almost translucent, with a kind of luminosity. That's the theory, anyway, but I've never tried it.

I tell Felix this and he says, blinking a sweep of dark lashes, "You know, I could teach you. If you want . . ."

The air is humming with possibility. My sisters' glares come back to me, along with Mum's words: *Here comes trouble.* Holy effing Gustav Klimt: Do they think . . . ? Did Felix knock on my door this morning for a reason? We're still staring at each other when a bus roars by, blowing dust and leaves across the sidewalk and sweeping my hair around, transforming me into the love child of a yeti and Cousin It.

Felix reaches out his hand and pushes the strands away.

As he tucks my hair behind my ear, his fingers graze my cheek. He leaves them there for a few seconds, his clay-dry skin against mine. I should say the words "I have a boyfriend," but I'm having trouble breathing.

Because this small moment feels enormous. Like a pin pushed into a map. A declaration. A flag planted on the effing moon. The beginning of something.

Brown
(An Ongoing List of Every
Color I Have Lost)

Sloe sister can't-keep-a-secret eyes, though it
turns out we can—I'm a treasure trove of secrets.
The acorns scattered in Meadow Park, burnished
gold. Leaves about to fall to the earth all over
London, like pennies from heaven,
and the same coppery color.

CHAPTER 15

The Color of Pigeons

A nonstop train goes zooming through Poets Corner, blasting its horn.

We both startle, the mood instantly broken. Felix whisks his hand from my hair and we stand up, smoothing our clothes and looking everywhere but at each other. In the aftermath of the train, a hush settles: pigeons coo-cooing, Full Moon Lane's constant quiet hum of traffic; footsteps of passersby and playful shouts drifting over from Meadow Park.

I stare at my feet, which are filthy with sidewalk grime. Perhaps I do have a little bit of Mum's impetuous joie de vivre after all . . .

After a minute, Felix scuffs his boot and says, "I'll never get over how noisy London is."

I look up, pulling my best *you're bananas* face.

"Are you joking? This is idyllic." I point through the

railway arch to Meadow Park. "And there's that greenery you were looking for."

"To a city slicker like you."

"Where did you live before, then, if not a city?"

"Holksea. It's a village about yay-big, in Norfolk." He holds his hands an inch apart. "The loudest thing I ever heard there was next door's chickens."

"Seriously? You're a farmer boy?" I smile at this discovery, a fleeting moment of joy—Big Bad Doc Martens Boot-Wearing Felix is a tractor-riding, pig-racing, field-plowing hayseed—before catching his eye again.

He's looking at me with the same desperate sadness as always, and I'm suddenly right back there with him. Perhaps the two of us are a separate species to everyone around us, one with turbulent sorrow written into our DNA.

Perhaps this is why, when he asks if he can walk me to school on Monday, I say yes.

. . . . .

As I wander home, I think about *The Kiss* and the way Rodin uncovered the glow deep within the marble, like an archaeologist of light. If Felix is right about recreating it in porcelain, I'll have to go back to Mum's studio.

I stop dead in the middle of the sidewalk. Duh, Minnie. Of course I'm going back to the studio! Where else will I unlock the colors and discover what was going through her mind in June? It's so stupidly obvious, I can't believe I haven't thought of it before. I don't know what stops me from running there right now, instead of pushing open the back gate and going into the kitchen, where the Professor and Emmy-Kate have vamoosed and Niko is mopping the floor.

The room reeks of bleach. The sink overflows with bubbles. Cupboards are hanging open and empty, their contents piled on the table along with the fridge-door detritus—magnets, notes, photographs, postcards. Alarm bells start ringing in my chest.

Niko ditches the mop and grabs a garbage bag. She flaps it open—it makes a noise like bats taking off—and turns to the table, sweeping almost-empty jars into it. Her arm catches a pile of postcards; one goes tumbling into the bag.

I march over to her and snatch it back from the brink. Mum's handwriting is on the back. I liquefy, as if I'm holding the goodbye letter all over again and not a photograph of Venice, sent during the Biennale a couple of years ago.

A fumbled finger click drags my attention from the smudged ink. Niko is wearing rubber gloves. She drops the garbage bag between our feet and yanks them off so she can sign, "Where the hell have you been, Minnie? It's not okay to walk out of the house without a word, in the middle of a conversation."

I ignore her—and the sour guilt in my stomach—and flap the postcard. "What's this? You're throwing away her things?"

"I'm not throwing away anything. That fell in by accident." She points to a can at random. "We've got chickpeas dating

143

back to before the *Rainbow Series I*, and the fridge magnets are covered in grime. Someone has to clean this place up."

"Don't throw any of her things away."

"Some stuff has to go, Minnie. We don't need a cupboard full of cigarettes." Niko stalks over to the sink and grabs a spray bottle of something caustic, squirting it on the counter. Then puts it down and turns around. "I'm not going to throw away anything important."

"You'd better not."

She tilts her head back, looking down her nose. "You're one to talk."

"What does *that* mean?"

I can't work out why she's being so extra until she signs bitterly, "Ash. He's in your room."

We stare at each other for a moment, then she turns away abruptly, starts scrubbing the laminate right off the counter. Chastened, I plod slowly up to the Chaos Cave, where Ash is sitting on the stairs outside my door. I remember what imaginary Mum said, about him being the reason I left the house. Is that true? Did I conjure her as an excuse?

Ash is wearing a blanket of bleak. His guitar is ignored at his side and he's staring off into space. It empties my insides out: He looks like an Ash without music, the same way I'm a Minnie without color. Fear arrives: Maybe he saw me with Felix Waters. What was I even thinking, arranging to walk to school with him? Confessing my monochromacy, letting him run his fingers through my hair! I didn't even tell him I have a boyfriend.

"Hey . . ." I poke Ash's knee with my toe. He looks up, and the freaky, music-less version of him is replaced with an unsmiling one.

"Hey, Min." He examines me from flushed face to dirty feet. It feels like he can see right down to my conscience. "Where've you been, mucky pup?"

"Meadow Park," I lie, sitting down next to him and resting my head on his shoulder. It doesn't feel right, and I sit up straight again.

"Yeah?" asks Ash uninterestedly. Almost . . . annoyed. "Did you forget I was coming over? I texted you."

"I left my phone in my room." This, at least, is true. "Sorry."

"Your phone, your shoes, me." He sighs, lifting my hand into his. Our fingers refuse to interlace, and sit there, lumpenly. "What's going on with you lately, Min?"

"What do you mean?" My voice is loud in response to what feels like an accusation.

Ash twists toward me. His round eyes are warm as they search mine. "I'm worried about you."

"I'm fine."

"I know you are. But this isn't the first time you've left your phone behind and gone wandering off. I feel like . . ." Ash chews on his lip. I chew on my guilt; it tastes like seawater. "Like you're avoiding me and that. That you're not all there. Like you're disappearing on me."

"Disappearing?" I can't believe he said that.

He screws up his face. "Bad choice of words. I mean, you're

always zoning out. And . . . Niko told me some dude was over this morning?"

I gasp, trying to turn it into a deep breath, my face burning. "That was Felix," I mutter. "He's new at school. We got assigned to be homework partners in art."

Ash frowns. "And you were doing this homework barefoot in the park?"

"Artist, remember?" I say, making my voice bubblegum like Emmy-Kate's. "We're nuts."

Gradually, the concern clears from Ash's face. "That's good, Min," he says. "I'm glad you're, you know, feeling better about stuff. Getting back into the swing of things." His spare hand begins drumming absently against his thigh, the music coming back to his body. "Listen, party at my house tonight. I'm DJing. You want to come?"

"I don't think so," I say. Ash's face clouds over, so impulsively I add, "But do you want to come with me to my mum's studio tomorrow? After school."

"All right. Yeah, can do. I mean, if you're sure," he says, not sounding elated about the idea. His hand is super-drumming now. Any minute now, he'll grab his guitar. I have about ten seconds left of his full attention.

"Ash, do you know a sculpture by Auguste Rodin?" I ask. "Called *The Kiss*."

"No, but I know a sculpture called *The Kiss* by me, Shashi Gupta." He smooches my cheek, holding the pose even when I start to laugh—I can't help it. When he pulls away, he grabs his guitar, starts tuning it. "You know me and art, Min," he adds, bending over the guitar. "In one ear and out the other."

I try again: "What would you say if I told you I couldn't see colors anymore? Like, everything was in black and white. Even you and me."

Ash doesn't look up. He chuckles softly to himself, adjusting the tuning pegs. "I'd say you're cuckoo," he says, shaking his head in amusement, but I can tell he's not really listening anymore. "Is this what they teach you in art lessons these days?"

Then, with a wink, he starts to play.

Duck Egg
(An Ongoing List of Every
Color I Have Lost)

Eggshells. Emmy-Kate's swimming towel.
Mum's eyes when she was starlit. A painting
I love called Blue and Green Music *by*
Georgia O'Keeffe.

CHAPTER 16
Blanc de Blanc

Rain steals into my dreams, pattering on the attic roof and tapping at the windows. On Monday morning I roll over and stick my head underneath the curtains, peer out at the garden, now underwater. The deluge knocks all energy from me.

I hide under the duvet until my alarm clock shouts a warning, then waste ten minutes banging on the bathroom door, where Emmy-Kate is busy steaming herself like a lobster. Then I give up, racing back upstairs and weatherproofing my hair: weaving it into two plaits, wrapping them around my head. In the mirror is a pen-and-ink-Heidi version of myself. Late, I throw on a dress and tights, pick up my bag, and grab the studio key. It falls from its ribbon again, clattering onto the desk. Eff. Carefully, even though I don't have time, I slide it back on the ribbon and tie it in a double knot around my neck.

Downstairs, rain has smothered the house in despair. The kitchen has a pallor that reminds me of gardens in winter, when the earth freezes over, roots go dormant, and not even weeds grow. Niko is at the table, slumped over a plate of burnt toast. She glances up, sees me hesitating in the doorway.

"Hurry up, Minnie, you'll be late for school . . ." The command is listless, with none of her usual regal authority. And she's distracted as she leaves for SCAD, abandoning her charred toast, drifting from the room.

The only sound is the rain's insistent thrum and the wind as it whips through Poets Corner and into every nook and cranny of the house. Then a knock at the back door.

It squeaks open to reveal Felix Waters and about half the sky. He's sopping, dripping all over the floor as he steps inside. It's as if the direct descendant of young Monet walked into the kitchen. (Dictionary definition of tall, dark, and smoldering.) How am I only just noticing this? Felix is gorgeous. My cheeks flame.

"Hey, Minnie," he says, shaking the rain from his hair. "You ready?"

I nod, speechless. We're walking out the back door as Emmy-Kate clatters into the room from the hallway. She takes in the scene—Felix and me, side by side—and tilts her head. "Is that your toast you've burnt, Minnie? Gosh, it's really *ashen*, isn't it?" She sounds like a human stinging nettle. She glares pointedly for a moment, then pushes past us, storming off to school.

"Have you thought any more about *The Kiss*?" Felix asks as

we start fighting our way through the rain as well. "And what we talked about on Saturday, about getting your colors back by making something?"

"Yes, actually," I tell him. I'm distracted, keeping an eye out for Em. But she's miles ahead and cloaked from view. It's one of those washout autumn cloudbursts that floods gutters and steams buses. Every car that swishes past sends up sheets of water. Without thinking, I say to Felix, "Actually, I think I'm going to go back to my mum's studio after school."

"Oh yeah?" Felix gives me a disconcerting look, then veers abruptly sideways, ducking under the awning of the Bluebird Bakery and through the door.

I follow him inside. The bakery smells of bacon and damp and heat; the steamy air instantly undoes my plaits. I fluff my hair out to hide my burning face, wishing I hadn't mentioned the studio when I'm meant to be meeting Ash there.

"What are we doing?" I ask over the clank of the coffee machine.

Felix replies with something I can't quite hear. I shake my head. "What?"

He leans down, cupping his hand to my ear. "Trust me," he says in a warm, low voice, like he's confiding a secret. "I discovered the chocolate croissants my first week here. Worth being in London for. And a girl can't live on ashen toast alone."

Felix straightens up, ordering croissants as though nothing has happened. I'm knocked sideways. I concentrate on listing the pastries behind the glass counter, trying to shake off the feeling of him whispering in my ear—how intimate it felt, like he was peeling off my bra. God. Where are these thoughts coming from? And what about Ash? Danish, cinnamon bun, iced bun, pain au chocolate, almond croissant, English muffin, muffin, palmier, Felix's hand on my cheek, his warm breath . . .

"Tell me about your mum's studio," he says once we're out in the rain again, croissants in hand. "You said go back there?"

"Um." I'm pushing my hood down to eat my croissant, and my huge hair starts blowing every which way; wet strands whipping across my face as I answer. "I haven't been there in a while. Like, all summer. But if I want to get my colors back . . ."

". . . it has to be there," Felix says, understanding immediately. "What do you plan on making?"

"I don't know yet." I take another bite of croissant, and my mouth floods with liquid chocolate. It makes my brain blur. I shouldn't be talking to Felix about the studio—an arthead who's a fan, who found our house easily enough. What if he shows up there? "She mostly worked in earthenware. But I thought I'd try porcelain, like you said . . ."

"Yeah?" Felix swivels, looking down at me, a dark smile forming. "You want me to show you how? I'm not saying I'm an expert, but I'm pretty good."

I take another bite of warm croissant to give me time to think. The chocolate tastes like leaf buds in spring. "I do," I say eventually, "but not today. I kind of need to go there alone."

"Got it." Felix nods, finishing his croissant and balling up the paper bag, drop-kicking it into the trash. We're almost at school, but I don't want us to be there yet.

Clearly, neither does Felix, because he stops dead in the middle of the sidewalk, and turns to me. I'm afraid to look at his face. I watch our feet instead. Our boots are being pelted with rain, shimmering white splashes of it.

"Minnie . . ." Felix says my name in a strangled voice, pulling my head up like a magnet.

Our eyes meet and lock. After a few thousand years of staring at each other, he swipes a hand through his hair, knocking his beanie into a puddle—I don't think he even notices. Water is streaming down his cheekbones, running over his lips. My rib cage contracts in a slow, painful squeeze.

"Jesus, you're so pretty," he mutters.

And in the last second before the bell rings and makes us both late, I hear the beat of my own heart, like a gleaming gold clock.

Gold
(An Ongoing List of Every
Color I Have Lost)

*Chocolate coins, the end of a rainbow, sunsets,
shooting stars, secrets, Felix.*

CHAPTER 17

The Color of Moonstone

By the time school finishes, it's no longer raining; the sky is scrubbed clean of cloud. I decide to walk the couple of miles to the studio. As I pick my way along Full Moon Lane, stepping between sidewalk rivers, I feel like I'm caught on a river of my own, swept away by Felix's reckless words to me this morning. During our art lesson, the tension between us required an exhibition title: *What Happens Next?*

And now here I am, on my way to meet my boyfriend.

Like half of south London, Mum's studio sits between overhead railway lines. She has a solo space taking up the whole of one of the arches—the others are shared by painters, furniture makers, jewelers, craftspeople, collectives. Soggy bunting snaps in the wind as I enter the huge, brick-walled yard. Each studio has a giant, semi-circular metal door, made for a supersize Bilbo

Baggins. Most of them are shut, light spilling from the cracks, reminding me of Niko and her candlelit séance-Ouija-whatevers.

Ash is loitering next to Mum's, wearing a ginormous sheepskin coat. He's bopping his head, tapping his foot, doesn't take off his headphones as I approach. Acting as though his first time at her studio is as inconsequential as queuing for a late-night kebab.

"All right, Miniature!" he yells.

I wince, gesturing at my ears.

"OH YEAH," he shouts, pulling them off. A drop of rain lands on his face. The afternoon is growing cooler, the air softer. I'm afraid Ash will read me like an open book—or a neon sign by an English artist called Tracey Emin, looping light-up handwriting saying:

MINNIE AND FELIX ARE . . . SOMETHING

But all he seems to see is my enormous halo of hair. "I like this look," he says, fluffing the curls with a finger. "Bananarama meets Bon Jovi."

I have no idea if that's a compliment, but I say: "Thanks." Another quick splat of rain lands. "How was your house party?"

"Banging."

Neither of us moves to kiss each other. Ash and Minnie have been replaced by robot versions, who aren't sure of the correct motions. I plonk my arms around his neck and he steps politely forward into my embrace. The hug feels hollow, like a tree. Our bodies are slotting into each other's angles automatically, but the rain has wiped out Ash's lemon-coconut scent and the essence of *us*. We're not quite fitting together.

I take a couple of steps backward. It's starting to rain again for real now and, all around us, it's transforming the yard into the scene from thirteen weeks ago. Puddles begin to ripple and polka-dot as the sky drops down, the air shifts, shadows coalesce.

"Brrrr. Are you ready to head inside?" Ash asks, tugging on his earlobe. I barely hear him. I'm looking into the past, at flashing red lights reflected in every puddle.

I'm seeing again the police car screeching to a halt, siren whooping, because on the phone all I said was, "She's dead, she's dead, please come."

"Min." Ash puts his hand on my shoulder, making me jump. "Easy," he says, the way you would to a runaway horse. "I don't want to rush you, but we're getting sopping out here . . ."

"Yeah, okay." I fumble for the key, jitters making their creepy-crawly way along my arms. What are we going to find inside? What if Mum didn't do it at Beachy Head? What if she doubled back and came here? What if she's inside? Stupid. She *wouldn't*. The worst I can expect is dirt. Three months of dust and cobwebs and that peculiar, damp coldness you only get in empty buildings.

I unlock the door and yank it across the asphalt with a rat-a-tat-tat boom that judders my ribs. A trickle of dread runs down my spine as we step inside and I click on the light. It buzzes once, twice, then floods the room in harsh, unforgiving fluorescence.

Ash coughs, wafting a hand in front of his face. "Sorry," he says huskily.

The dust is at Sahara levels. This is normal, an unavoidable side effect of ceramics—clay, plaster of Paris, powder glazes. They're all, essentially, dust. It's a crematorium.

I step slowly past Ash, who's still spluttering. My body stirs the surprisingly warm air, which gives off a waft of her perfume. Jesus. It's like walking through her ghost. I'm already lifting up my arms, wanting to embrace her, wanting to touch her, but there's nothing to hold on to.

I turn away, trying not to breathe.

There's a dirty coffee cup on a worktable, the rim still printed with her lipstick mouth. Black against the white china. Tiny fruit flies buzz around the syrupy dregs. I waft them away and lift the mug up, carrying it to the kitchenette, arms trembling.

The tap is dripping into the metal sink. It makes a faint, creepy echo that brings me out in goose pimples. The room doesn't feel empty and dank, the way you'd expect after three months; it's warm and dry. Everything is so exactly as she left it—from this mug to the blinking light on the kiln—that walking through the space is like reading a book full of unfinished sentences. The drainboard is heaped with buckets and jugs and jars, paintbrushes. I reach out and squeeze one. The bristles are damp, like it's only been recently used. My heart scurries and skips.

Carefully, I fill the mug with water to get rid of the coffee without removing her lipstick. I catch sight of my reflection—a bonkers girl with voluminous gray hair, holding an ocean of foolish hope in her hands.

"Is it always like this?" asks Ash curiously.

"Like what?" I turn round, trying to see what he sees, if he can see evidence of her the way I'm starting to.

The concrete floor is swirled with old mop marks and thick with dust. There are miles of shelving lining the walls, bowed beneath test pieces and experiments and jars of glaze powders. There are cloths over the out-of-action kilns, turning them into squat, square ghosts. Milk crates holding equipment are stashed under every table and workbench; books are piled and strewn haphazardly. In other words, it's mayhem. She could have been here the minute before we arrived, mixing up a glaze or kneading clay, before rushing out to grab cigarettes or food.

Seeing her space so casually abandoned is a sharp knife to my heart.

"It looks like your room," Ash says, giving me a tentative smile. He's been prowling around the studio, carefully avoiding touching anything. Now he waits in the doorway out of the rain, watching me.

I turn away, trying to tune in to this peculiar sensation the studio is giving me. I want so much to believe that Mum has been here.

There's a book open on the workbench, cigarette ash scattered on the pages.

A picture is forming in my mind, of her climbing out of the sea—like Botticelli's *Birth of Venus* painting—and returning. Throwing out *Schiaparelli* and starting over with a new series.

I pick up a smooth, prekneaded ball of clay from a stack of them, each wrapped in a plastic sandwich bag, and weigh it in my hand. Didn't I feel her presence watching me in the walled garden? Aren't I seeing her all the time? And hasn't it always been a too, too ridiculous concept that such a helter-skelter of a human isn't coming back?

It feels indescribably good to believe she's in another room right now, instead of totally and forever gone.

"I can still smell her perfume . . ." I say.

Ash gives me a tight smile, clearly unsure how to respond. "You ready to go?"

I shake my head, putting the clay down on my wheel and picking up the book. It's photographs: wiggly bronze sculptures like alien life-forms, by an artist named Sir Tony Cragg. Some pages are marked with Post-it notes. I sit on my stool and start turning the pages, then stop, not wanting to lose Mum's place.

"You won't," she says, leaning over me. Her hair brushes my face, tickling. "You should open the kiln, though."

"No way," I say, grinning with relief that she's shown up. "No snooping, remember?"

"You can if you like." She cups a cigarette in her hand and

lights it, taking one single drag before flicking it to the floor and snuffing it with her work clogs. Then she starts gusting back and forth across the room. When she blows past Ash, I swear I see him twitch. He pulls his headphones on.

"That's okay," I tell her, starting to pump the wheel into a lazy spin. I dump the clay ball out into the center, make a hollow with my thumbs. "I'll wait for you. What's even in there, anyway?"

"You'll find out," she says. "It's something I've been working on for a while."

"And it's finished?"

"Mmm, as finished as anything ever is," she says, tilting the flat of her hand back and forth.

"What do you mean?"

"Minnie, not every story has an ending—"

She blinks into nothing as Ash walks over and rests his hand on mine. The clay quivers and collapses. I stop the wheel, feeling—irrationally—like he's stolen something from me.

"Whoops. Not the first artwork of yours I've ruined." He tugs at my hand. "You're not going to start working on something now, are you?"

"Well . . . that's why we're here." I look down at the wheel, then up again. The studio is bright with artificial light, but through the open door the sky is gathering, dusk sinking into the corners, rain tumbling down. The truth is, now that I'm finally here I could happily stay all night—sleep here, even. I tell Ash this, and he smiles worriedly.

"Don't be daft. Come on." He pulls me upright. "I'll buy you something to eat that isn't microwaved."

Before I shut the door, I glance back inside the studio. Like the house, it's in stasis, waiting for her to return. But it's also different. The studio is alive, buzzing. As if any second now, she's going to tap her heels together three times, and come home. I think of the dregs of coffee and the damp paintbrush, and wonder if maybe, she already has.

Belief in this idea is washing over me, like I'm swimming in a sun-drunk sea.

"Min?" Ash tilts his head at me, frowning. "You're drifting off again. Sure you're okay?"

For the first time in forever, the answer isn't a resounding *no*. Hope lifts me up like a balloon, carrying me through the rain, back into Ash's arms.

Silver
(An Ongoing List of Every
Color I Have Lost)

*Her earrings. Metallic marker pens. The mirror,
tarnished with watermarks and crud from weeks
and months and years of art.*

CHAPTER 18
The Color of Chalk

When we emerge from the yard, the city's nighttime yell has arrived.
Up and down the main road, buses scream their horns, the
last call to prayer rings out from the mosque a few streets away,
and music blares from hipster bars beneath the station, filled
with crowds of SCAD students. London is alight.

We run through the rain and win a table in the window of
a family-run Italian place Mum and I used to come to sometimes after the studio. I'd try to make my half of the tiramisu
last for hours, watching the clock, counting down to the point
I'd have to share her with Emmy-Kate and Niko again. But
there was always a moment when she'd reach out with her fork
and scoop up the last bite, ready to get moving.

Ash and I sit side by side in the radiance of twinkling Christmas lights and hundreds of candles, choosing buttery garlic

bread and pizzas the size of bicycle wheels from laminated menus.

"Min!" Ash beams brighter than the candlelight as our table is overloaded with food. "Look at all this. Makes me want to go to Italy."

Caught in the spotlight of his brilliant Ash-meets-Elvis smile, I'm right back to being the girl who met his eye in the National Gallery. And the cinder block in my chest becomes a little less heavy. It's strange. I keep expecting it all—grief, sadness, hope, happiness—to happen in a straight line. But life lately is more about tiny moments like this. Pockets of ups and downs.

I say, "Imagine, Italy. We could visit Rome, and the Uffizi Gallery in Florence. See Botticelli. And da Vinci, Raphael, Michelangelo . . ."

"All four Teenage Mutant Ninja Turtles, if you like," Ash teases, and there it is, moment gone.

Because I immediately start thinking about Felix in the kitchen on Saturday, raving to Emmy-Kate about Michelangelo and telling me he wished he could see *The Kiss*. If I went to Italy with Felix, we would lie underneath a hundred sculptures.

I'm unforgivable. I'm on a romantic date with my boyfriend and I'm thinking about someone else.

Ash hums happily, sucking butter from a piece of garlic bread and discarding the crust. Between each bite, he drums the fingertips of his other hand on the tablecloth. "This is fun, Miniature. Pizza was a good call."

"It is fun," I manage to say. At least, it beats the frozen version, eaten at Niko's mandatory sit-down Saturday nights. "Thank you."

"Good. And you're welcome." He smiles to himself, body-bumping me gently, then lifts a slice of pizza. It trails white cheese strings that remind me I once had a macramé-making phase but didn't finish a single piece then, either. "So, we should go to Italy for real, though."

"Obviously," I say through a delicious mouthful. "Everyone should go to Italy."

"Yeah?" Ash starts chair-dancing. "We could do the back-packer thing through Europe. Italy, and there's this banging music festival in Paris every August, one in Barcelona too . . ." He's off, his hand full-on slapping the tablecloth in a frenzied drumbeat. Both his legs are bopping up and down. It's the happiest I've seen him in ages. I put down my pizza, no longer hungry, and break off a chunk of soft candle wax, molding it in my hands as Ash continues: "We can get cheap flights, leave well after our exams. I could carry my guitar as well as a back-pack, make money on the road by busking. You want to? You could take a gap year before SCAD. I could put off getting a real job after graduation; that'd thrill my parents."

"You're not serious." I drop the wax back into the candle, where it starts to melt and pool, and stare at him. "Ash, I can't go on holiday. Or backpacking."

He stops tapping, wiping his fingers on a napkin before taking my hand, giving me his full attention. "Why not? It might be good for you, Min," he says. "We don't have to do the full gap-year thing. But a holiday might help. Some time off. Come to a party. Go out."

"We're out now," I say, bewildered. What more does he want from me?

"Yeah, and it's fun. Going away might be even better. Give you something to look forward to." He knocks his knee against mine. "Think about it: you, me, spaghetti, gigs, when the moon hits your eye like a big pizza pie."

I take my hand away and flap it miserably around the restaurant, trying to tell him telepathically: I can't go anywhere. Not as long as Mum's not here. Which, okay, I might end up stuck in Poets Corner for a lifetime. But so what? I've got whole worlds on my doorstep: the *Rainbow Series I*, a gingerbread cottage of a house, an overgrown back garden, the studio, Meadow Park, galleries galore, dinosaurs. Who even needs Italy?

My sigh says everything I can't, and it hits Ash like a gale-force wind. He drops his head, looking down at the grease-stained tablecloth. "Min. I know it's hard, but—"

"You *don't* know," I interrupt, appalled. How can he?

"True. But . . ." He starts chewing on his lip, watching me warily. Then he sighs almost as loudly as I did, makes a decision: "I don't know because you don't tell me."

There it is. I shake my head, lips pressed together.

"And I wish you would, Min," he urges, taking my hand back and holding it between both of his. "Tell me it's hard. Tell me everything. Tell me something at least? Tell me we both reek of garlic right now, I dunno . . ."

He huffs a laugh, and I give him a tiny smile, one that hurts my face.

Ash returns it. He looks like he wants to say something else but doesn't. Instead, he lets go of my hands and turns back to the table, picking up a slice of pizza. He drops his other arm around my shoulders with a *clunk*, and we eat the rest of the food that way, awkward and silent.

When Ash pays the bill, I stare out of the blobbed-with-rain window and try not to think about the other boy who's somewhere beyond it, as lonely as I am.

. . . . .

Later, I take the train alone back to Poets Corner. Here, the streets are still slick with rain and striped with neon reflections from the halal-burger-chicken-BBQ-ribs-chips-fried-everything place opposite. There's one every ten yards in south London.

Above this scene towers the spiky castle silhouette of the Full Moon Inn. The windows form squares of light, like a pop art painting by Mondrian. I linger on the corner for a second, looking up at the second floor and wondering which window is Felix's.

I have no idea whether I like him, or if I like the fact he likes art—and Ash doesn't—or whether I'm an unholy mess of a girl and he's an unholy mess of a boy.

My footsteps beat slowly on the cobbles. I pass the Bluebird Bakery, shuttered for the night, and realize I'm in no hurry to go home. I'm in no hurry to go anywhere. I stop, turn around, drifting, aimless—and see Felix coming round the corner.

He cups his hands to his mouth and yells: "Minnie!"

This startles a fox from the garbage spillage outside the kebab shop; it goes slinking into the shadows. Felix skirts round it, lumbering toward me. I retrace my steps until we meet in the middle, a lamppost casting an umbrella of light over our heads.

"Going for a walk?" I ask, tilting my head back to look up at him.

He shakes his head. It's silhouetted. "Looking for you. I saw you from my window." His shadowed face is swimming with sorrow, and I wonder what he was doing up there in his bedroom. Actually, delete that last thought: I don't want to know.

"You were looking for me?" I repeat, unable to keep the happiness from my voice. Even though I should be pouring cold water all over this, walking away, mentioning my relationship.

Felix nods. "How was your mum's studio?"

"Good," I say, wrapping my arms around myself. "And bad. Well, more like weird. Strange."

"It was adjective-y?"

"It felt like she was there," I tell him. Out loud, it sounds bonkers.

Felix nods. He's holding me in his dark gaze, and my whole body is vibrating imperceptibly with something—misery, want, calm, intensity, lust, all at once. I don't know. I only know that if I don't look away, I might thaw into this puddle I'm standing in.

"Did you try doing porcelain?" he asks.

"Not yet. I'm kind of out of my league as far as that goes." *Not to mention, Minnie, your boyfriend was there.* Only I don't mention him. I continue to not mention Ash.

"Well . . ." Felix smiles. Kind of. More like a glimmer at the edge of his mouth, like the moon emerging from behind a cloud. His melancholia is beguiling me. "I did say I'd give you lessons."

I do want to try porcelain—I want to try everything—but it would be impossible. I can't go to the studio with Felix—it's too near to SCAD and Niko; to Ash's house. It's too big a betrayal of my sisters, who I've never offered to take.

"But—" I say, at the same time as Felix says, "So—"

He bops the toe of my boot with his. "You go."

The Meadow Park clock tower strikes ten, a countdown to what I'm going to say. Even the fox comes creeping back out of the shadows, pricking an ear. But I can't seem to make myself speak, can't make my mouth form the word *no*.

"Minnie, you want me to teach you how to make porcelain?" Felix asks slowly.

And I nod, a mute marionette.

"What about tomorrow. After school?"

"Tomorrow," I repeat. Then I think of how closely Ash brushed by Felix yesterday. He's pretty dedicated to university;

he wouldn't be anywhere near the studio in daytime. I add recklessly, "But not after school. During."

Felix gives me a quick, searching glance, then says, "It's a plan, then. Tomorrow."

I think he's going to say good night and walk away, but he doesn't. He hesitates, then slides his arms around my waist, bending me backward so our bodies curve together like double quotation marks. I close my eyes and inhale, drinking in his bonfire scent: a mixture of cedarwood and mint. However much I tell myself it's body spray, this hug is conjuring swollen rivers and thunderstorm skies, nights lying on the grass in Meadow Park as sheets of lightning break across my head.

It's not a kiss. But if anyone saw us, I'm not sure they'd be able to tell the difference.

Pale Yellow
(An Ongoing List of Every Color I Have Lost)

The sun in midautumn, casting primrose light through increasingly bare branches. Petrol-scented London smog. Brioche and croissants in the window of the Bluebird Bakery. The quiet beehive hum of jealousy between me and my sisters.

CHAPTER 19
The Color of Snow

"Don't forget, I'm off on my school trip today," I tell my sisters the next morning.

My hands move too joyfully as I sign; too exuberantly, too not-Minnie. I can't help it, though. I'm walking on air. Actually, clunking—I snuck into the Museum of Mum before breakfast and liberated her most teetering pair of shoes: what I remember as bright green suede, with a chunky heel and hundreds of straps. They feel correct on my feet, like the baby bear's porridge, and exactly the way she ought to be mourned, or enticed home. With bold, bodacious gestures. Skipping school and breaking rules for the first time in my life, going to her studio, making art. Conjuring starlight.

Emmy-Kate's head tilts, regarding me like I've announced I'm joining the circus. She's surrounded by a small fortress of sugary cereal and reading matter—an art book, her sketch pad, a magazine, her phone; the attention span of a mosquito—but ignores it all in favor of narrowing her eyes at me.

Niko frowns, putting down her book—*A Matter of Life and Death*, by the Professor. Is she having trouble sleeping?—and giving me her full attention. Eff. My plan was to breeze in and out of the kitchen with the lie, acting as though this trip was mentioned ages ago. In retrospect I should have pulled a sick day instead.

"What school trip?" she asks.

Emmy-Kate echoes, "Yeah, what school trip?"

"Mind your own beeswax," I tell her, then turn to Niko and try to look innocent, deliver the speech I've been practicing for the past ten minutes up in the Chaos Cave, my hands wavering. "My art class is going to the National Portrait Gallery. There's this Cézanne portraits exhibit Ms. Goldenblatt wants us to see. We're getting a guided tour, then we're supposed to imitate his style and techniques. I told you about it ages ago, at the start of term."

I can't stop signing, embroidering the lie. Technically, there *is* a Cézanne exhibition on at the NPG—and Ms. Goldenblatt has been known to take us out of Poets Corner High and into galleries. Just not today.

"I lurve Cézanne," signs Emmy-Kate dreamily, forgetting she's currently not talking to me. "Did you know he astonished Paris with an apple? Get me a postcard from the gift shop."

"Are you sure you asked me about this, Minnie?" Doubt clouds Niko's fine features. "Where's the permission slip?"

"I'm over sixteen."

"You could still ask me." She shakes her head, hurt, pushing back her chair and taking her plate over to the sink. Beneath her T-shirt, her shoulder blades stick out like little bird wings, and it makes me want to cry.

"You look *nice*," Emmy-Kate blurts out loud, suspicion tainting her voice. "You're wearing lipstick . . ."

I blush, from the strappy shoes to my hair, which I've ironed into a Lady Godiva-esque sheet. Overall impression: probably not going on a school trip. But did I overdo it with the lipstick? I thought I chose a neutral color, but the way Emmy-Kate is glaring, maybe I'm accidentally pouting in fluorescent tangerine.

"One more word and I'll put a lock on your window," I tell her.

"What was that?" Niko turns around, catching our mouths moving. Emmy-Kate looks mortified at speaking behind her back and retreats into her Sugar Puffs.

"Sorry," I sign to Niko, genuinely. "We got carried away talking about Cézanne. So, I'm going to go . . ." I tell them, creeping backward toward the kitchen door.

"Straight home afterward, please," Niko orders, as I hear the sound of mail hitting the doormat out in the hall.

I nod, tripping on the shoes on the way out of the house, falling over all my lies.

Chartreuse
(An Ongoing List of Every Color I Have Lost)

*A color halfway between yellow and green,
named after a French liqueur Mum drank when we
went to Paris and saw the* Venus de Milo *and*
The Kiss. *The floral dress I'm wearing, if
I remember its color correctly. Algae on the
duck ponds. This sunglasses-bright feeling as
I walk to meet Felix, like the world is one
incredible discovery after another.*

CHAPTER 20
The Color of Milk

Uh-oh, I think, as I arrive on the platform of Poets Corner station and see Felix Waters leaning against the wall. The sunshine he's basking in is marmalade thick, with the same bittersweet taste. It's on my tongue, a combination of yearning and foreboding. Like Mum said, he's trouble, overwhelmingly so. I should walk away right now.

But my feet must have a mind of their own, because they start wobbling along the platform. When I arrive in front of Felix, he jumps to his feet, dark eyes skimming over my shoes-dress-hair-mascara-lipstick-nervous-smile-everything. He leaves a blush in the wake of his gaze—I can feel it radiating from my face, rendering me silent.

"Hey." He thrusts a Bluebird Bakery bag into my hand, not taking his eyes from mine. "Breakfast."

"Thank you," I manage. Then I have to look away. I perch on the wall next to him and take tiny nibbles of croissant as we wait for the train. The air crackles with anticipation.

When we get to the studio, I take a deep breath. With Ash, I felt afraid of what I might find inside. With Felix, it feels like I'm about to unveil my soul. After I open the door, he glances at me for permission, then starts prowling the room. His shoulders unhunch and his posture straightens. It's like looking at an evolution chart, watching him go from monkey to Cro-Magnon to upright human.

"Holy shit," he says over and over again, taking in each new piece of art.

I walk over to my wheel, disappointed to see the lump of clay I left on it yesterday is dried up. Mum hasn't been back here overnight. Of course she hasn't. No one falls from five hundred and thirty-one feet, then climbs back up the cliff and makes art. So why do I feel disappointed? Maybe it's because I believe that if anyone could pull off such a stunt, it would be her.

I prize the clay off with a knife, throw it into the recycling bucket.

Dehydrated clay is never wasted. You can let a pot dry out until it's ready to be fired, then smash it to pieces instead and reform the dust with water. Stir it up, and it makes the same wet clay you started with. Reincarnation. I stare into the bucket. It's filled with broken pieces once destined for the *Schiaparelli* series, destroyed before they ever made it to the kiln. Mum was looking for the shape of something in this clay, and didn't find it.

"Minnie," says Felix. I turn around. He's standing next to the original *Rainbow Series I* test bubble, a prototype piece not quite as enormous as the finished work but somehow as gob-smacking. He sweeps an arm around the room. "This is amazing. Everything . . . Wow. Thank you for showing me. I feel like Frida Kahlo invited me behind the scenes, you know?"

I nod, swallowing around the clay lump that's forming in my throat. This. This is how Ash should have responded yesterday. With reverence.

"I'm going to make tea," I say, and scurry to the kitchenette.

Yesterday's coffee mug is upside-down on the drainboard. I twitch, remembering only that I filled it with water, then boil the kettle and make tea. There's no milk in the fridge, not even a spoiled and moldy bottle left over from Mum's last days here. Only an Emmy-Kateish selection of snacks in the near-empty cupboard, Golden Oreos and pink-frosted store-bought sugar cookies.

When I turn around, clutching two mugs, Felix is standing among the kilns, resting his hand on top of the one that holds Mum's last artwork. His eyes are closed, his head bowed. Has he looked inside? Has he seen it? With a lurch, it occurs to me that this piece is the closest thing we'll get to a gravestone.

"Tea!" I yelp.

Felix looks up, raising his eyebrows at my Muppets voice.

"I was thinking," he says, moving over to the small test kiln. "Would it be all right to start heating up one of these? We could—" He breaks off, taking in my trembling self, and makes it over to me in two strides, lifting the mugs from my hands. "You okay?"

"I'm fine," I say, even though I'm careering between horror and hope. Yesterday I was so convinced that she was here. Now I'm convinced her body is being pecked by seagulls. The croissant threatens to make a reappearance. I'm completely out of control.

Felix puts down the mugs on the nearest workbench, then comes back to me, shaking his head. "You're not fine."

He's examining every brushstroke of my face. And I am so tired of imagining her death—or not—and the way it's drawn fault lines in my brain. I'm tired of craziness and drowning and disappearing, and of the imprecise words of her goodbye letter. Why couldn't she, for once, have gone about her life in the normal way? Even the potential ending of it had to be extraordinary. It makes me want to lift up the kiln, last-ever artwork and all, and throw it over Beachy Head. Let *Schiaparelli* drown along with her.

"You're crying," says Felix, gruffer than billy goats. He lifts a hand to my cheek and starts smudging tears away with his thumb. "Don't. Don't, Minnie. I know it's fucking shit."

His words soothe me like a lullaby. How is he the only

person who understands, the only one who can sum it up so clearly? It's all so indescribably awful.

"Fuck this," Felix is saying, both of his hands cupping my face now, and somehow his mouth is murmuring into mine and I'm crying into his, a cataclysmic mix of my shuddering sobs and his calming words, the taste of cigarettes as his lips crash into mine. And then I am cry-kissing.

But with each second our mouths are glued together, I leave my despair behind. Wrapped in Felix's bonfire scent, there's only stillness—like someone pressed a PAUSE button on my torment. And when our tongues finally disconnect, I think: *Felix is delicious*. Then I'm instantly mortified that my first thought wasn't about Ash.

My hand flies to my mouth in shame.

"Sorry, I shouldn't have . . ." Felix trails off, misunderstanding the gesture. He shoves his hair this way and that in distress, then mutters, "Let's start making the porcelain. I mean, if you still want?"

"I want," I say, before realizing what a breathy, double-entendre, Emmy-Kate thing that is to say. Felix's pupils flare. He frowns, confused.

Then his arthead self takes over—he has two identities, Batman–Bruce Wayne-style. This one summons all the creative energy in the studio and announces, "Okay, it's mad-scientist time. Here, take this." He rummages in his pocket for a scrap of paper and hands it to me, then descends on the workbenches and begins hoisting ingredients up from the storage boxes. "You don't mind?"

"Yes. I mean, no, it's okay." I'm caressing the paper scrap as if it's a love letter. These are the words I'm swooning over, in Felix's scratchy handwriting:

dry clay powder, hot water, darvan 7, soda ash, barium carb

He's so at home in Mum's space. It reminds me of her at her most uncontainable, this whirlwind of measuring out clay and boiling water and mixing chemicals, finding her equipment, bringing this place back to life. Felix hurls everything into a bucket and turns on a drill with a vroom-vroom-vroom, then stops.

"Wait," he says. He rests the drill on the table, wiping curls from his eyes and leaving a smear of dust on his forehead. "I'm supposed to be showing you. I have this tendency," he explains, "to get carried away with things too quickly."

Is he talking about the kiss or the clay?

I peer dubiously into the bucket. Inside is a soupy mess of recycled clay pieces, weird-looking chemical powders, steamy hot water.

"Do you want an apron?" I ask, then shake my head, point to his sweater. "Stupid question."

"You might, though." Felix hands me the drill. There's a spiral whisk attachment at the end, one that Mum usually uses for glazes. "Mix this, and we've got porcelain."

I dip the drill into the bucket.

"Sure you don't want an apron?" Felix asks.

"I'm okay," I say, and I am.

I put my finger on the drill trigger and it roars to life, drowning out everything else. I can feel the tremor through my hands, arms, legs, the way I imagine a chain saw feels. And the mess in the bucket is swirling in circles, gradually resolving itself from lumpy soup to liquid cream.

I start thinking about this American artist called Anne Patterson, who has synesthesia. In her work *Graced with Light*, she listened to a Bach concerto, then suspended twenty miles of colorful silk ribbon from the ceilings of San Francisco's Grace Cathedral. Twenty miles of color! I'd give my left thumb for a single inch.

The porcelain is turning lighter and lighter. It looks almost weightless. It makes me want to take the sun in my hands like a ball of clay.

My whole body is shaking as I drill deeper, tapping into lunacy and loneliness. Everything shudders: the bucket, the table, my arms, my legs, the whole effing studio. I'm drilling into unsaid words. Into disappearing mothers and secretive sisters. Into faltering relationships and charismatic new boys, bumbling professors, the chasm in my heart that I will never ever fill, and this aching worry I have: that my brain is as effed up as Mum's and there's no way to be an artist, no way to be *her*, without our stories ending the same way.

"Holy shit," says Felix.

Or at least, his mouth forms the words. I can't lip-read the way Niko can, but I get the gist.

"What?" I ask, taking my finger from the drill's trigger. The room falls silent, except for a ringing in my ears like church bells.

Felix is staring at me. He's newly bespattered. I look down. I'm covered too. There's porcelain everywhere. Thick globules up and down my dress, tiny freckles all over my arms, liquid clay pouring down my tights and onto Mum's platform shoes and pooling around my feet, spreading out in a shiny lake all over the floor.

I've drilled a hole right through the bucket.

"Yes, yes, yes!" Mum's voice in my head.

This is the first time ever, in my whole life, that I've hit her genius-zone.

I don't know if this is a good thing.

"Holy shit," says Felix again, awestruck.

I say, "Sorry. I have this tendency to get carried away with things too quickly."

Then I start to laugh.

He's still staring at me. I recognize his expression. It's the same one I exchange with my sisters whenever Mum stumbles into a sinkhole or announces some new bizarre notion, bathed in starlight. Felix Waters thinks I've lost the plot.

It's terrifying. As scary as applying to SCAD and not getting accepted, or losing my virginity, or following in my mother's footsteps (right off a cliff). The porcelain splashes look like *The White Album*. Unease slides its way into my stomach.

I put down the drill and walk over to Felix.

"Forget it," I say as lightly as I can, putting my hands on his chest. His sweater is splashed and wet. "I'm an idiot. I can't see in color, remember?"

He nods, wrapping his arms around my waist, pulling me closer. "Yeah, about that . . ."

"Don't," I say. "I don't want to think about it."

I want to think about blue. The rich lapis lazuli of Renaissance paintings. The shiny cobalt glaze of Dutch delftware pottery. Yves Klein inventing a brand-new shade of it. Or literally anything except what I just did. What I am doing.

I look around at all the Day-Glo sun that's bouncing into the studio, illuminating weeks and days of dust and mourning and absence, then back at Felix. Then I stand on my tiptoes, press my mouth to his, and forget.

. . . . .

"So what happens next?" I ask.

It's a couple of hours later and we're walking back to the studio from McDonald's, a meandering route that skirts far away from the SCAD campus. There's a new porcelain mixture resting in the studio, waiting for us. According to Felix, porcelain is like pancake batter—you can't use it right away.

"Not much until the kiln heats up," says Felix, tipping the last fries into his mouth. "We can practice making molds. Or I brought a few along; we can make greenware."

Greenware. This is what it's called when a piece is dry but before it's fired. After the first firing, it's called bisque—when the clay melts and hardens into a ceramic. The final step is glazing and firing again. Then it's finished.

Felix and I are greenware. There's still time to break down this tentative thing between us, whatever it is, and reshape it. But Ash and I are glazed. If I smash what we have, there's no gluing back together the pieces.

The neighborhood is quiet, wiped of last night's noise and activity. The only movement is the breeze and a couple of pigeons fighting over Felix's discarded McDonald's wrapper. As we turn a corner, he lights a cigarette and asks, out of nowhere: "So, what happens next, with your mum?"

"Nothing." I stuff the last piece of hamburger into my mouth and tuck the wrapper into my pocket. "What do you mean?"

"Well . . ." Felix prowls along, blowing out smoke. "I don't know how someone going missing works. You wait it out?"

"Pretty much." We come to a stop outside a church and lean against the wall, looking into the graveyard. We're next door to the Italian restaurant, and the enormity of it wallops me. I almost choke on the burger. Last night I was eating candlelit pizza here with Ash; today I'm kissing Felix. More than once. Who does that?

"Sorry," Felix tells the wall. "I thought . . . I don't know. You'd have a funeral or a memorial, or . . ."

"I'm not sure it would help."

"It wouldn't." Felix blows smoke over the wall. I watch his profile. "People say stuff like 'It will get better with time' or 'You'll feel better after the funeral.' Closure or whatever. Because they want to believe it. But when my mum died it was shit, and it was shit the day before the funeral, and the day after, and it continues to be shit."

"It didn't even help a little, on the day?" I ask, unsure if I want to know the answer.

"Nope." Felix clenches his jaw. "Sorry, but funerals suck. They suck donkey balls."

"That's . . . eloquent."

He drops his cigarette and grinds it beneath his boot, turning to me. "Yeah, well. Ever had twenty grown-ups put you on sympathy blast?"

"Sympathy blast?"

Felix does a pity pout. "Like that. My mum's friends falling all over themselves to say, 'Poor *you*. How *awful*. You must be so sad?' Like they wanted to be the first to make me cry. And they all rub your arm in the same place, like this." He demonstrates. It reminds me a little of Ms. Goldenblatt's shoulder squeeze and Ritika's shoulder punch, but it's different, because this hand on my arm belongs to Felix Waters. I can't believe I'm noticing the weight of his fingers, even as we're talking about the worst thing ever. "And all the sympathy cards are

187

pink: 'There's nothing worse than losing a mum.' Eurgh. Fucking awful."

I nod, thinking of the teddy bears at the walled-garden memorial, the Hallmark card sentimentality.

Felix folds his arms. Sun streams down behind his head, shooting out glittering rays that prevent me from seeing his expression. "Minnie, I know you want to feel better, but that's the thing. You can't. *I* can't, unless she magically gets not dead. The trick is . . . You work out how to live with feeling terrible for the rest of your life."

This is so unbelievably depressing. But it's reassuring, too. Like a safety net. Felix's intensity makes me feel less insane. Ash keeps asking me if I'm all right, trying to tell me things will be okay. But it's nice, for once, to admit that maybe they won't be. That this hurt is permanent.

We walk on, into the sun. The light is blinding-bright, blending the street and the sidewalk and the trees into one white canvas. Up ahead of us, near the entrance to the studio, there's a blur of movement. A thin figure with long glowing hair, turning to look at us—

"Oh my God." I stop walking abruptly.

"What?" asks Felix.

I shield my eyes, wishing I had my sunglasses—wishing I had those EnChroma sunglasses I ordered already, but they won't arrive for weeks.

It's Mum. I'm sure of it. For real.

In the days after the letter, I saw Mum everywhere. On street corners, on the Tube and the bus; walking through Poets Corner or browsing in the bookshop on Full Moon Lane. I heard her, too—a crash from the kitchen or her key in the lock in the middle of the night, the Beatles floating faintly up the stairs. And, of course, now I see her all the effing time.

But this is different. This isn't my imagination. This is finding evidence of her in the studio yesterday: the damp paintbrush and the full ashtray. Lipstick marks and coffee dregs that haven't dried out the way they should have if they were from weeks ago; her perfume hanging in the air.

She's two hundred yards away, fading into the sun.

She's dead, I think.

She's here and she's dead in the same moment.

I believe in both. I like it that way.

I know the way I'm thinking isn't right. But I don't want to give it up, either. What a crappy choice to have to make: Mend my brain and never see her again. Or tumble forward into this burgeoning madness and get to be with her all the time.

Now I see what a great metaphor a sinkhole is. A cavernous space is opening up at my feet; I'm teetering on the brink.

"Minnie, what?" Felix's voice rumbles through me as Mum flees round the corner. He places his hand on my arm, gently shaking me from my walking coma. "Minnie. What's up?"

Felix moves in front of me, blocking the light.

I blink away the sunspots in my eyes, taking in the streaks

of white porcelain on Felix's navy sweater; lavender clouds against a buttercream sky.

I blink again.

The sun is glazing everything apricot.

Color.

Paler than pale.

But there.

This is what it looked like in August, right before it all faded. Somehow I've hit a button, pressed REWIND, gone back through these aching days and found the world again. Almost. The colors aren't absolute: Imagine the world's smallest, itsy-bitsy, teeny-weeny dab of rose-violet paint diluted by a gallon of white. Or a photo on your phone with the saturation turned almost down to nothing. The faintest wash of watercolor across the paper.

But there's no mistaking the blue-lavender-rose-violet-yellow sky.

Or Felix squinting down at me with charcoal eyes, brown hair.

A haze of color.

Lavender

(An Ongoing List of Every Color I Have Lost)

The plant that woos hundreds of bees to the garden each summer. Tired shadows under Felix's eyes. A late-September afternoon haze.

CHAPTER 21
Tombstones Are Gray

I'm standing in the back garden, trying to decide between scaling the wall or going in through the kitchen like a normal person—where I'll end up in trouble. It's obvious I haven't been on a school trip: there's clay dust billowing from every pore, porcelain streaked across my dress.

As I'm staring up at her window, Emmy-Kate's flamingo legs emerge, followed by the rest of her. She starts clambering down, wreathed in long strawberry-blond hair. Halfway to the ground she spots me and stops, then goes scrambling back up the wall like a spider. Her window slams.

It shakes half the climbing roses from their stems, depositing a carpet of petals at my feet. Dusk creeps across the garden as I lift one from the grass to examine it.

The petal in my palm is bruised. And it's the wrong color. I look up at the trellis. These roses should be apricot, and they're not. They're . . . some other color. Only, I can't name it. I can't even describe it, because it doesn't exist. It would be like trying to explain birthday cake to a Martian—there's no common reference.

I run through the mnemonic: ROY G BIV. Red, orange, yellow, green, blue, indigo, violet. A rainbow. The full spectrum.

Except now I'm seeing an extra color.

Ummm.

There's no blue in the Bible. Mum whispers in my ear: *There are more colors in the world than you'll ever know about.*

Worry clenches a fist around my heart. I look at the grass, then the sky, reconsidering their pale pastel hues. I've been so happy to have color, I've convinced myself they're green and blue. But they're not. They're vast great canvases of weirdo nonexistent new Minnie-vision.

This is not how normal brains work.

I crush the petal in my fist and bang open the back door.

The first thing I notice is how quiet the kitchen is, like a breezeless day. After Niko's marathon cleaning session it's sterile and bare, too. It feels entombed.

The next thing I see is Niko herself. She's sitting bolt upright behind the table, her face stony and flat. In front of her is a sheet of paper, unfolded, with three creases in it. The fold pattern immediately makes me think of the goodbye letter—but the police have that. Then I think it's a note from school about my absence. My sister is quivering with rage, but she can't be this annoyed that I've skipped school . . . can she?

Finally, I see that the Professor is here—a-freaking-gain—perched on his usual chair in his jogging outfit, drinking chai and working at a laptop. He stands up when I come in. Niko flicks her eyes toward the movement, then back to me.

"What the fuck, Minnie?" Her hands snap-snap-snap. "You used her credit card."

Oh no. My eyes drop to the paper in front of her. She pushes it toward me. It's a statement for Mum's Visa, showing one item only. Enchroma.com. The stupid magic sunglasses.

Niko's fist hammers on the table for my attention. I'm expecting her to stand up and condemn me, but she stays seated, shoulders flopping in defeat. She starts signing lethargically, speaking at the same time for the Professor's benefit in the deep voice she rarely uses:

"Do you even know what you did, Minnie? I called the police this morning. I had to stay home from SCAD all day and clear up your mess." Niko's hands move like broken birds, but all I can think is, *phew*. She was nowhere near the studio today, nowhere near me and Felix. She hasn't witnessed my epic boyfriend betrayal.

"This letter arrives," Niko continues, "and I thought it was her, and I called the police. Then the Missing People hotline. And I had to knock on the Professor's door and ask him to come round because the police always take it more seriously if there's a grown-up. And it wasn't an emergency, so I had to wait in the house all day thinking: Is this it? Is she actually out there somewhere? The whole day, I had this stupid hope."

She's tearing up behind her glasses, hunching over her hands: "Do you know what that was like?"

I'm so horrified—I didn't even consider this as an outcome—and so overwhelmed by this weirdo day I say exactly the wrong thing. Which is: "How did you know it was me?"

Niko's face crumples. She looks crazy vulnerable for a second—almost like Felix at his most despairing. "The police finally came round a couple of hours ago with that inter-preter woman I can't stand. They explained that they spoke to the credit card company, and then they spoke to"—she glances down at the bill and spells out—"E-N-C-H-R-O-M-A, and finally they found out this transaction wasn't her. It was you."

The two of us stare-off. Me coated in porcelain and panic; Niko in a headscarf and charity-shop cardigan and *Battersea Cats & Dogs Home* T-shirt she's amended with a Sharpie to read *& Rabbits*.

"I'm sorry, okay?" I sign, but my words don't breach the wall between us. By this point it's impenetrable, like Sleeping Beauty's thorns-and-all barricade.

Two rosy spots of annoyance appear high on Niko's cheek-bones. Her vulnerability vanishes and she's tense again. "That's it?" she signs. "You're sorry. God! How could you, Minnie?" She takes in my soaked-in-art appearance, and her nostrils flare.

Then she shakes her head—in disgust or disappointment, I can't tell—and goes rushing from the room.

I slump into her chair, staring at the Visa bill. Okay, but so what?

I open my eyes every day to monochrome. I go to school. (Albeit not today.) I chew my way through every microwave meal. I wash my hair, brush my teeth, do my homework; I plod on and on and on through these endless empty days and I don't tell on Emmy-Kate and the boys in her room, and I don't confess to my sisters the exact words I read in the goodbye letter, because no one needs to carry that weight on their shoulders, and I see Mum everywhere and now I'm seeing colors THAT DON'T EFFING EXIST, so tell me this:

Where's my Get Out of Jail Free card to do one tiny thing wrong?

I've forgotten the Professor is here too until he sits down opposite me and clears his throat repeatedly. He spins the bill toward him between finger and thumb, the same way he twirls his bow tie, then clasps his fingers together under his chin. It's instantly clear: He and Niko have discussed this ambush. They're in cahoots. I don't get her at all, why she keeps inviting him over.

"Er—Minnie, er, perhaps you could . . . explain," he waffles. "Why you've used Rachael's credit card to, ah"—he squints, peering down at the page—"spend, uh, three hundred and fifty pounds?" The Professor starts squinting around the kitchen, as if looking for a Cadillac or a diamond ring or a yacht, some evidence of my spoils.

Holy Botticelli, to steal a phrase from Emmy-Kate. But who cares? In the grand stupid scheme of things, does any of this even really matter?

"Three hundred and fifty pounds?" I repeat.

"Mmm."

Silence reigns. It strikes me that it's not only one tiny thing I've done wrong, not only one person I betrayed today. By kissing Felix, I'll have upset or disappointed or pissed off Ash and Emmy-Kate and Niko and even the Professor—weirdly, even this last one bothers me.

"Look, I'll pay the money back or return the glasses," I mutter, humiliated.

The Professor nods. "I don't think that's your sister's issue," he says gently. "I think perhaps she wants an explanation."

The way he says it, I can tell he doesn't mean about the credit card. Niko wants an explanation for Mum's disappearance.

"Don't we all?" I say, and he smiles in a shipwrecked fashion.

After an hour of sitting in silence and the Professor's disappointed sighs, I apologize again and high-tail it upstairs, where Mum's bedroom door is ajar. I hesitate outside, listening to the banshee wail of music seeping from Emmy-Kate's room, then peek through the gap.

Niko is stripping the bedsheets.

Quick and methodical, she shakes the duvet from its cover, yanks off the fitted sheet, pulls pillows from pillowcases, and in doing so, deletes our mother's last dreams. She piles the sheets on the floor and tips out the contents of the laundry basket on top. Then she grabs the dress from the chair and adds that to the pile on the floor, places the sandals inside the wardrobe. I bite the inside of my cheek so hard I taste blood.

The ashtray gets tipped into the bin and both relocated near the door—I shrink back—to be taken downstairs, along with the lipsticked wineglass. Books are reshelved. Niko unwinds her headscarf and uses it as a duster, swiping over my words on the mirror without noticing them, cleaning the dressing table of its history. She screws lids onto jars and tucks them into drawers.

Pretty soon the room looks hotel-neat, void of any personality. But Niko keeps moving around: straightening and restraightening any remaining knickknacks, pushing at the books on the shelves until they're in perfect alignment, twitching the curtains into neat pleats.

When she finally runs out of things to organize, she stands in the center of the room, biting her lip. I know what she's going to do before she does it, as if I'm watching my life on replay. She sits on the edge of the unmade bed and reaches underneath, pulling out the shoebox and lifting it onto her lap. There's an inch of dust on top. Niko blows it off, then runs her hands back and forth across the lid.

My whole body begins shaking. This is a pact I can't watch

her break. I slip away from the door and dart up the stairs to the Chaos Cave, heart exploding because the last living traces of Mum are being deleted from the world.

And as I sit in my room, the pastels begin to drain away.

I watch them for hours, each new and strange color fading from view, like paint down a drain. Until all that is left is a black-and-white that's much, much darker than before.

Lime
(An Ongoing List of Every
Color I Have Lost)

Niko's sketch pad cover—an Aquarelle watercolor block. Tic Tacs. Tulip stems and the garden in early spring. Some of Ash's more outré sneakers. The parakeets that flock through London's parks.

Violet

(An Ongoing List of Every Color I Have Lost)

Stocks and wallflowers and sweet peas, spring flowers she will never see again. The winter pansies and violets that are about to bloom and she will miss. Purple shampoo for super-blond hair, which used to sit in our shower caddy and has now been relocated by Niko to the bathroom cabinet.

CHAPTER 22

The Color of Shadows

The sunset beams light through the skylight and all over my bed. I've propped the window wide open to listen to the trains, and every now and then I catch a waft of traffic fumes mingling with the sweet scent of the roses. The combination reminds me of this afternoon's illicit cedarwood-and-cigarettes kisses with Felix.

I'm still wearing my porcelain-covered dress—I can't bring myself to take it off—and every time I move, I want to be back at the studio with him. Or underneath a bubble in Meadow Park. Or at school. Basically, anywhere but trapped here in the house of heartbreak, where any minute Niko will summon me downstairs for seitan fingers and Bird's Eye potato waffles and a lecture.

I close my eyes, hoping to escape my life and relive a

moment from this afternoon: when Felix Waters put his arms around me in the lee of the Full Moon Inn and kissed me goodbye. But with my eyes closed, all I see is Ash's face, contorted with shock.

How could you, Minnie? Niko's words reverberate through my skull.

Ugh. Disgrace chases me from the bed. I go to my desk, where I idly pick at a blob of porcelain on my sleeve and revisit the floral drawings from the other day. Each one is unfinished, a cautious pencil rendering to be painted or inked or crayoned. Without color, there's no way to decide which. They'll remain incomplete, like everything else in my portfolio.

That's it. I'm incomplete. Monochromacy will stop me from applying to SCAD or being an artist. Mum made *The White Album*, and quit. I'm not even going to get started, not going to have a chance.

The clay blob comes off in my hand, flat and round like a pebble—or one of the rose petals from earlier. I fiddle with it, the porcelain thin and delicate. It's dry, ready for the kiln— my cardigan has soaked up the water and created accidental greenware. And when I spin my chair around and hold the piece up to the window, it glows.

I feel on the brink of some huge discovery, the way Rodin found the light in the stone. Maybe these porcelain scraps and splashes on my dress are what I'm supposed to make?

I start agitatedly peeling and picking at my dress, jabbing my nails in the fabric and prizing off the clay shards, piling them carefully on my desk. I'm thinking that this is the closest I'll ever come to being Mum—wearing my art on my sleeve—when of course she strides into the room.

"Fleas?" she jokes, waving her cigarette at my disassembly.

I stop yanking at my cardigan. Mum is wearing a chartreuse frock like mine, and scarlet stilettos. As always, she's the brightest thing in the room. She's also soaking wet, and there's seaweed hanging from her hair. Her skin is waxy and blue. Cold sweat springs up on my skin.

Every time I imagine her, she looks more and more dead. The trouble is, I don't know if I'm doing it on purpose or not. Am I holding on to her, or letting her go?

"What's going on, Min?" she asks.

"I had a slight porcelain accident at the studio," I say. "Sorry."

"Pah! Who hasn't?" She dismisses this with another wave of her cigarette, and I giggle. For all her morbid appearance, she's still acting like Mum.

"That's right, I forgot. You saw it already. I kind of felt like you for a moment," I tell her. "When I was stirring—well, exploding—the porcelain."

Mum tilts her head, gives me a Professor-ish "hmm" as she wanders to the desk, brushing the porcelain pieces aside. They make a soft clattering noise. Each is an off-shape oval, gently concave: not petals but seashells. She ignores them, holding my flower drawings up to the light.

"Forget those," I say, embarrassed. What must my Turner Prize–winning artist mother think of my inability to finish anything? Even today in the studio, Felix had to finish mixing the clay. "I was experimenting."

"What do you think of them?" she asks. "What do you see when you really look?"

I walk over to her. When I try to breathe in her Mum-smell, I can't catch a whiff of Noix de Tubéreuse or clay or glycerin or even her cigarette. Only salt and seawater.

"I see someone who hasn't decided on anything yet."

What is the art I want to make? I only know I want to undo the dark, discover the secrets I'm keeping from myself. Looking at the porcelain flower-shells, I know, with absolute certainty, that they aren't it. I'm not going to find the colors this way.

Mum blows a smoke ring. "Min, remember how there's no blue in the Bible?"

"We've been through this already," I say, frustrated. "I don't know what that means, remember?"

"It means what it means."

"Holy vague, Batman." I throw up my arms in annoyance. I'm kind of wishing I had Ash's headphones and some of Emmy-Kate's noisy rock music so I could tune Mum out. The more I see her, the more it feels like she's daring me to go nuts.

"In *The Odyssey*, Homer calls it 'the wine-dark sea.' Not blue. *Dark*," Mum explains. She's waving her arms too. "And in the ancient Hebrew version of the Bible, there's still no word for blue. Don't you see? People didn't have a name for it, so they couldn't see it. Blue was dark. And you know there are communities who can't distinguish blue from green? To someone without the word *green*, it's the same color."

She spins toward me, sizing me up like I'm a lump of her clay. This is Mum in starlight mode. She's acting the way she does when she's been up all night, researching some new idea. Speed-talking and giddy, not quite making sense, a supernova. She's me today, drilling through the bucket. We're becoming the same person.

"Okay," I say, trying to be logical. "How in the world did no one have a word for blue? Behold, the sky."

Mum doesn't answer: closes her eyes instead, swaying on her feet, dripping seawater.

I sit down on the bed, watching her. Then perhaps I fall asleep, because the next thing I know, it's pitch-dark outside, Mum is gone—like she always, always is—and Emmy-Kate's window is opening with a ghoulish shriek.

I poke my head out into the night air to discover my sister hanging half-in, half-out of the house, resplendent in a shimmering dress. She doesn't appear to be going anywhere this time: staring at the sky, blowing smoke at the moon. Since when is Emmy-Kate a smoker? The Beatles drift from her room, a song called "I Feel Fine," which couldn't be more wrong.

I get this gut wrench of nostalgia for her, for us. Not the Emmy-Kate who's smoking like a chimney, ten feet below, but another, long-gone sister.

"Pssst," I hiss.

She swivels around and peers up, silvery in the starlight, her eyeshadow as sparkly as her dress. I'm wearing Mum's shoes, but Emmy-Kate is wearing her effervescence. She looks like a sugarplum fairy. The kind of girl who's the heroine in the story. Unlike monochrome me.

She scowls, but at least speaks to me. "Did you see the Cy Twombly sunset?" she asks, her voice less piano-y than usual, even as she accesses her mind thesaurus. "Way *Quattro Stagioni: Autunno*, you know what I mean?"

"Rarely," I say, which prompts a begrudging smile. "Are you going out?"

"Thinking about it." She shimmies, and the sparkly dress rustles like wind through the trees. "You missed dinner," she adds, curious.

"Wasn't hungry."

"Did you get me the Cézanne postcard?"

"The what?"

She squints up at me. "Your. School. Trip."

Oh. This morning's lie feels like a lifetime ago. I blink down at her for approximately eons before saying, "Sorry, I forgot."

Emmy-Kate's lip curls. I think she's going to accuse me of not going on the school trip but she only inhales, coughs, and says, "Have you heard of something called super amnesia?"

I shake my head, pulling my duvet around my shoulders. "What about amnesia?"

"I read about it on the internet." Emmy-Kate lets her cigarette drop and wriggles further out of the window, holding on to the top of the frame to keep her balance. I want to tell her to be careful, but I know she won't listen. "About a woman who disappeared? Twice. Anyway, the first time was, like, ten years ago. In New York. She went for a run and poof! Vanished. Turns out she had this super amnesia. They found her three weeks later, facedown in a river, and when she was rescued, she had no memory of going missing at all, even though she'd been to Starbucks and the Apple shop and the gym. And swimming . . ."

Emmy-Kate trails off, her eyes making planets in the dark. It's obvious why she's telling me this. She wants me to say that Mum is coming back, that she has super amnesia.

I could. I could tell her that Mum's already back; that she visits the studio all the effing time, but hasn't made it to Poets Corner yet. I could tell my sister that I see Mum everywhere, that I saw her earlier tonight. But the thought of admitting this to anyone terrifies me. Is that why Mum never acknowledged her sinkholes? We never spoke about them. She would simply emerge from the despair and act normal again, for a while, before winding herself up into a frenzy and then plummeting again. She was loud and proud and bold in every other aspect, but she denied this element of herself like a shameful secret.

I get it. When I think about telling someone what's going on, my skin grows clammy with embarrassment. My stomach churns, my face flushes, I dry heave.

Or I could tell Emmy-Kate the whole story: that Mum left a suicide note. I wonder what painting she'd talk about then.

Something surrealist and macabre, probably. A Hieronymus Bosch, with bloodied demon heads and hellfires.

"What about the second time this woman disappeared?" I ask. "Super amnesia again?"

Emmy-Kate gives her head a tiny, unhappy shake. Then she swings one long leg out of the window. She's also wearing Mum's shoes: a too-big pair of high heels that dangle from her feet. It takes me a moment to recognize them as the sandals that Niko tidied into the wardrobe.

I have a horrible feeling that they were never thrown on the floor by Mum; that the dress on the chair wasn't left by her. That the mess I wanted to preserve was Emmy-Kate's klepto-mania. It doesn't matter now anyway; Niko has cleaned it all up. When someone is gone, they're truly gone. Holding on to their hairbrush or clothes won't make any difference. Nor will holding on to their shadow, the way I'm doing. But I don't know how to stop.

"So, where are you maybe-going?" I change the subject, pretending it's entirely ordinary for one's fifteen-year-old sister to escape the house night after night.

"None of your beeswax," she says automatically. Defiantly, daring me to say anything, she starts speaking in capitals. "There's a party on campus at SCAD. Have you SEEN the boys there? Some of them are so CUTE they need to be CENSORED. Holy Michelangelo!"

Her voice hopscotches in fake enthusiasm, and it occurs to me, a thousand light-years after it should have, that

Emmy-Kate is pretending to be a person too. She's a big faker.

The night we found the shoebox rushes into my head.

It was a few years ago, before Emmy-Kate became this fully fledged adult. Mum had dragged the Professor out to some razzle-dazzle art-show-gallery-opening-awards-whatever, and the three of us sisters were home alone, having a fright night. Scary movies. Afterward, we brushed our teeth side by side, quaking and giggling with pretend terror until Niko dared to yank the shower curtain back to prove there wasn't a psycho killer behind it.

None of us wanted to go to bed alone, so we climbed into Mum's instead and stayed up talking, finger spelling on each other's palms. Every time the old house creaked, we'd shriek and double-dare each other to creep out into the dark corridor, or peer under the bed for monsters.

Then Niko actually *did* look under the bed. There was nothing there except for a box we'd never seen before. An ordinary shoebox, beige and old. Something about the way it was hidden, pushed far back out of sight, frightened me more than any of the imaginary monsters we'd been conjuring. It reminded me of the nursery rhyme:

In a dark, dark wood there was a dark, dark house;

And in the dark, dark house there was a dark, dark room;

And in the dark, dark room there was a dark, dark cupboard;

And in the dark, dark cupboard there was a dark, dark shelf;

And on the dark, dark shelf there was a dark, dark box;
And in the dark, dark box there was a . . .

"Secret," Emmy-Kate signed, eyes wide with intrigue.

"Should we open it?" Niko asked. I shook my head, but in customary fashion, she went ahead and did it anyway.

Inside were medicine bottles. Plastic jars that rattled and shook with complicated-sounding drugs: citalopram and carbamazepine and lithium and quetiapine and valproate and zopiclone; prochlorperazine and a syrup called trifluoperazine that came with a measuring spoon. The bottle was three quarters full and sticky. There were half-used blister packs labeled with days of the week, but the occasional empty pill spaces didn't correspond to any pattern. A stack of unfilled pharmacy prescriptions was stuffed in the corner of the box. The name on each of the bottles was Mum's. The dates went back years.

Somehow, we absorbed all of this information in seconds, and what it might mean. That the tidal ebb and flow of Mum's sinkholes and starlights might signal something serious and medical and real and forever. She wasn't a magical mother after all: There was something wrong with her. My stomach flipped. All I knew for certain was that I didn't want to know what. It was too much.

Emmy-Kate grabbed the lid from Niko's hand and grappled it back onto the box, her fingers shaking, then shoved it out of sight. On wobbly legs, I climbed from the bed. We all did, clearing our throats and finger-combing our hair. Niko tweaked our shapes from Mum's duvet, and we crept from the room, closing the door behind us as gently as possible, not speaking of what we'd seen, more frightened than we had been all night, watching the horror films.

When the police asked me if Mum was on any medication, I answered in all honesty that I didn't know.

Emmy-Kate has made it halfway down the trellis.

"Are you going to tell on me?" she asks.

"No." For some reason I sign it, don't say it.

Emmy-Kate clambers down the roses and lands on the grass with a soft little *whoomp* noise, then looks up, surrounded by thick night.

"Good." She signs too, her hands half-invisible in the dark. "Were you really at the Cézanne exhibition?"

Worry glides through me. "Emmy-Kate, what—"

"Listen," she interrupts. "You weren't at school, and neither was Felix Waters. And I know you weren't on a field trip. I saw Ms. Goldenblatt."

Then, very carefully, she finger spells it out, each letter hovering in the air like a star:

"W-H-A-T A-B-O-U-T N-I-K-O?"

Emmy-Kate slinks through the garden, a streak of glitter, then gone, leaving her words behind. For a while, I watch for her to come back, but she doesn't. Nor does Mum. All that's left of this day is the pile of porcelain flower-shells, and this inescapable truth: Emmy-Kate is right.

I think of the impenetrable fortress between me and Niko

in the kitchen earlier, how it's been there ever since I stole Ash with a kiss. *How could you, Minnie?* And it will only get worse if we break up. I will have betrayed my sister for nothing—a relationship of less than a year. She'll never speak to me again. And I can't afford to lose another Sloe.

Apricot

(An Ongoing List of Every Color I Have Lost)

*Niko's nubby winter coat, the one that makes
her look like a teddy bear. The roses Emmy-Kate
shakes from the trellis each night when she
goes who-knows-where.*

CHAPTER 23

Clouds, Gathering

I wake up when the first train comes rattling through the garden and cringe under the covers for a while, listening to the soft, musical chatter of birdsong. The grays have become darker overnight, as if I slept inside a smokestack. Things are supposed to look better in the morning, after a good night's sleep, but they literally don't.

Over breakfast, neither of my sisters communicates with me, and I leave the house alone, texting Felix to meet me outside the bakery. He's there ahead of me, leaning against the wall, two paper bags clutched in his hand. Dawn is still clinging to the morning, and it's strangely quiet. We're the only two people on the street.

"Hey, Minnie," Felix says, his voice somber and sweet in a way that instantly undoes my resolve to end this thing.

His vampiric unhappiness reflects my own. Whether I like it or not I'm drawn in, walking toward him. Felix pushes himself upright and I rise onto my tiptoes, our two sadnesses colliding before we even touch each other. There's a split-second opportunity for me to say something, like—

I can't

I have a boyfriend

my sister

we need to stop

but then it's gone and Felix's mouth is crushing mine, the bakery bags smooshing between our out-of-control bodies. This kiss isn't like yesterday's. It's pure commotion. We're entangled, his fingers bruising my waist and simultaneously running through my hair; our teeth and tongues mashing together. We've barely said hello. Come to think of it, I barely know this person, and I've never made out in public before—not like this. But I can't seem to get a grip on myself. Because as long as we're kissing, nothing else matters, because there *is* nothing else. It blanks out my brain, disappears all thoughts of medicine or madness.

We finally come up for air and the world rushes back in. I step away so quickly it's almost like a shove and teeter, losing my balance. The croissant bags tumble to the sidewalk. Bending to grab them lets me catch my breath, hide my flushed face. That wasn't a kiss: It was an exorcism. When I'm upright again, Felix is shoving his hair to and fro. He looks feral, totally effing unhinged—which is how I feel. I stare back at him, my heart threatening to burst right through my rib cage.

I think we're never going to stop staring at each other, when his eyes flick across the road and he says, "Your sister."

Sick adrenaline kicks in. My legs wobble. I turn around in super slow motion.

On the other side of the road, Emmy-Kate is trudging to school, a snail under the shell of her enormous backpack. The glitzy, glittering girl of last night is gone. My sister looks like isolation personified. It makes me want to hurl these croissants I'm clutching into the sky.

I have no idea if she saw us kissing. Possibly not—her eyes are on the sidewalk, and she's not screaming at me or setting my hair on fire—but bile floods my mouth anyway.

Delirious, and not in a good way, I turn back to Felix. He's a charcoal sketch of a boy, hawk eyes watching me from beneath thick brushstroke curls. Together, we form a deep shadow. A place where nothing exists but loss.

And I don't want to be there anymore.

I don't want to believe that I'll feel this terrible for a lifetime, or that being with Felix is the only way to retrieve my colors. I don't want Emmy-Kate to look like a cloud, or for Niko to hate my guts. I don't want to kiss a boy who knows my mum's art but doesn't know *her*, doesn't have any idea that she did ordinary things too, like cook grilled cheese. When Ash came around to dinner he'd say happily, "Student food!"

Before I know which words are going to spill from me, I've said them: "We have to stop, I can't kiss you again. It's not—" I thrust the croissant bags at him, as if this is explanation. "I can't."

Felix's jaw tenses. His eyes grow darker, trying to work out what's changed. I don't blame him: Twenty-four hours ago, we were skipping school in marmalade sunshine. Two *minutes* ago, we were practically having sex on the sidewalk.

"You're serious?" he asks, tugging at his hair again so hard I'm amazed he isn't bald.

"Yes." No. I don't know.

We're standing in the exact spot under the lamppost where we hugged two nights ago. I look away from Felix's desolation to Meadow Park. Beyond the gates, the hill is veiled in a damp, spooky fog, as though a piece of deepest winter has been cut out of some other year and transported here into this September day.

Far in the distance, Emmy-Kate is drifting to school, a speck of dust blown through the landscape. I want to go back to the beginning of the story, play the song again, tear up the drawing and start over. There are some things you can't undo.

"Why?" asks Felix.

"I'm sorry," I whisper. This is the perfect moment to explain to him that I have a boyfriend, but I still don't say so. I don't want to admit out loud what a monster I am. Instead, I edge away on shaking legs, walking backward, then turn and head toward home. The thought of school, art, seems beyond impossible.

Waiting at the traffic lights, I take gigantic gulps of London smog, wishing-hoping-wondering if Felix will follow and try to talk me out of this. It's not absolute: There's still a small part of me that wants to run back into his arms and carry on merrily smashing my life to pieces. But when the lights change, I make myself cross the road.

When I finally look over my shoulder, he's not even there.

．　．　．　．　．

I'm still standing on the corner of Full Moon Lane like this—unraveled—when a bus pulls up to the stop ten yards away. Impulsively, I run to catch it and collapse into a seat on the top deck, resting my heavy head against the window.

I've no idea what route number this is, but it doesn't matter. I used to do this all the time: take any bus at random and ride it across London, watching the city flow from neighborhood to neighborhood. Crossing the river transformed my town into an entirely different place, making me feel like I'd fallen down a rabbit hole.

My breath mists the window and I squeak my finger through it, writing:

Then huff on the words and rub them out with my fist. Beyond the erased sentence, brittle sun shines on rapidly emptying trees. It's six days until October, over three months since the goodbye letter fragmented our lives, and winter is sending out feelers. Stretching ahead are foggy mornings. Snow. Bare trees, icy sidewalks, empty skies. In a month it will be half term. Then Diwali, Bonfire Night, Advent, Hanukkah, Christmas. Niko's birthday, then mine. New Year. Always.

Year after year after year, days will roll on and on. I will leave school, become an artist or fail, fall in love, travel and, ultimately, become a completely different person. And she will always be the same.

I don't know how I'm supposed to survive each of these minutes without her.

If I so much as deadhead a rose or cut my hair or break up with the boyfriend she knew or go somewhere other than SCAD, I will change the world in some small, incremental way. I'll make it into a place she won't recognize and can't come back to. She'll never know about any of these new choices, and that is unacceptable to me.

By some cosmic coincidence, the bus route I've chosen is trundling around the outskirts of the SCAD campus. There's my future.

I hunch down in my seat, turning my back on the buildings, and text Ash: *Hey.*

Three little dots appear, then nothing.

I swipe out of my texts and punch in Mum's number, hoping against all odds and judgment she'll answer, say, "Honey! I'm at the studio. Come on over, let's open the kiln."

But instead she climbs the stairs of the bus and sits next to me, dressed in the summer outfit she disappeared in. Smock bestrewn in ten thousand glaze colors, bare legs, yellow sandals, pink toenails. Clothes too cold for late September. I know, I know: Her clothes don't matter, because she's not coming back. But why is it so wrong to want her to?

No one answers the phone, but next to me, imaginary Mum says, "What's up, Minnie?"

With the phone still pressed to my ear, I ask, "Why did you do it?"

She makes a game-show buzzing sound. "Wrong question. You should be asking . . . why did I think I *could* come back from that?"

"Okay, so why—?"

She leans her face in front of mine, rolling back her irises to show the whites of her eyes and waggling her tongue grotesquely, like a medieval lunatic. "Because I'm craaaazy. That's what you believe, isn't it?"

"I don't know *what* to believe," I mutter. The passenger ahead glances over their shoulder; I scowl back at them.

Then I hear Mum's voice mail cut in, and her melodious voice sings in my ear—literally—ten times as real as the one in my imagination:

"This is Rachael Sloe—fast talker, fifth Beatle. Don't let me down: For commissions, please contact my agent; we can work it out. For everything else, love me do."

When it beeps, I croak: "If I'm as crazy as you are, what happens to me at the end of the story? After years of this—do I end up going over Beachy Head too?" Then I hang up, pressing both hands across my face, trying to hold in the howl of outrage that's been building in me ever since the colors disappeared.

"That's your question?" Mum shakes her head, peering over my hedgehogged body to press her face to the window. The bus is still noodling around SCAD, shadowed by its squat square buildings. They look like kilns.

"I noticed you haven't applied yet," she says. "How come? You're a shoo-in."

"Why are you so sure about that?" I mutter into my hands, squeezing my eyes shut.

"Duh, Minnie. Because you're my daughter."

"That's the only reason?"

No reply. I peep through my fingers. Mum is swinging from the seat, ringing the bell, and dashing down the stairs. I leap up and follow her off the bus, trying to figure out why I'm imagining her all wrong. My mother was, is, a thousand things—suicidal, mad, gifted, obsessive, focused and vague all at once, messy, starlit, a terrible cook—but never cruel.

She endlessly encouraged us, right from when we were little kids and our portfolios were finger painting and potato printing, macaroni art and toilet paper roll angels on the Christmas tree. She would never tell me I could coast on being a Sloe: She wanted us to earn it, live and breathe it.

I'm no longer imagining her; I'm haunting myself.

When I step from the bus Mum is nowhere to be seen, and I'm a couple of streets from the studio, so I walk there and find the porcelain still splashed across the floor.

It looks like the sea roared its way up the Thames and threw a rave in here. The kind of wild party Emmy-Kate sneaks off to each night, where she kicks off her shoes and shakes out her hair.

I wish my sisters could see this.

Actually, Niko would flip her lid if I brought her here and it wasn't cleaned up. But when I fetch the mop and bucket from the kitchenette, her coffee cup is back in the sink, filled with water. I close my eyes, gripping the edge of the counter, losing my stupid mind. Did I do that, or was she here?

Don't go crazy, Minnie, I tell myself. At least, not yet. Not until you have some answers . . .

I need to talk to Mum. Need to hold her hand, hear her voice, be hugged by her, be told that everything is going to be okay. The unrequited want convulses through me.

I abandon the mop and try to invoke her, rubbing glycerin hand cream into my palms, hitting PLAY on the stereo. There's a CD in there already and as the Beatles song "I Saw Her Standing There" rings out, I tie on one of her smocks over my dress, exchange my boots for her clogs, start the wheel spinning out of pure habit. The whole time, there's a *rat-a-tat-tat* of fear and heartbreak breaking out all over my skin, because no visions of Mum appear. I don't think I'm going to see her, not ever again, whatever I do.

Blown by the motion of the wheel, a scrap of paper goes fluttering across the floor. It's Felix's instructions on how to make porcelain. The only evidence that he and I once had a beginning. But I don't want to make porcelain, or clay for that matter.

I want to think about the time Mum first decided to bring me here to the studio, the year after she returned to full-time art. It was the end of the Christmas holidays, a few days after my thirteenth birthday. We were all in the kitchen, going stir-crazy from being cooped up with weeks of rain—especially Emmy-Kate, who was practically bouncing off the walls.

"Dare me to go to the pool," she challenged, making her signs supersized.

Niko shook her head. She was scissoring at a piece of paper, sending tiny flurries into the air. I watched them through a brain fog.

"Not on your own," Mum told Emmy-Kate.

"Minnie, come with me?"

"I've got my period." Truth. Not that it stopped me swimming—the fact that it was January stopped me swimming. But ever since getting my first period a few months earlier, I'd had these fuzzy moods. I was in one now—it felt like someone had switched my brain for molasses. My signs came out in slow motion.

"It's going to be reeeaaally cold," Emmy-Kate taunted. When no one answered, she threw her hands up with a "Whatever!" then stomped out into the garden under the angry winter sky. Through the window, she immediately came to life, jumping about on the sodden grass.

Niko dropped her scissors and announced, "I'm going to clean out Salvador Dalí's hutch." She clomped outside to boss Em about.

I put my head down on the table. My skull was so heavy, it seemed as if it should sink right through the wood. For no reason and every reason, I wanted to cry.

"Quick, while they're all gone," Mum hissed, her hand stroking my brow.

I tried to answer. But words weighed so much, and my mouth and hands didn't move.

"Honey, when did you last wash your hair?" she asked, taking her hand from my head. "Never mind: I've been waiting for this moment. Minnie." She hauled me upright like a sack of potatoes. "We're going to the studio. You and me."

This drew a word from me: "What?"

The Alpha Centauri gleam in her eye told me she'd throw me over her shoulder and drag me there if she had to. Also: seriously? She was taking me to the studio now? This was on par with announcing we were going to visit Aladdin's cave or Disneyland. But in my sludgeville state, I couldn't understand it.

When I thought about it later, I assumed she'd plucked the

concept from the night sky like any other of her whims—
buying Salvador Dalí, returning to art in the first place, painting the floorboards pink, befriending the Professor.

I missed the obvious. Mum hadn't spied some latent ceramics ability I had, or singled me out as the heir to her talent. She
was keeping an eye on me, keeping me close, studying my
moods.

She saw the sinkholes in me before I did.

Almond

(An Ongoing List of Every
Color I Have Lost)

*Bisque-fired porcelain, not quite white yet.
Marzipan. Flaked and toasted slivers on top of the
perfect croissant from Felix. The pale, strained
look on his face when I walked away from him.*

CHAPTER 24

The Color of Shrouds

I race home from the studio through thick velvet air. The clouds seem close enough to brush against my skin, justifying my decision to skip school. (Again.) This is the kind of day made for lying on your back at the top of Meadow Park, swimming in the sky. But first, I'm going to ransack Mum's room once and for all. Open the box, face up to her medical diagnosis, stop calling it sinkholes and starlight, determine why she dived into the sea. Summon her one last time and have a real conversation.

The house is empty. With Emmy-Kate still at school and Niko at SCAD, it's desolate as dirt. The distinct unearthly absence of anything living or breathing—with apologies to Salvador Dalí, who emerges from under the sofa as I close the curtains against the Professor's prying eyes.

He—the rabbit, not our neighbor—hops slowly behind me as I wander from room to room, finally winding up in Mum's doorway.

The emptiness is infinite. Niko hasn't emptied the place, but she's stripped the life from it. There are vacuum marks striping the rug, and the mirror shines spotlessly. Even Mum's fingerprints have been wiped out. I open the wardrobe and gather her dresses and smocks into my arms, inhaling and inhaling and inhaling, but Niko has hung them with a lavender sachet and propped the window open, vanishing Mum's scent.

Every day, she's really, truly gone a little bit more.

I sink to my knees, peering under the bed. Salvador Dalí blinks back at me from the vacant space. The shoebox isn't there. WTF?

"Mum?" My voice echoes, but she doesn't show.

I stand up, unsure what to do, and my eye falls on the empty surface of the dressing table. When I open the bottom drawer, it's filled with neatly rolled sweaters, wrapped in tissue paper and tucked beneath mothballs. No room for a box. I leave the drawer open, like a burglar, and pull out the middle one, then the top two. Nothing but her cosmetics and an almost-empty bowl of broken earrings.

I think about Emmy-Kate plundering Mum's shoes, wearing her jewelry, smoking . . .

Back out in the hall, I peep through Emmy-Kate's keyhole. Her window is wide open. Next to it is a huge canvas propped on an easel, covered in handprints. She really has been painting with her fingers. The door opens with a soft *click*.

Pact, schmact: Stepping over this threshold feels revelatory. I'm rediscovering my sister, like an art historian scraping back years and centuries of paint and varnish and dirt, breaking down these walls between us. No more secrets.

"No more secrets!" I yell out of the window, then remember the Professor working on his magnum opus next door, and duck back. When he doesn't appear, I poke my head out into the morning again and breathe in whopping great lungfuls of the garden, my chest filling with the pine smell of the sun, as if Poets Corner has landed on the beach.

Then I turn to Emmy-Kate's desk.

It has more in common with mine than Niko's: The drawers are half-open, overflowing with dried-up felt-tips—minus their caps—train tickets, makeup, old birthday cards, candy wrappers, notepads, an empty vitamin bottle. I sift through it all, find nothing but glitter. The wardrobe reveals little except that most of Mum's most glamorous clothes have migrated here. I bury my face in these sequined dresses too, but they now smell of Emmy-Kate—cherry-vanilla perfume and malevolence.

The medicine box isn't hidden in any of the places you might expect, like under the bed or in the wardrobe. It's not under a heap of shoes or in the rank-smelling laundry basket. But when I slide my hand under her mattress, my fingers land on something. I pull it out.

A condom packet.

Unused.

Oh my God.

I sweep my arm underneath the mattress again, as far as it will go, and retrieve more condoms, a foil packet of birth control. I think of all the times I saw Emmy-Kate creeping from the garden in a teeny-tiny dress, or sneaking a boy from her room, or blinking at me, desperate to talk—and I didn't say a word to her.

But I'm totally out of my depth!

There's no one to tell about the condoms and the pills. So I put them back under my baby sister's mattress and burst out of her room like I'm being pursued by spiders, crash straight into Niko's—ignoring the invisible sign on her door saying KEEP OUT, MINNIE—because if Emmy-Kate's having underage sex, what the heck is Niko hiding?

My pulse drums in my ears. Niko's bedroom is neat as ever. No dust bunnies or eight thousand half-drunk glasses of water or underwear on the floor here. Only dozens of candles, burnt to stumps. There are no clues, and no box—in light of the Emmy-Kate discovery, I've almost forgotten about the original purpose of my search.

Her chest of drawers reveals nothing but T-shirts, ironed and folded into stacks, headscarves wedged into neat triangles. A rail holds identikit dungarees. The desk drawer holds scissors and scalpels and knives, all safety-capped and bundled together with elastic bands. I brush them aside, and something shiny beneath them catches my eye.

It turns out to be a stack of glossy brochures for non-London art schools—the Ruskin School of Art at Oxford, Glasgow School of Art—and normal universities, faraway options like Manchester, Newcastle, Leeds, Edinburgh.

What the heck? Niko never told us she'd thought about applying anywhere but SCAD.

I never even knew it was an option. Going somewhere else. Not going to art school at all, studying English or history instead. There are artists who don't have art degrees: Frida Kahlo, Basquiat, Yoko Ono . . . And she married a Beatle! *I* could go to—

I slam the drawer on the brochures and that thought simultaneously, stomach churning. Clench and unclench my fists, open the next one.

It holds a mystifying selection of religious and superstitious stuff. An actual rabbit's foot—this, despite vegetarianism and love of Salvador Dalí; a plastic light-up Jesus figurine; rosaries; a maneki-neko lucky cat; joss sticks; a tiny Ganesh idol. This is stuff I'd expect to see in the Professor's home office, not here.

Turns out, I don't know either of my sisters half as well as I thought.

The next drawer proves it. It's overflowing with watercolor paper, pages fluttering out to the floor.

Instead of being cut into pieces, the paper is covered in words. Niko's handwriting, in ordinary ink pen, front and back, upside-down and all over. Inky lines crisscross each other, scrawled up the margins. Niko is writing with

words standing on end

& CAPITAL LETTERS IN THE MIDDLE OF THE PAGE

and tiny sentences squished against the edge of the paper

Bone-chilling fragments leap out at me: *Mum* and *SCAD* and *the dark is not what I am afraid of* and *coffin is the smallest word*.

I'm standing in her room, but in my mind, I see her at the kitchen table, scribbling these frantic essays, flipping shut the pad whenever I walk in. I see her locked in this solitary room for hours, writing inexplicable Sylvia Plath–meets–e. e. cummings poetry with her eyes closed and all these candles aglow. Forget Emmy-Kate's condoms—this is definitely not what I expected.

I can't be in the house for another minute. Not with the walls closing in on me, secrets rattling like skeletons. No longer caring about the pact, I take Niko's poems from the drawer, gathering them in my arms and racing to the *Rainbow Series I*, where I coil like a snake under my favorite bubble, and start reading. Start making my way home to my sister.

Hello

Listen. Not even light can escape.
I went to church, temple, mosque,
synagogue, monastery, looking for
the answer. It was somewhere else.

Niko has inked out a reflection of the words, backward, as if there's a mirror on the page.

I forget about the reality of what I'm doing—reading my sister's diary!—and instead fall in love with her poetry. Hours of afternoon go by, the sun growing longer and later as I let Niko's bleak words envelop me, mingling and jumbling together.

And the surprises keep coming: Niko hates SCAAAAAD. She's as jealous of Emmy-Kate's beauty as I am. And losing Mum has made her more desperately miss a father. She resents being our guardian. That's why she keeps inviting the Professor around, hoping he'll discipline us so she can give up.

It's early afternoon by the time I read the last poem, and stop breathing.

Confession

My sisters are not the only ones with secrets.
I watch Minnie and Felix through my window,

suspended between orange lampposts.
It's a golden-hour sunset—
the Hollywood kind where light seems like a miracle
and you want to catch time in the palm of your hand.

But I am not looking at the outrageous sky.
I'm looking at them.
The baddest boy in Poets Corner,
and the saddest girl.
Except Minnie isn't sad. She's smiling.
I turn away as the sky burns down,
leaving behind nothing but ash.

Even my dunderhead-moron-doesn't-understand-poetry brain gets it: Niko knows about Felix. Seeing it this way, in my sister's unhappy, candle-smudged words, my guilt swells to astronomical proportions.

How could I be so cavalier with her heart? With Ash's?

No wonder I can't see in color. I'm not a girl who deserves green. Or pink, or yellow, or any of the rainbow. This is why this should-be-turquoise bubble above me is black.

I roll onto my back, thumping my fists on its glazed surface, wishing it would shatter into a hundred pieces, rain down clay, and bury me in dust. Every bone in my body moans and breaks as I think about Niko's acute unhappiness and Emmy-Kate having sex with ten thousand boys.

Why has life turned out so awfully?

Here to answer that question is Felix Waters.

He's prowling into the walled garden, giving off seriously intense caged-tiger vibes. Exactly like the first time we encountered each other, he goes striding past my bubble, then doubles back, staring down at me through disheveled hair, utterly overwrought. Wow, he's beautiful.

"Minnie," he says, all anguish. "You . . ."

"I'm sorry." I shake my head back and forth in the soil. I'm not talking to him but to Emmy-Kate and Niko. The revelations are exploding like fireworks now, my family falling apart and the one person who could fix it, gone.

Felix comes closer, casting a cool shadow over me. As I stare up at him, this thought dawns: The connection between us is because we're both walking around with our insides ripped out. We're both half people, trying to be whole. That's the love story for a girl who is broken: another broken person.

Part of me wants to give in to this idea. Give in to the sinkholes, to being damaged, because I am so effing tired of fighting it. But another part of me thinks, *Holy Botticelli, this is depressing.*

"Minnie," Felix says, his voice raw. I start wriggling out from underneath the bubble. "I'm not okay. Look, I'm sorry, or whatever. If I did something . . ."

"You didn't do anything." I shake my head again. We're standing opposite each other, surrounded by ridiculous roses and these impossible floating ceramics. There's a paintbrush sticking out of his jeans pocket, smears all over his hands. Maybe there is more to us than misery—there's art, too.

"So, then, why?" asks Felix. "I don't understand, and . . ." He ducks his head, giving me one of his X-ray-vision looks. "You were supposed to be my grief twin, you know? The other half of all this crap."

I'm enthralled by his batwing darkness, spiraling toward it. I don't understand Mum's choice to walk off a cliff, or let us think she has—who does that?—but I'm captivated by the idea of surrendering to misery the way Felix does. But then I think of Emmy-Kate and Ash and Niko and every reckless, stupid error I've made since school started, and say, "You don't even know me. We've known each other, what, three weeks?"

"I do . . . ," he says, his voice sending shivers through my chest even though I tell myself to resist. "I *do* know you. I know you want to have a tea party inside a dinosaur, you own a surrealist house rabbit, and you wear those boots so often I think they're glued to your feet." I look down. My feet are back in their allotted footwear instead of Mum's platforms. When I got dressed this morning, I wanted to look like me. "On the rare occasions you actually draw, you stick out your lips like Donald Duck. When you eat croissants, you close your eyes, like a little kid. Your hair always looks bizarre, and I don't think I've ever heard you swear, you say 'eff,' and you have all these weird cardigans you're constantly tugging down over your hands. And—" He breaks off, his shoulders hunching into a frown.

Meanwhile, I'm on the *effing* floor. Ash has never given me a speech like this. (But, Minnie, hasn't he given you enormous pizzas, cheesy Valentine's cards, astounding smiles, hundreds of love songs on his guitar?) *Shut up*, I tell myself. I don't want to hear it. I want to stay in this single moment, with the clouds whizzing by and Felix's mournful face echoing my own so exactly, we're no longer mirror images but one mega-sad person.

That's the crux of the matter: We are both so stupidly sad. I step forward and press my hands flat against Felix's chest, discover the slow drum of his heart under my palms. His forehead drops to mine, and already I'm breathing a little easier. We fit. I don't know why, but we do.

And I know that kissing him will break Ash's heart and Niko's in turn, like dominoes, but I do it anyway. I kiss him. And let him kiss me. Felix tastes of cigarettes and salt, and he's the one stupid thing that makes this monochrome girl feel close to being understood.

"Holy Michelangelo."

When I hear the words, I know it's Emmy-Kate—only she could sound so cotton candy and so appalled at the same time.

Felix and I freeze, then inch apart. Our lips puffed, our faces panicked.

I swivel my head and discover I'm wrong; it's not Emmy-Kate. Or not only her, anyway.

They're all here.

Emmy-Kate. Ash, for once minus his guitar. Niko, with her hands pressed to her mouth.

My heart goes on display at Tate Modern. Pinned out wide like a butterfly behind glass, wrapped in a gold-gilt frame and spotlit, accompanied with a gallery-wall caption:

Minnie Sloe (b. 2001)
"I AM SO EFFING LOST" (2019)
Mixed media—muscle, veins, and blood
An ongoing performance piece
after the artist's mother disappears.
Minnie behaves unforgivably.

I lift my eyes to Ash's. Even if by some miracle he missed that almighty kiss, he knows. The truth is there in my every weird mood of the past few weeks, hiding under the bed, ignoring his texts, coming home with dirty feet and a song in my heart, pulling away in every conversation. It's all over my Sloe sister can't-keep-a-secret eyes.

But of all the things to say, I choose: "How did you know where to find me?"

Emmy-Kate stomps her foot. She's close to tears, but signs what I said to Niko.

Niko snorts. "It was here or the studio. We were going there next. You went in Emmy-Kate's room?"

I can tell by the unruffled way her hands move that she (a) doesn't know what I found in Em's room and (b) hasn't yet noticed her missing poems, which are on the ground by my feet. Of course, the breeze chooses this moment to come to life, stirring the roses and rustling the paper.

"Ash deserved to know," signs-says Emmy-Kate, her voice quivering. I glance at her. She's cocking her head defiantly, and I know without a doubt that this is her showdown. She brought Ash along as witness, on purpose.

"Minnie," Felix says behind me, his hand on my sleeve. "What's going on?"

I ignore him, don't sign what he said, and tell Ash, "I'm sorry," taking a few unsteady steps toward him. My sisters clear a path, Niko with an unreadable glance at Ash before she fades into the background.

Ash doesn't say a word. Stares at me with folded arms, face a brick wall, no way in. Not so much as an Elvis sneer. There's no sign of the boy who is eggs sunny-side up, a winning lottery ticket, a human four-leaf clover. Only this angry version of my boyfriend—no, not even angry. There's no revulsion. There's nothing. Just, ugh, disappointment.

"I'm sorry," I say again, pointlessly. "I . . . Me and Felix. He. We're not. It's not like that. We're nothing, but . . ." I start and finish a thousand aborted sentences, none of them an explanation, because what explanation is there? "He understands." Then I bleat: "My *mummy*." The closest I can come to the pathetic truth.

I try to step forward, into his arms, but there's no space for me. Ash lurches away, as if he can't even bear to share the same air. And the worst part is, even as I'm watching the realization flood through him, I'm also noticing Felix brush past me, his face a mask of disgust, storming from the garden.

"Felix!" I shout, but he only runs faster, and then is gone.

I shatter. The breeze is building, blowing around this last gasp of summer weather. Niko's poems swirl at my feet. There's this poem we had to read last year in school, about hope being the thing with feathers that perches in the soul. It probably means parrots, flamingos, Disney bluebirds—something cute, with rainbows for wings. I've got a crow perched in me. It sinks its claws into my stomach, pecks at my chest, flaps its furious wings against my ribs.

"I'm sorry," I mutter again, to Ash's continued stonewalling. I know I'm in the wrong here, but the silent treatment is beginning to grate. "At least let me explain?"

He stares, and stares, and stares, and still doesn't say anything, and then this head-spinning-hell-beast roar of frustration emerges from me:

RRRRRRRRRRRRRRRUUUUUUUUUUUUUUUU UUHHHHHHHHHHHHHH!

And uh-oh, wait, there's more, rage bubbling up after weeks and months of holding it back. I can't stop myself, Monster Minnie opens her mouth and goes on a rampage, letting Ash really have it—all the rage that should be directed at my stupid baby sister for not knowing about the goodbye letter, for being happy; at Niko for bottling up her feelings into these poems, now flying through the sky around us like confetti; at the Professor for his bumbling intrusions; and most of all at Mum, for leaving us when she shouldn't have, when she had a choice:

"Uuuuuhhhhh, why aren't you speeeeaaaaaaaking," I rage, sounding like Emmy-Kate at her absolute whiniest worst. "And what are you doing here, anyway? It's like you're always turning up at the house and acting as if I can be cheered up by you playing that stupid guitar, la la la la la, pretending everything's okay, ooh, let's go to Italy, are you aight Minnie? and no, of course I'm not all right, Ash, of course I'm not, so why would you ask such a stupid effing question and why aren't you talking now? *God.*"

I stop abruptly, chest heaving. Equal parts exhilarated and aghast. Where in the world did all that projectile word vomit come from?

Strangely, shouting everything out has made me feel a little better—until I see that Ash's head has drooped under this onslaught. For a moment it looks like he's praying, then that he's angry. His shoulders heave up and down like mountains. Then I see it: He's crying. He goes stumbling from the garden, not looking at troglodyte-werewolf-Grendel me.

Remorse rains down on my head.

I've almost forgotten my sisters. I turn to see them both glaring at me.

Poems are snowflaking all around us, white against the blackening sky.

"You went in my room too?" Niko asks. "When Emmy-Kate texted me, I—"

Her hands part to say something else, then she stops, shaking her head, giving up on me, turning away without another word.

Emmy-Kate follows, spinning on her ridiculous platform shoe. Niko puts an arm around her shoulders, and the two of them walk away.

I drop my head into my hands, and the whole of me beneath the bubble, shutting out the entire stupid world.

CHAPTER 25

Every Single Color in the Universe at the Same Time

My sisters do not come back to claim me. I lie beneath the clay, waiting for a night that doesn't arrive quickly enough. Sun ribbons across the sky for hours, chasing feathers of cloud.

Every bubble in the *Rainbow Series I* is black. Not shiny and reflective but matte, forming a hole in the world. And inside each one, a memory. Felix and me trying to outrun each other's demons. Ash, defeated. Lonesome Emmy-Kate having sex the whole summer, and I didn't stop her once. Stealing Niko's private poetry—now littered all over Meadow Park—and worst of all, the fact that I pushed the self-destruct button on purpose. Why else would I ransack my sisters' rooms and leave the evidence behind, kiss Felix in such obviously public places? Some part of me was pushing for this to happen, looking for a way out.

Then there's this memory, over and over: Mum waving joyously goodbye without a single hint of what she was about to do.

I can't bear to see her leaving, so I roll into a ball and close my eyes.

But that makes me feel like I'm falling, so I open them again.

Color slaps me across the face.

Click-your-fingers quick. Like God flipped a switch and blasted the world with full-on-lurid-rainbow-migraine-inducing-fluorescent-neon-highlighter Technicolor.

I screw my eyes shut again, bury my face in my hands, try to blank it all out, try to wish myself out of existence, out of this stupid garden, out of my life. Can't. Blink open my eyes and see evil-nightmare-clown colors.

It's a fauvist painting. Matisse himself has opened a packet of Sharpies and gone to town, coloring everything incorrectly: tree trunks are lime-green, the grass blue, and paths electric orange. The colors turn the air loud, a crash of cymbals. I can hear them.

Ash and Felix and Niko and Emmy-Kate and Mum.

How could you, Minnie?

The truth.

Eyes open: color.

Eyes closed: me.

And her.

This is what I've been afraid of for months, ever since I saw the locked kiln and the goodbye letter addressed to me alone, because she knew I of all people would instantly understand what she meant by Beachy Head and the words *disappear into the sky.*

I can't escape it.

Stepping off a cliff isn't the normal thing to do, is it? Nor is talking to imaginary mothers or seeing in black and white or walking around sometimes with a rock-heavy weight inside your chest.

I close my eyes again and see her, falling from five hundred feet.

In slow motion, her clothes fly off, launched into the clouds. Her smock, her shoes, her dress. Then her skin peels away. Each bone breaks free, then her luminous hair until, halfway through the empty sky, she disappears altogether.

My mother vanishes.

And without her, there's only me and this horrifying truth: I'm as crazy as she was.

White

(An Ongoing List of Every Color I Have Lost)

Rodin's The Kiss—*a boner in Pentelic marble. The thick, textured Daler-Rowney paper of Niko's poems. Porcelain splashed across a floor. New paintbrushes. Blank canvases. And paint and glazes: Titanium, Zinc, Transparent, Flake, Cremnitz, Iridescent, Mixing, Chinese, all these different whites, all of them gone.*

Gray
(An Ongoing List of Every
Color I Have Lost)

*Sidewalks. Rain. The Professor's conversational
gambits. Drawing pencils. Sometimes everything
everything everything. The color of forever.
Loneliness. Waiting for her to come back.
My vacant heart.*

Black

(An Ongoing List of Every Color I Have Lost)

Hope. The sea at its deepest point. A coffin underneath the dirt. Night. Shrouds. Crematoriums. This endless endlessness. Me.

PART TWO

A Mad Girl's Love Song

CHAPTER 26

The Color of Starlessness

After a few hours spent cringing in the corner of the walled garden, fear slowly relinquishes to calm. My breathing steadies. The topsy-turvy colors fade back into deep and dark monochrome. I wriggle out from my hidey-hole and look around. It's a lovely evening: the gray sunset gleams, coaxing shadows from the roses. I'm not all right—I'll never be truly all right again, or even *aight*—but I feel something like stable.

Niko's poems are scattered across the walled garden: nesting in trees, floating among the flowers, clinging to the *Rainbow Series I*. I start gathering them up, my foot crunching on something. I lift my sole and see a hard pastel stick in a paper tube, crushed between the paving stone and my boot. Felix.

But my thoughts turn to Ash, and how we're finally, truly over. Irretrievably, irreparably doneso. There's a whoosh of relief, like jumping into an enormous pile of crunchy leaves, followed fast by regret so strong it knocks me sideways. Ash is so lovely and so kind, and I've played yo-yo with his feelings, his kisses, pushed him away, bawled him out. I've severed all hope of reconciliation, of ever speaking. And he's one of the few people I know outside of my sisters who knew Mum—it's like losing another part of her.

Briefly, I consider hiding out with the *Rainbow Series I* for the next, ooh, forever. But I'd rather face the music than have Niko stomp back up here and drag me out, so I start walking home. The sun is sinking rapidly, and at the bottom of the hill, the Full Moon Inn is radiant against encroaching night.

Felix Waters. Yearning tumbles through me as I recall that tumultuous cyclone of a kiss. His speech, the way he's seen the details of me and possibly fallen in love with them. But I broke him too. Two boys' hearts in one night, it must be a record—I bet even Emmy-Kate and her millions of condoms hasn't managed that.

A train passes by below with a donkey hee-haw honk, pulling me from my thoughts. This is when I see the Professor standing halfway up the hill, à la the grand old Duke of York. He has one hand to his brow, scanning the horizon; the other holds a flashlight. Oh—he's sending out a search party for me. Knowing that the Professor cares enough to come looking gives me an inkling of belonging, of safety. How weird is that?

I plod toward him, and he coughs into his fist, sticks his hands in his pockets.

"Come along, come along," he mutters, like Alice's White Rabbit. I trail him home in shameful silence.

The Professor ushers me into my own kitchen. There's no sign of Emmy-Kate and Niko, but the lights are on and the room is a cocoon of warmth and welcome. It smells like pizza, and there are boxes folded up by the trash can. I've missed dinner. The Professor motions for me to sit, then makes tea in a slow, ponderous fashion. He places a mug in front of me, then sits opposite, resting his hands on the table, on either side of his tea.

"Well." His voice is creaky, the sound an old church door might make, as if he's opening it up to give me a sermon of some kind.

I lock eyes with my mug, mortified. After a few fidgety minutes, in which I wait for another *well* that doesn't come, I peep up. The Professor is sipping his tea. There are deep grooves around his mouth, practically engraved. He's aged about a hundred years since summer.

Eventually he says, "Your sister sent me to find you. Asked that I talk to you. Again."

I'm confused, then I remember the Visa bill speech—and the poems of Niko's where she wished she could pass her guardianship to the Professor. I brace myself for the Ash lecture, but instead he asks, "How go the university applications? All set for SCAD?"

I squirm. I haven't even signed up for a SCAD log-in to apply, let alone finished a single piece in my portfolio. Not to mention I've skipped school two days in a row. The deadline isn't until January, anyway, but the thought of the work it will take makes me want to lie down and sleep for a hundred years.

"Fine," I lie, wrapping my hands around my mug and shivering. I hadn't realized until this minute how cold I am. This has been the longest day.

The Professor nods. Uneasily, I observe the droop of his face: jowls, beard, shoulders, all slumped together in an avalanche of dejection. He doesn't look like he wants to give me a lecture on Niko's behalf.

"The Prof—" I cut myself off in time and say, "Professor Gupta?"

"Yes?" He blinks at me the same fluttery way Ash sometimes does, with a small smile. It almost makes me laugh, how briefly alike the gesture makes them. Perhaps there is some great reason—I mean, hidden *really* deep down—Mum chose the Professor for her best friend.

"What, um," I continue. "Did Mum . . . Did she ever talk to you about . . . her—about being ill?" I stutter and stammer to a halt, unsure how to phrase the question. "Like, her being crazy, I mean."

"Crazy?" he barks, misunderstanding ruffling his face as he peers at me. More gently, he adds, "Er—Minnie. I'm not sure . . . Your mother was sometimes unhappy, definitely complicated, often . . . erm . . . an upsy-downsy sort of person."

I think about *The White Album* and the *Rainbow Series I*, amazing and opposite artworks that have drawn worldwide acclaim. The spectacularly selfish act of going missing and leaving three teenage daughters. The interview in which she called synesthesia a kind of madness; the box beneath her bed filled with prescription medications I'm not sure she always took; starlit days and sinkhole ones when she had no use for smiling. *Upsy-downsy* doesn't begin to cover it.

"Do you think . . ." I ask hesitantly. I've known the Professor almost my whole life, and we've never had a conversation like this. It's like trying to talk to a briefcase. "Do you think she was only successful . . . I mean, do you think her art was good because she was, um, complicated?"

The Professor yanks on his bow tie, looks for an escape route, blows on his tea even though he's drunk it all. This is the kind of conversation Mum might have rejoiced in—the origins of art!—but he looks like he's being slowly strangled. Finally he harrumphs, "Rachael's talent was separate from her . . . hmm, humph, her mind. She had her moments, but she never made art when she was unhappy, did she?" There's a little "ha" of triumph on his face at this argument.

"No, she made art when she was a bit"—I wave my arms above my head, then try to talk the Professor's language, change *unhinged* to—"overenergetic."

He strokes his chin, going into what I recognize as one of his academic theology lectures. These usually happen over too-long dinners with Mum, and I tune them out, but now I listen attentively as he says, "Ah, here's the rub. What is crazy, really? Perhaps it's simply behavior that we don't understand. Historically, martyrs have been accused of insanity—and, then, of course, there's the witch trials . . ."

I tune out his unhelpfulness. Because there are artists who are definitely mad: Vincent van Gogh—not only that whole severed-his-own-ear thing, but he also shot himself in the chest. Michelangelo slept in his shoes. Edvard Munch had visions and hallucinations, Georgia O'Keeffe was hospitalized with anxiety, Francisco Goya was delirious, graffitiing the walls of his house with the *Black Paintings* series, surreal images of despair.

Each one totally certifiable. But also geniuses.

Perhaps the two always go hand in hand, the way you can't have joy without sorrow, can't have love without risking your heart a little bit, can't wake without sleeping; winter and summer, failure and success, Emmy-Kate *and* Niko.

Then again, plenty of my favorite artists manage to be stable as suburbia, so who the eff knows?

"Now, er—Minnie." The Professor concludes his ramblings, pushing back his chair with a squeak. "I must say good night. Tomorrow," he adds, "I have a whole day researching in the British Library!"

"Er, good?"

"Indeed, yes." He beams, rocking on his heels. I'm surprised to feel a sudden rush of fondness for his out-and-out nerdiness.

I walk him to the front door, replaying our conversation, no closer to any answers. He's halfway down the path when I blurt it: "Were you in love with Mum?"

"Oh." The Professor turns, tugging on his bow tie. "Wouldn't that have been something?" He stares off into the night, years and years into the past. "I was in awe of your mother. Who wouldn't be? And I loved her . . . but not in the sense you think."

When he says this, for once he doesn't stutter or waffle or stammer. It's the truth.

"So, then . . . why else do you keep coming around here?" I ask.

He waggles his head, perplexed. "Minnie," he says gently, for once minus the *er*. "Why would I not? Your mother was a lovely woman with very little practical sense. She left you no guardian, Niko made it known she was in difficulty, I am here. What on earth else would I do? It's simply my, er, responsibility."

We're staring at each other, equally bemused. To him, this clearly makes perfect sense. But he's the only one of Mum's friends who's behaved this way. The glitterati art crowd, the Young British Artists, SCAD professors: They've all been interviewed on the news about her art, but they've never once checked in on us. Not asked us about school and eaten fried eggs each Saturday and scolded us about Visa bills.

In a cheesy Hollywood film, this would be the part where I discover I've had a father figure here all along. But, no. It's not that simple. He's just the person who is here. And I find myself astonishingly glad that he is. It's enough.

"Well, there we are," the Professor says, more or less to himself. He shuffles out onto the sidewalk. A moment later, I hear the creak of his own front gate, then the sound of his door opening and softly shutting. I linger on the path for a minute or two, staring up at the starless sky, then I turn around, and go inside.

Beige
(An Ongoing List of Every Color I Have Lost)

Life without a whirlwind mother. Life without these high-highs and low-lows, probably. And that might be what I'm really afraid of. If I fix my broken brain, switch off the monochrome sinkholes and the neon wildness somehow—won't I be a little bit beige? The color of a shoebox beneath a bed.

CHAPTER 27

The Color of Smoke

A cool wind blows in the next morning, ushering normal life back in. I should probably go to school.

At breakfast I collapse at the kitchen table, staring blankly up Emmy-Kate's abstracts. All night long I've been contemplating Mum and madness. The Professor is certain that she was merely complicated; the mysteriously missing shoebox suggests that she has or had some specific diagnosis. I think I'm still more comfortable thinking of it as sinkholes and starlight, something uniquely her, not medicalized.

Although, perhaps if she suspected I had it too, she should have left me with some answers.

Emmy-Kate stalks in and I swivel my head, waving hopefully: "Hey . . ."

She stops, narrowing her eyes until they're two little slits. I can't believe she's having sex.

Hand on bony hip, she says, "Ugh, take a picture, Minnie, it'll last longer."

I take a deep breath, say, "Emmy-Kate, I'm sorry—"

"My room's free now, if you want to go and rummage in my private things," she interrupts, sounding like a poisoned apple, one that speaks.

"I don't, I promise. But can I talk to you about it?"

I'm too late to take on the role of responsible big sister—especially since sex is a topic I know next to nothing about—and Emmy-Kate chirps, "Nope!" while miming zipping her glossy lips. But a confession is bubbling. Her eyes bulge, the proverbial fairy-tale frog sitting on her tongue. Then she thinks better of it, shaking out a never-ending bowl of Frosted Flakes, conspicuously ignoring me as she sits on the counter, kicking her long legs and fiddling with her phone.

I look down at my own lifeless phone. Last night I texted Felix to explain, but he didn't reply, or call, or swoop down the road looking like a beanie-wearing Count Dracula. And no wonder: I did all that with him, when I had a boyfriend. Speaking of whom: I dial Ash's number, but it goes straight to voice mail, the same way it did last night. Over and over again.

Emmy-Kate is slurping and I'm despairing when Niko walks in. She bashes around, loudly charring her toast and crashing into a seat opposite me, arms folded, glaring into space. I try and fail to catch her eye. Last night, I left the salvaged poetry pages propped against her door, along with a note of apology. They were gone this morning, but that's probably more to do with her aversion to clutter than forgiveness.

I'm almost grateful to leave the house. Emmy-Kate runs off till she's miles ahead of me, stomping along on too-high heels, hair swinging from side to side like an angry Shetland pony. And I come face-to-face with the Full Moon Inn. I stop and stare up at the second-floor windows, where I swear I see a curtain twitch. Felix wasn't in the bakery this morning. He's up there watching me, I know it.

The pub's front door is closed, barred shut, but down the side alley, a smaller staff door is propped open. A man with an undertaker air and masses of salt-and-pepper curls is slumped against the fence, eyes closed; the only clue that he's not a statue the smoke curling from his cigarette. Felix's dad, I bet: They both look like life has knocked the stuffing out of them.

I skulk in his direction. Leaves eddy on the sidewalk as I duck past his closed eyes and dart through the door.

The pub is empty, chairs hooked upside down on tables. Sun floats in through leaded windows, illuminating armfuls of dust motes. The air looks like a pointillist painting. Behind the bar is a glass door marked PRIVATE. I swallow my nerves and go through it, then up the stairs beyond.

Each step creaks creepily as I climb. I'm ready to abandon this stupid cloak-and-dagger pursuit when I reach the top and see Felix's bedroom straight ahead.

No question it's his.

The wide-open door reveals walls smothered in art. I walk inside, mesmerized, my fourth bedroom snoop in as many days. Every inch of wall is stuck with sketches, the ceiling too. The dinosaur studies, *The Kiss*—and our kiss (!), the *Rainbow Series I*; portraits. Depressing ones. There are thick, jagged lines through each face. My broken-people theory comes back to me, Felix's claim that I'm his grief twin.

The desk is equally a riot, piled with sketch pads and jars and jars of brushes and pens. Here, there's a self-portrait: Felix in crisis. Black lines streak across the page, capturing his curls and flat mouth in a lion roar of grief. Wowsers. It's entirely possible he drew this with the charcoal in one hand and the other stuck in an electric socket.

And there are portraits of me. Hundreds of them, actually: on dinosaur day, under the willow tree, lying beneath the bubble, slumped on the bench, covered in porcelain, even running from the classroom that first day. Is this a tad stalky for a boy who's known me all of three weeks . . . ? On the other hand, I'm the one sneaking into his bedroom uninvited.

This is when I hear Felix's unhappy rumble from behind me: "What do you want, Minnie?"

I spin around. He's leaning in the doorway: the self-portrait come to life, rebel without a cause, shadows circling his wary eyes. His hair is wet and shoved to one side, dripping onto his T-shirt and jeans, his feet bare. "Hi . . ." I say hesitantly. The last time I saw him, our tongues were locked around each other. Actually, the last time I saw him, he was turning his back and running away without a word. "You weren't answering your phone."

His eyes flick away, then back to mine. A heartbeat passes. My feet start moving toward him, acting on their own accord, when Felix holds up a "stop" hand.

"Don't."

I come to a faltering halt. "I wanted to talk to you," I say.

Felix brings his shoulders up around his ears, then scrubs at his chin with one hand. With his face screwed up, eyes closed, squeezing out the sentence, he says, "Nothing to talk about. You have a boyfriend."

I shake my head. "Actually . . . not anymore."

Felix tilts his head back and says to the ceiling, Adam's apple bobbing, "But you did. And you never said. You let me think . . . And now, what?" He drops his head, eyes blazing. "Let me guess: He saw us kissing and he broke up with you. You're here because there's a Minnie's-boyfriend gap to fill."

"That's not exactly what happened. And I'm not looking for a boyfriend." At least, I don't think I am. "I wanted to explain."

"'Me and Felix. He. We're not. It's not like that. We're nothing,'" he recites. The words I said to Ash at the *Rainbow Series I*. "And," he adds, in a tight, strained voice, "you're right. We're nothing. You're with him. So what is it that you want from me?"

"I want . . ." I trail off.

And therein lies the problem—kind of a huge one. I don't have a clue what I want, and Felix knows it. I bite my lip, looking around the room. Now that I'm accustomed to the ferocious art surrounding us, other details spring from the mess. T-shirts leave a Hansel-and-Gretel trail across the floor—Felix is as allergic to laundry baskets as I am—and his unmade bed is filled with books cracked open at the spines. It makes me want to tell him about the way Emmy-Kate marks her place: tearing off the corner of each page and eating them as she goes along. I don't want things to end before we can have stupid conversations like that, tell each other everything.

"I want you." I can't pull this sentence off the way Emmy-Kate could.

"No, thanks," Felix says, like he's kicking a stone.

Euuuurrrrgh. Some of yesterday's rage comes back to me in the face of Felix's moodiness. A tidal pool of emotions opens up—misery, jealousy, confusion, annoyance, lust. Why can't he be kissing me right now, instead of staring morosely at the carpet? Or at least talking to me, telling me what's on his mind.

I don't know because you don't tell me.

Ash's frustration at me, mine at Felix.

Another meltdown is rising, but I swallow it, say "Forget it," mostly to myself, and inch past an immobile Felix because I can't take another confrontation.

I retrace my steps down the ancient, creaking staircase, along the narrow corridor, through the empty, dusty pub—where Felix's dad jumps, doing a double take—and out into the blustery black-and-white morning, legs shaking all the way.

I want to take the world apart at the seams.

Vanilla
(An Ongoing List of Every
Color I Have Lost)

*Vanilla. What I've always suspected I am. Niko
makes art with sharp cuts, and now grief-stricken
poetry. Emmy-Kate paints in a five-star league
of her own. My mother is famous. Felix draws
like a clenched fist. I still don't know
what I'm supposed to be doing.*

CHAPTER 28

The Color of Night

School holds zero allure so again, I don't bother with it. I phone the office and tell them I'm ill and won't be coming in. Although my coughs on the answering machine are fake, I do feel poorly—there's a lump in my throat.

The house hums with silence, with the same forsaken atmosphere as yesterday. And when I retreat to the Chaos Cave, the mess kicks me to the floor.

I tidy half-heartedly, scooping armfuls of dirty clothes downstairs to the washing machine and piling art materials on the desk. I put the clay tiles outside in the shed. The whole time, I think: *Even if Mum did lose all her colors, why did she leave? Why weren't we reason enough to stay?*

I'm facing a lifetime without purple. If I go to SCAD

in this state, try to become an artist when I can't see properly . . . will my sisters be enough to keep me tethered to the earth?

Under a cardigan, I come across the books I retrieved from Mum's room. I cocoon myself in bed with them and Salvador Dalí, sliding the Georgia O'Keeffe hardback onto my lap. "*Aight*," I say. "Let's see what Mum was up to."

O'Keeffe painted flowers in extreme close-up: irises and lilacs in pink-lavender-yellow-teal. Mum's Post-it notes mark so many pages, it's impossible to tell what she was bookmarking—these flowers can't all be pink, this can't all be research for *Schiaparelli*.

One painting is completely covered in Post-its, all emblazoned with her handwriting, saying things like "YES!!!" and "THIS IS IT!" The caption beneath says:

Blue and Green Music (1919–1921). Oil on canvas. The Art Institute of Chicago. O'Keeffe believed music could be "translated into something for the eye."

It's been one of my favorite paintings since forever, but I never thought about the title before. Blue and green music . . .

"Sounds a lot like synesthesia, doesn't it, Salvador Dalí?"

The next book is the Yves Klein. He was famous for inventing a brand-new shade of blue. A synthetic ultramarine he named International Klein Blue. This dude invented the *sky*.

Woke up one day and announced, "The blue sky is my first artwork."

Imagine inventing a new clay, inventing the world, or a different color—the way I did last week after kissing Felix, when the sun transformed into yellow-violet. I would make

INTERNATIONAL MINNIE SLOE ORANGE

Maybe this was what Mum was planning to do with *Schiaparelli*. She was looking for a new pink—and in doing so, she lost her colors. That's the risk, isn't it? If you lean into art, open yourself wide, look for the glow in the stone or embrace the starlight moments, it leaves you vulnerable.

A vast tsunami of grief comes crashing in.

Before I know it I'm tearing the books apart, breaking their spines, ripping off the Post-it notes, trying to shake the colors from the pages so they fall into my hands. And I hear a thumping-great orchestra, getting louder and louder; soundtracking the frenzy, playing scary *Jaws*-style violins that sound exactly, *exactly*, like green-and-blue music should—

Black-and-white music.

The air seems to laugh at me, at how idiotic I'm being—to think there are possibly any answers—but tears don't come. So, after scooping up the ruined books and stuffing them into the bin, I run around the house, throwing open all the windows; letting autumn flood in. It's midmorning, the sun high in the sky, shining off the skyscrapers in London's financial district and, distantly, the buildings of the SCAD campus.

I'm going to go there now, I decide, finally.

Find out what I've been so afraid of all my life.

. . . . .

Seeing the artheads en masse is a jolt, even in monochrome. There are undercuts and nose rings and glitter; disco leggings and leopard print. I try to picture myself walking among them next year; can't. It's too far in the future, too alien. Like imagining myself as a giraffe, or speaking Russian.

I follow signs to the Ceramic Design building. The place where my mother studied, invented the *Rainbow Series I*, graduated, taught. A plaque above the door proclaims her fame. I wait for her to stride from the double doors and jump down the steps two at a time, her blond hair flying as she dismisses admirers, saying, "Not now! I've got to get home, to my girls."

But she doesn't. It hits me with horror that I haven't visualized her since that awful moment on the bus yesterday, when she told me I'd only get into SCAD because I'm related to her. She's right: Everyone else is armed with portfolios, cameras, instruments, and, in one instance, a blowtorch. I didn't even bring so much as a pencil. Since school started I've drawn a few flowers and that's it.

And this is prime Niko territory: I could do without her finding out I'm skipping school.

Drifting from the campus, I wander; not wanting to go home but not drawn to the studio either. Predestination, or lingering guilt, brings me to Ash's side of the neighborhood. At least, I think this is where he's living. He texted me the address over the summer.

How awful is that? He's folded himself into my life and I've never even visited his new student digs.

I ring the bell, crossing my fingers until Ash answers the door. He's in bare feet and skinny jeans, a flannel shirt pushed up at the elbows, as cute as the day we met. But totally different too, his face the opposite of a smile.

"Ash," I blurt. "Hi."

He keeps one hand on the door and leans the other arm against the doorframe, putting a barrier between us. Message received loud and clear: I'm not invited in.

"I wanted to say sorry," I begin, already trembling.

"So then say it," he challenges.

"I'm sorry."

"Wicked, everything's fine now, then."

I look down. His feet aren't tapping. There's no song inside him. Who invented the word *sorry*? Five letters, not nearly enough of an apology.

I stumble on: "Professor Gupta, your uncle—well, you know that." Am I imagining things, or was that an eye roll? It's no smile, but it's better than the blank face. "He lives next door, which . . . well, you also know." I'm wringing my hands, which are sweating. "I don't want it to be weird, if you want to come to Poets Corner." No response. "Also, Emmy-Kate is bereft, Salvador Dalí too." I don't dare mention Niko's feelings.

Ash raises an eyebrow in disbelief. "That's your fault, Min."

I take a deep breath, wishing this were easier, even though I know I have no right to want that. I broke his heart, and what's worse, I did it on purpose.

"I shouldn't have spoken to you like that," I tell him. "I hope you know it wasn't about you, though."

"I know." His face is softening. "Can't say it was fun, Min," he says, "but at least you were finally talking. That part I understood. But that boy you were with . . ." He shakes his head.

"Felix."

"I don't want to hear it," he interrupts. "You—"

"I'm so unhappy," I interrupt back. There it is, the truth. I *am* so unhappy. "That's it, that's all I have. I'm unhappy and I'm sorry. I wish it was more, but I . . ." I cover my face with my hands, groan into them. "All those things I said to you, I— I'm so messed up," I finish, not sure if I'm making any sense.

When I emerge from my hands, Ash is leaning his head heavily against the doorframe. "I might have understood all that if you'd have ever talked to me," he says at last. "About anything. Ever."

Puny autumn sunshine dapples our surroundings with its soft light. This is it. He's not going to forgive me, and I'm not sure I deserve to be forgiven. This terrible conversation is all there is left.

"I'm talking to you now," I offer, suddenly so, so eager to talk to someone. "And—"

"*Min*," Ash interrupts, firm but not unkind. He lifts his head. "It's too late."

He looks at me for a long, sad second, then closes the door gently in my face. And I walk home. Sunshine behind me, shadows ahead.

Blue-Gray

(An Ongoing List of Every
Color I Have Lost)

*Twilight. A steely blue that appears for less than
an hour on a handful of evenings. The Latin name
for the color is* livid, *meaning black-and-blue,
a bruise, a cold body in a morgue.*

Peroxide Blond

(An Ongoing List of Every
Color I Have Lost)

Somewhere between white and yellow, like
Marilyn Monroe. Her glow-in-the-dark hair.

CHAPTER 29

All the Colors in the World at the Same Time (Again)

It's the middle of the night and I'm stretched out with Salvador Dalí on the newly tidy floor of the Chaos Cave, thinking about the time Niko and I practiced kissing on our wrists and gave ourselves hickies. When she taught me how to apply liquid eyeliner and poked me in the eye so hard I saw stars for a week. The hand-me-down C-cup bra she bestowed on me with the advice "Stuff it with socks"; the day in Meadow Park when Emmy-Kate was being completely unreasonable and Niko pushed her in the duck pond, midsentence, barely breaking her stride.

I take out my phone and do something I haven't since the disappearance: google "Rachael Sloe." Famous-her is a different person from Mum, but tonight I need to see her, hear her voice, even if it's only on grainy YouTube videos of awards ceremonies. I scroll through image after image, noticing how there's not a single photo where she looks at the camera.

Always, her brilliant white hair blows across her face, her eyes are crinkled in amusement, she's laughing at someone or something out of shot, a blur moving toward the edge of the frame, disappearing.

Missing is as gone as dead.

I wouldn't dare voice this out loud to anyone—definitely not to Felix Waters—but I think that missing is a little bit worse. There's nowhere for me to stash these runaway emotions I have. I can't claw the earth over her grave, because there isn't one. There's no stone to hammer my fists on. I can't tear petals from funeral flowers or hurl handfuls of ashes into the wind or even stand in the sea beneath Beachy Head and catch her body in my open arms. I can't blame this monochrome existence on cancer, or old age, or a drunk driver, or anything but her.

And it hurts too much to do that.

I don't want to hate her.

The way Ash and Felix both hate me in different ways, the way my sisters hate me.

Thinking about Niko's expression in the walled garden yesterday makes me want to crawl out of my window, climb a ladder into tonight's starless sky, and yank Mum back down to earth, where she should be.

She is the only person who could make things better between us. She'd know unquestionably that I'm awake, and would drag me from my room to eat ice cream in the kitchen, even though it's 2 A.M. In the morning she would refuse to let us go to school until we'd fixed ourselves. She'd solve this with a Beatles song.

Or maybe she wouldn't do any of those things if she was in the middle of making art.

Ding. The idea lands in my head like a pebble thrown at my window.

The perfect paean to my rabble-rousing, peroxide-brilliant, glow-in-the-dark mother, who at twenty-one years old hand-built a brick furnace so she could make a clay bubble as big as a horse; *and* the way back to my sisters.

I rummage through the supplies on my desk and gather what I need, then creep down the stairs. Candlelight seeps from beneath Niko's door; no doubt she's writing an I-hate-Minnie haiku.

A big button moon floodlights me as I fly down the road, as fast as I can to my future. I duck under the railway arch to the start of Full Moon Lane, a vast sprawl of lamppost-lit black-top, take out my paints and brushes and pastels and oils, then spray-paint across the sidewalk in letters as large as I can: I CAN'T BEAR THIS.

I can't see the color, but I know it's an eye-popping, lemony-green citrine, a shade to stop my sisters in their tracks when they leave the house tomorrow.

I turn to the chalks, checking the labels to scribble I'M SORRY in turquoise, periwinkle, navy, azure, indigo, cyan, International Klein Blue. Halfway through my fifteenth *sorry,* a taxi comes crawling up the road, radio blasting. I dart into the shadows until it goes by.

When the music fades, I use pink to ask my sisters, *Where is the love story for the girls who are broken?* Green for gardens and dinosaurs and jealousy. I cover bins, traffic lights, road signs, the bus stop, sidewalks, even the railway arch, stopping only to check the shade names by the lampposts' thick glow: fuchsia, copper, mint, lavender, coral, buttercream, silver, yellow, more citrine.

As I work, I imagine the poem I'm creating, how it will make a lackadaisical exploration of Poets Corner:

> *Out of the blue.*
> *I can't bear this.*
> *Sorry, sorry, sorry.*
> *Where are you?*
> *We miss you. Come back.*
> *Where is the love story for the girls who are broken?*
> *Did you know it was forever?*
> *Listen. Not even light can escape.*
> *International Minnie Sloe Orange.*
> *LET'S FILL THIS TOWN WITH ARTISTS.*

Chalks become stubs in my fingers, paints dry up, spray cans rattle and run out of color. I use the remains of the final one, labeled BLOOD ORANGE, to add a last-minute FELIX + MINNIE on a table outside the pub. Then I close my eyes and turn around toward the road, picturing the colors: red-orange-yellow-green-blue-purple.

In my head, the poem glows neon against the sidewalk. It's not gray but Technicolor, a vivid explanation of everything I have lost, and the first piece of art I've ever completed. Something I could photograph for my portfolio, a companion piece to the *Rainbow Series I*, the kind of shock-to-the-system debut that makes me a true artist.

I open my eyes, immediately want to vomit.

There's no color. There's no genius, either. The minicab has smeared *sorry*s across the road; and with everything in gray, most of my words aren't even visible to me. They blend with the sidewalk, disappear. But here and there, individual letters stand out in bright, false white against the dark background. Spelling out:

Out of the blue.

I can't bear this.

So**rr**y, sorry, sorry.

Where are y**o**u?

We miss yo**u**. Come b**a**ck.

Whe**r**e is the lov**e** story for the girls who are broke**n**?

Did you know it wa**s** forever?

Listen. Not even light c**a**n escape.

International Minnie Sloe Ora**n**ge.

L**E**T'S FILL THIS TOWN WITH ARTISTS.

My reaction is instantaneous. I take off down Full Moon Lane to the studio, trying to outrun my own accusation. I'm going bat-out-of-hell-style, feet pounding across my stupid poem and leaving this mess behind. And as I run, the anger swells. Bigger than any of the mini-Minnie rages that have come before: Why am *I* the one who inherited Mum's madness?

Fury transports me fast to the studio, where I burst through the door—I've left it unlocked, unbelievably—and charge to the kilns, pummel at the control panel, lift the handle, jump back as the kiln door swings open, revealing—

Nothing.

It's empty.

This whole effing long and lonely time, it's been empty.

Where there should be a behemoth Rachael Sloe ceramic— one enormous, ethereal, punk, cool, out-of-this-world artwork; ferocious pink—there's nothing.

I spin around, panting, still furious. The fluorescent lights are buzzing like bluebottles—I don't remember turning them on, but whatever—and glinting on the shelves full of test pieces, including stacks of my abandoned tiles. My eye falls on the recycling bucket of dried clay.

I pick it up, oofing at its heft, then swing it at the shelves.

The crash is so satisfying I do it again. *Smash.* For being mad. *Smash.* For graffitiing that poem. *Smash.* For thinking I could make astounding art.

Soon the bucket is as empty as I am and stops being effective. I grab a plaster-of-Paris mold instead and sweep it along another shelf, almost experimentally. Pieces tinkle to the ground. The sensation is awesome, so I lift up a whole pot and hurl it across the room. My hands take on a life of their own, throwing and smashing and breaking and tipping and destroying, storming through my crappy life. *Crash.* I take a swipe at my missing mother, who could have left a goodbye letter anywhere but chose to deliver it here, where only I would find it. *Bang, bang, bang, bang*—I work my way along a test series of terracotta, hurling the pieces at the wall one by one, for my secretive sisters. For gifted and gorgeous Emmy-Kate breezing so easily through life. For Niko being in love with Ash. For Ash no longer being in love with me. I crash through ceramic after ceramic for Felix's hot-cold tempers, send piece after piece to the floor for sex and SCAD and love and madness, and then I turn my raging hands to this terrifying monochrome that I'm afraid I'm stuck with forever.

This is the big one.

All that's left intact: a huge, unglazed pot and a test bubble from the *Rainbow Series I.*

I try to lift the pot but I can't, it's too heavy. So instead I put all my weight and all my wrath behind it and SHOVE, pushing and pushing and hating and crying, until it goes crashing to the cold concrete floor and breaks into a million huge and ugly shards, along with my stupid, hopeful heart.

I'm turning to the *Rainbow Series I* bubble, a Christmas bauble almost as tall as I am, the one Felix called "wow," when a blur comes racing out from behind the kilns, waving its arms and shouting, "Stop! Minnie, stop it! What are you doing?"

I pause, chest heaving. Emmy-Kate is in the center of the room in a too-tiny dress, mascara smudged across her face, staring around at the disaster I have wrought.

"Stop it, Minnie," she says again, with a tiny, pathetic stomp of her high-heeled foot. And the words make her suddenly shrink, until she's my baby sister again.

Rose Gold

(An Ongoing List of Every Color I Have Lost)

Emmy-Kate.

CHAPTER 30
The Color of Sloes

My every molecule is pressed into the last existing bubble of the Rainbow Series I. *Hands and glaze united as one, ready to heave and push and smash it—down to the effing ground. Break. It. All. I want to drop a meteor on the studio and wipe it out like the dinosaurs. Delete our history, delete ceramics, delete my mother, scorch her right off the map. Smash and smash and smash this whole wretched life into dust, until there's nothing left—no memories, no impossible art to live up to. I can be free.*

But Emmy-Kate is trembling a few feet away, eyes overflowing, and these pieces are as much hers as mine. Mum belongs equally to my sisters. The same way her things weren't Niko's to tidy up, the same way I have as much right to the stolen clothes Emmy-Kate is wearing. She's in Mum's sequined cocktail dress, her most outrageous snakeskin stilettos, a lipstick-slathered cigarette shaking in her hand.

Along with the ludicrous outfit, I see the truth of the past few weeks.

The studio key falling from its pin in my room, even though it's my prized possession.

Emmy-Kate must have stolen it, had a copy made.

It wasn't Mum I saw running around the corner that day. The ghost who left wisps of Noix de Tubéreuse in the air, Beatles songs on the stereo, pastel-pretty sugary biscuits by the kettle—drank her coffee, smoked her cigarettes—was Emmy-Kate. It's all over her tearstained face.

I take a step back from the bubble, hold up my hands in apology.

But this small movement is the tipping point. Literally. All the weeks and weeks of rage I have heaved into our mother's most priceless heirloom sends it toppling to the ground. I watch the ceramic break apart in slow motion, shattering into a hundred unfixable pieces.

I join the devastation on the floor. There's nothing left. Not one iota of Rachael Sloe remains. Emmy-Kate begins keening, a low, unearthly wail that sends a chill up my spine, frightens me back into my own skin. The furious Minnie tornado of moments ago, gone. I take a deep breath and stand up, walk over to my little sister, touch her arm.

"I'm sorry," I say.

She shakes me off, sniffling, looking past me to the yard. It somehow seems inevitable that Niko is racing toward us through the dark. Clearly, some Bat-Signal from on high has brought us all here tonight. She windmills to a halt, hands flying to her mouth, absorbing the scene: Emmy-Kate dolled up to the ninety-nines, the fragmented art, me—the diabolical destruct-o-gremlin architect of it all.

Barely a blink goes by before she advances on me, hands whirring.

"Jesus, Minnie, are you insane?" *Yes*, I think, but she's not done. "Let me guess, dicking over Ash wasn't good enough, being the only one allowed in the studio wasn't good enough, you had to destroy it too." She's all up in my face, nostrils flaring, emitting steam, shaking her head, slapping her hands. "You really hate us that much?"

I'm too startled by the question to answer. She thinks I hate them? I try to process this, but I'm fixated on Niko's coat-flung-over-pajamas outfit. "How did you . . . ?"

"Emmy-Kate texted me!" she tells me, furious.

"Weren't you asleep?"

She purses her mouth. "I'm always awake."

I think of the candlelight seeping from around her door when I left. Emmy-Kate holding solo sleepovers here at the studio. The way Niko manages to find time for SCAD and poetry and her control-freak cleaning schedule. Of course I'm not the only Sloe family insomniac. All these nights, the three

289

of us have been awake together, alone. I could so easily have gone downstairs and shared my burden with them. I can't believe I didn't do that.

"I don't hate you," I tell Niko.

She waves me off, pawing at the floor with her sneaker, trying to find a safe place to step. It reminds me of a horse preparing to trot. Eventually she gives up and stomps straight through the debris to Emmy-Kate's side, puts her arms around her. I swallow and look away, at the ruins of the studio. Smashed and wrecked pots—smashed and wrecked everything—surround us. Worse than the Blitz. I don't even recall doing half of this. Perhaps I'm possessed.

Nothing is fixable; it's too broken. There are some things that can't ever be mended. My sisters and I might fit into that category.

"Emmy-Kate?" I say. "Niko too?" She presses Niko on the arm, indicating me, and the pair of them turn to me, whey-faced.

"I'm sorry," I sign for the thousandth time this week. "Really."

Emmy-Kate crosses her arms, pressing herself into the kilns. Niko snorts again.

"You're sorry?" she repeats, face full of sarcasm. "Sorry?" She's coming toward me again, shards crunch-crunch-crunching beneath her shoes, face flushed, eyes smoldering, about to blow. "I'm sorry," she mimics, screwing up her face in imitation of me, even tugging her pajama sleeves over her hands for the full Minnie effect. "Change the record, Min, I've heard this one before."

Her scorn knocks the wind out of me. This whole night (this whole entire life) knocks the wind out of me. Gravity goes full throttle, pulling me backward as Niko bears down on me, hands flying.

"What am I, what's Emmy-Kate, supposed to do with your 'sorry'? Sorry doesn't fix this, Min! How could you do this? How could you be so selfish?"

The first train of the morning comes through overhead, making the walls pulsate. I'm pulsating too, some of my earlier adrenaline making a comeback. Niko is holier-than-thou, but I am not the only selfish one.

"What about you!" I sign.

Her eyebrows crawl up, amazed. "Me?"

"Yeah, you. I told you I didn't want you to clean up Mum's room and you did it anyway. It doesn't even smell like her anymore, and what gives you the right, Niko? What if I wanted to keep her room exactly the way it was?"

"It wasn't exactly a shrine," she counters. "You and Emmy-Kate made sure of that."

"I took, like, two books!" Pissed-off tornado Minnie threatens to make a reappearance. "I can't help it that Emmy-Kate's been treating Mum's bedroom like her own personal Topshop, and what about the box—"

"Hey!" Emmy-Kate interrupts, skittering across the pottery shards, stilettos slip-sliding on the flotsam and jetsam. She yanks at the huge silver hoops in her ears and throws them at me. I'm too surprised to catch them, and they bounce and roll on the floor. "Take them, then, if they're so important. Take them and go back to not talking to me."

"They're not *yours*, Emmy—" Niko begins, but Emmy-Kate isn't done.

Her hands shake as she signs, "You get to go to SCAD every day, and Minnie's allowed to come here, but I can't have anything of hers?" She kicks at a nearby piece of bubble-rubble with her stiletto—Mum's stiletto. The clay ricochets off my ankle, annoying me.

"Oh, please," I tell her, ignoring the fact she recently witnessed me go berserk. "You have everything, everything! E-V-E-R-Y-T-H-I-N-G. And I've seen your wardrobe, it's full of her things—"

"That's right, you went in my room—"

"I know you went in mine too, dimwit. You stole the studio key—"

"I didn't *steal it*, I borrowed, and—"

"Tell me, Emmy-Kate, did you come here every night, or only the nights when you didn't have boys over?"

The two of us have been circling each other in a slow prowl, teeth bared, hands going at warp speed, but now we stop. I've gone too far. Niko's eyes are wide open—I can tell she doesn't know this detail.

"WHAT?" she asks.

"Big fat hairy deal." Emmy-Kate pouts. "I'm not having sex with any of them, if that's what you're worried about."

"That's exactly what I'm worried about, Emmy-Kate!" I sign, letting my frustration emerge in my hands.

She cuts me off before I can mention the birth control. "Fine, don't believe me, just because you're having sex with Felix and Ash."

As soon as she signs this, Emmy-Kate goes from malicious to horrified. She looks at Niko. So do I. Niko is drained, her skin as chalky as the night Mum didn't come home, the tendons in her neck sticking out. In my mind I'm reading all those hidden-drawer love poems again, seeing his name: *the sky burns down, leaving behind nothing but ash.* She loves him, and she thinks we're sleeping together.

"Niko, we're not," I try to tell her.

But she isn't looking at me. The floor shifts and grinds beneath my feet as I walk over, touch her arm. She flings away my hand, biting her lip. I have to duck down into a crouch, force my words into her unhappy face. "No. Niko, we're not having sex."

She looks skeptical. "You're not?"

I straighten up, shaking my head, and sign, "Never," thrilled to be the last virgin on earth. If I'd ever been ready to have sex, I might have lost my sister for good.

"N-E-V-E-R," I tell her again, fingerspelling it. Her face sags, a look I recognize: relief.

Niko slides into a seat at the workbench. She starts pulling pieces of pottery toward her, fitting them together like a jig-saw puzzle. I sit down next to her. After a moment, she drops her head onto my shoulder with a heavy *thunk*. We breathe in and out.

With my palm open on the table between us, I finger spell, "I'm sorry. I wish I'd never kissed him in the first place."

She shifts toward me. "Well, you shouldn't have."

I bite my lip. She's wrong, but I'm not sure I want to point that out: The anger in the room isn't gone, it's only on hold. But I can't keep any more secrets.

"He didn't belong to you, Niko," I tell her gently. Her face sours. "Look, perhaps I shouldn't have kissed him, knowing you liked him . . . But you never actually told him. You can't call dibs on a person."

Niko presses two fingers to the bridge of her nose for a mo-ment, the same way she does when she gets a headache, then signs, "I wish . . ." Instead of completing the sentence, she lets her hands fall into her lap, where she forms guitar chords with them.

"I don't know what to do now," I tell her.

"That makes two of us."

We examine each other, hovering at the edge of understand-ing, then Niko yawns. She makes a pillow of her arms and I do too.

Night is almost over. Dawn is beginning to creep through the yard, transforming the shadows into misty blue London morning.

Real blue, a powdery light.

Nothing weird or faded about it; no watercolor pastels or freaky-deaky neons. In fact, looking back over this entire argument, it's *all* been in color. From Emmy-Kate's red lipstick to Niko's rusty Hollywood hair. Despite my exhaustion, my heart swells.

The where and when of the colors' return is ironic: a concrete yard, an overcast day. But my sisters are as colorful as a pair of parrots.

When was the last time we were all here together? When we were little, probably. On rainy days, Mum occasionally brought us here to run around and paint and make potato prints and playdough sculptures. Back when art was fun and not a noose around our necks.

"Niko." I tap her arm for her attention. "Remember Mum trying to teach you to use the wheel?"

"Yeah. She kept squashing my hands."

"And you flinging her off and signing, 'Let me sign!'"

"I miss her." Niko exhales, blinking rapidly at the ceiling.

Emmy-Kate gasps. My bones crumble. Unbelievably, this is the first time we've signed this.

"You do?" I ask.

"God, don't you?" She sits up, reaching for a pottery shard, spinning it, the shiny red glaze catching the light. It's a piece from the *Rainbow Series I*. Words flow like water. "I've been going mad," she signs, and I think, *You're not the only one.* "Sometimes I turn my room into a séance, try to channel her.

I kept writing poems with my eyes closed, pretending she was there, having a conversation with me. Thinking, okay, well what would she say now, and what would she think about this? Only I can never quite capture what she was truly like, you know?"

This is astonishing: her story so closely resembling my own, both of us trying to bring Mum back to life, any way we can. Emmy-Kate too, with her clothes and perfume. We've all been searching for her.

Niko adds, "Well. I suppose you do know. You had to read every single one of my poems?"

"Sorry." The sign is thumping your hand to your chest, rubbing it in a circle. I'm going to erode my boobs if I have to say the word much more, but I'd do it. I'd say sorry a thousand times if I could.

Niko stands up, kicking her way toward a huge piece of ceramic that somehow missed the tempest and only got pulverized into two, not smithereens. A concave curve like a shallow saucer, which she pokes with her toe. It rocks gently back and forth.

She bends down and lifts it up, high above her head. I understand right before she does it: launches it at the ground, where it explodes.

Emmy-Kate's gasp echoes in the silence.

"Sloe sisters," Niko signs, turning to us with a semi-apologetic shrug. "Hive mind. God!" She gazes round, taking in the destruction again. "I feel like we cleansed this place of evil spirits."

I'm reminded of all the paraphernalia in her drawer. "Yeah, about your new religious experimentation . . . I think you've been hanging around with the Professor too much."

Niko smiles mysteriously. "Oh, if only you knew . . . Now. I'm going to go and get coffee. Then we're going to talk. Really talk. No more secrets, Min. I mean it, okay?" She glances down at her pajamas. "Going out like this feels like such a Mum thing to do."

"It does," I agree. We smile at each other.

After she leaves, I watch Emmy-Kate. She's tottering around the studio, examining the remains. Every now and then she bends over, hair trailing in the dust, and picks up a piece of pottery. She encloses each one in her palm before putting it back, as if she's found the very last seahorse in the world.

With her makeup streaked off from tears and laughter, she's back to looking about twelve years old. It makes me think we did the right thing, not telling her about the goodbye letter. The only trouble is, we can never tell her the truth. She can't ever know.

When Niko arrives back laden with recyclable coffee cups and pastries, she reads my mind. She slides into the seat next to me, hands me coffee and a cinnamon roll, and says telepathically, bossy even inside my own head: *We can't tell her. Can we?*

I say back, silently: *I don't know.*

"Why are you two doing eyes?" Emmy-Kate stops sliding around and scuttles over, grabbing her food then putting it down again to sign, "Well?"

"Nothing," Niko signs, concentrating on blowing through the lid of her coffee.

"Mum," I admit, using our Sloe-sister shorthand sign.

Emmy-Kate nibbles on her pink-polished thumbnail instead of the pastry. She perches on the table, starts unpeeling the roll into a long, sticky rope of dough.

"I know she's not coming back," she signs eventually, not looking at us. "I listened to Minnie's voice mail. But don't tell me any more, okay?"

"Minnie's voice mail?" Niko asks, glancing between the two of us. "Do I want to know?"

"Probably not," I tell her. "Em. I'm sorry. Did you . . . did you take her box?"

I don't have to specify what I mean. She nods. "I haven't opened it yet. It's under one of my floorboards. I just wanted something . . ."

Her hands falter and Niko reaches out, squeezing them. She lets go and signs, "It's okay." Then she shakes her head, standing up and kicking a path to the kitchenette. When she returns, she's carrying the broom.

"You don't always have to be clearing up, you know," I tell her.

She hands it to me. "I know. You're going to do it."

Dawn makes way for true morning as I start sweeping up,

thinking what a stupid end to my mother's story this is. Or perhaps it's the perfect one. The sun is shining down on the cacophony of colors, tiny droplets of white and purple and pink glaze, making them look like one badass flower bed—blossoming into thickly scented hibiscus and buddleia and geraniums.

This is what *Blue and Green Music* sounds like. It's a symphony for a mother.

Red

(An Ongoing List of Every
Color I Have ~~Lost~~ Found)

*Emmy-Kate's underwear and clown lipstick,
matching Niko's cheekbones when they're splotched
with annoyance. The original, very first* Rainbow
Series I *test piece. Priceless. Invaluable. Worth
way more than a crummy pair of magic sunglasses
(debt still outstanding). And now nothing
left of it but dust.*

CHAPTER 31

One Hundred and Twenty Crayola Colors

Minutes later we catch the bus home. I lean my head against the window, nonstop marveling at every color we pass and thinking what a dumbass Mum was to miss out on all this. Orange-brick Victorian houses forming a parade route along Full Moon Lane, pink-cream-yellow-lilac roses foaming in gardens, front doors standing to attention in mustard and black. Zingy red pillar boxes dot the gray sidewalks, pedestrians wear navy-blue winter coats.

When we tumble off at our stop, the early-morning air has bite. So does this thought: You can undo monochrome, but you can't undo death. I don't know if I'll ever be able to stop rewinding her split-second decision, watch her fly up through the sky instead of down. It kills me that it didn't have to end this way.

If only she had said something. To us, to the Professor, to anyone. Called her doctor, or the help lines that came up when I googled, gone to the ER. I wish when we opened the shoebox we'd kept it open, instead of stuffing it out of sight. I wish she had made any other choice but the one she did.

I don't blame her, but, quietly, I'm beginning to understand I have a choice too. Mum and I might share a brain, but that doesn't mean our stories are the same, with the same ending. And it's not as though I'm completely out of my mind. I started thinking about this the moment I saw Emmy-Kate at the studio and realized I was never being haunted by Mum. Grief made me a crappy detective: I interpreted the clues all wrong. So perhaps it's as the Professor said: Madness is simply behavior people don't understand.

Niko elbows me out of my thoughts. "Minnie . . . what is this?"

She's staring aghast at my street poem, gloriously garish in daylight. Rich blue apologies are scribbled all over the sidewalk, crawling up the brick walls of the railway line. It puts the blue right back into the Bible. Commuters queuing to enter Poets Corner station are taking photos; Felix's dad is mopping orange from the table outside the pub.

Okay, maybe I'm a little nuts.

Emmy-Kate is overjoyed. She grabs hold of a citrine lamppost and twirls around it, then jumps down to sign, enormously, "What a totally Toulouse-Lautrec thing to do!"

"You didn't stop to look at this when you came running to the studio?" I ask Niko.

She shakes her head. "You and Emmy-Kate were in trouble: I didn't stop to check for traffic."

I think we're having a moment, here, but then she moans. "But did you have to write your name on it? Your full name . . . You're going to be in so much trouble . . ."

Her face is paling rapidly—quite a feat for a Sloe; our skin can't get much whiter.

"In trouble with whom?" I ask. "You're in charge of me. You love bossing me about; this should be like a treat for you. You could ground me! You should tell me to go to school right now."

"Minnie—" Emmy-Kate objects.

"You don't have to go today if you don't want to," Niko signs, then breaks off, yawning. "I'll write you a note."

"Yes!" I crow, knowing I can fudge the dates on her note, get away with this whole week of absence. Every now and then, the universe surprises me. Niko frowns and I sign more calmly, "I mean, yes, please, and thank you."

She nods, vaguely, staring across the road. The Professor is joining the queue for the train station, shuffling along with his nose in a book. Another exciting trip to the Boring Library clearly beckons. He hasn't even noticed the graffiti.

I nudge Niko. "Is this why you keep asking the Professor round?"

Niko shakes her head and nods at the same time. "He's actually been helpful with all the legal stuff," she signs. "And, I don't know, I kind of like him. He's quirky. It's a lot, being your guardian. I thought about asking the Professor to take over . . ."

"Omigod." Emmy-Kate detaches herself from the lamppost, flailing her arms like a Muppet. "Do not let him adopt me!"

The Professor lifts his head from the queue, finally spotting the colorful landscape. He wobbles with confusion, looking around and noticing us. We must make a ridiculous sight: Niko in her pajamas, Emmy-Kate in cocktail wear, me paint-stained. Not one of us on our way to school or SCAD the way we should be. But rather than lift his hand in a wave, he darts his head around unconvincingly, as if he's being bothered by a bee. Then he ducks away: Pretending not to see us, he pushes past the crowd and scurries into the station, clearly refusing to be associated with our eccentricity. I'm definitely warming to him: He is human, after all.

"Did he just . . ." asks Niko, her mouth dropping open.

"What a load of Jackson Pollocks!" declares Emmy-Kate.

I'm the first to crack up. Next, Niko lets fly a huge goose honk of laughter. She squawks away, doubled over with hysteria, flapping her hands. Emmy-Kate joins in with her Tinker Bell giggle, click-clacking on the too-big heels until we are together, wheezing and giddy and leaning on each other for support.

The three of us have our arms spaghettied together,

Emmy-Kate's va-va-voom body wriggling between both our skinny ones. I catch a whiff of Em's cherry-vanilla scent layered beneath Mum's perfume; see the sunlight play through Niko's bare eyelashes—it's strange seeing her without the cat's-eye black liner—feel like I'm in my own skin for the first time in ages. We're a six-legged, three-headed, sad-happy girl who's laughing and crying and mourning and rediscovering her sisters: all at the same time.

. . . . .

The dust of this strange day settles. Afternoon light is leaking from the clouds when Niko finds me in the Chaos Cave. I'm sitting at my desk with Mum's laptop, trying to drum up the courage to go online, google this peculiar brain of mine. See if there's a solution. I've got as far as switching the computer on. Current status: staring at the screensaver, a painting by Vanessa Bell called *A Conversation*. Three red-haired women with their heads together, exchanging secrets.

Niko barges in, both hands occupied by mugs of tea. "Sorry," she says, not seeming it, as the door ricochets off the wall. Her pajamas have been replaced with a green Vauxhall City Farm T-shirt and jeans adorned with Biro scribbles, her hair in two ribboned horns.

I'm still in my graffiti-stained dress. Wearing this multitude of colors against my skin makes me feel as though I'm channeling the best parts of Mum, instead of bearing the weight of her body the way I have been.

We settle on the bed, mugs on the windowsill, Salvador Dalí stretched out between us, and Niko signs, "I want to ask you something."

"Okay . . ." I know what's coming, grab my tea for moral support, take a sip, and dribble it back out. Yuck—herbal.

Niko gives a curt nod, drumming her fingers as she takes in the rare tidiness of my room, examining everything in it but me.

"I know you know I like Ash." Her cheeks revolve through the full spectrum of reds—crimson, carmine, cerise—and if it were any other topic I'd revel in the colors. "I want to ask him out."

I blow ripples in the surface of the pond-water tea, unsure what to reply.

"Not that I need your permission," she adds waspishly.

Perhaps Ash and Niko always made more sense than Ash and Minnie: They're closer in age, neither of them cares that much about art, they've always had something of a simpatico. I can picture Ash studiously learning sign language; somehow teaching her the guitar—after all, Beethoven was deaf. It would sting, though, if he said yes to her so quickly after me. But if he says no, Niko gets hurt.

Maybe she intends to. All I know is this: You don't always get a neat ending to your own story. You can't control the outcome, however much you relive a moment. I can go back to the National Gallery and Bonfire Night in my mind over and over again, but I can't change the past—or stop the future getting messy.

"Yes, of course, go for it," I tell her, privately thinking, *Ick, ew, second-hand tongue.*

Next thing I know she's wrapping me in a boa constrictor hug, spilling tea across the duvet. My sister smells like a cathedral, all incense and essential oils. It's as comforting as home, as Mum's cloud of amber and glycerin. Or the way Felix smells of cedarwood . . .

Niko reads my mind and pulls back to sign, "What about you and Felix?"

I shake my head. "I don't think he wants anything to do with me."

"Don't believe it. You two were like . . ." Niko whistles, eyes wide, and makes kissy noises. Then she rearranges the pillows, gets comfortable, cradling her mug in one palm. The old imperiousness makes a return as she issues sweeping, one-handed commands: "Talk to the boy. With words, not graffiti— something legal, Min. Tell him you like him."

I give up on the lukewarm tea, tipping it out of the window. A small, outraged shriek tells me Emmy-Kate is hanging off the trellis below.

When I look back, Niko is staring at the SCAD motto on the wall. The letters are bubble-written in Junior Minnie's green felt-tip penmanship:

307

We believe art and design can change minds and move worlds. Immersive, imaginative, and hands-on—because theory without practice is like learning to swim without water. Let's get messy.

"You're still planning to go?" she asks.

"Oh, that." I peel the note from the wall, rereading the words that have watched over my sleeping body for hundreds of nights. *Art can change minds . . .* It changed mine; it changed Mum's. "I don't need to go to art school; I'm messy enough. Anyway, don't you hate it there?"

Niko exhales, stretching out on the bed. I lie down beside her. The sun is sinking low and the room glows gold. This bed could be a flying carpet. It makes me think of days spent at Meadow Park's pool together, staring up at the sky while Emmy-Kate swam, the clouds moving so fast we could feel the earth spinning beneath us, time rolling forward the way it does.

"I don't hate it. I hate the students who ask me about her, and that there's not a big Deaf community the way there is at some other unis. And . . ." She takes my hand, switches to spelling: "I W-A-N-T T-O W-R-I-T-E." She smiles. "I don't think I'm an artist. Not the way Emmy-Kate is, or you."

"Me?" I roll over onto my side, goggling.

Theory: Is it possible that everyone sees everyone else differently from the way we see ourselves? That we're all walking around misinterpreting each other and having no clue what our family and friends are even thinking? People definitely should come with art gallery captions, subtitles for the soul.

"I don't even know what it is I want to do," I tell her.

"That's what art school is for, you moron," she signs. "You've always done a bit of everything—you're multidisciplinary. That's what it's like, your first year. You dive in, try things out, learn."

She waves at the windowsill, at our empty mugs, gilded by the evening. That's what I made the first day Mum took me to the studio. The stripes look like a jaunty sunset, but they lack the mystical pizzazz of the *Rainbow Series I* or the peculiar melancholy of *The White Album*. They're not world-shaking-genius-ambitious-wow. They're mugs.

I always thought you made the portfolio to get into art school, then once you were there, you specialized. But what if I could go to learn? To work out what kind of artist I'd be if I wasn't Rachael Sloe's daughter. I don't think I'd choose clay. It's too close to the edge of the cliff. But an idea is taking shape: a life more ordinary. Calm, not loopy. Moving at my own speed, trying to determine who I'll be, not racing to get there the way she did. Oddly, this doesn't feel like failure. It feels like a fresh path emerging on the map, pushing aside trees and buildings as it wends its way somewhere altogether new.

"Hey, Min." Niko nudges me. "What are you thinking?"

"I would like to go to SCAD . . ." I confess. As soon as I sign it I know it's true. "But not ceramics. Fine art. No special focus yet." The words are coming out of my hands faster than my brain can keep up. "And maybe not SCAD, but some other art school . . ." I add, thinking of the brochures in

Niko's desk drawer; dozens of possible outcomes on their glossy pages . . .

"Oh!" I say it, then turn to Niko. "You were planning to leave SCAD and go away this year, weren't you?"

She nods. "Edinburgh uni has a sign-language society. Durham is supposed to be amazing for English literature. A friend from Poets Corner High is at Newcastle; she signs. A few people at SCAD do, but it's not great."

"But then Mum . . . and you became Emmy-Kate's guardian . . ."

Niko nods again. "I can't go anywhere."

This is huge. And it means I can't leave either, but it doesn't matter: I can't picture any other me than the one who loves south London. There's nowhere else I'd rather be than here, now, for as long as my sisters are. Conclusion: "Or, actually, yes, SCAD."

Niko's beaming at me, might even fall off the bed with pleasure. I hide my face in my hair. "This is *good*, Min," she signs. "So what's the problem?"

"The problem is I don't have a portfolio. I used up all my paints on that stupid graffiti, everything else of mine I smashed, none of my drawings are finished . . ." *Of course they're not*, I think, finally understanding. Completing something would have meant admitting to myself that I want this. Can't fail if you don't even try.

"Better get organized, then." Niko is stroking Salvador Dalí's fur with her toes.

"Says the neat freak."

"Which is why I'm not suited to art school—let's get messy, remember? Also, if you want to get in anywhere at all, you should probably go to school at some point . . . Today is a one-off," she warns.

I nod, staring out of the window at the fierce sun, clouds rearranging the red-orange-purple into streaky bacon. The *Rainbow Series I* must look beyond wow right now, what with this epic sky-bonfire. My hands itch to sketch it.

Niko moves her toes from the rabbit to me. She foot-drums on my leg, her toenails a shiny aubergine purple.

"What?" I swat her away.

"You have your art pout on," she signs. "Whatever it is you want to draw: go."

Clementine

(An Ongoing List of Every
Color I Have ~~Lost~~ Found)

*My hair, a solid Pantone ginger. An early series of
Mum's,* Terracotta Tigers. *The line of the London
Overground on the Tube map, from Poets Corner
to her studio. International Minnie Sloe Orange.
This sunset, this moment, here, now.*

CHAPTER 32
Metallic Gold Marker Pen

Color intoxicates me as I jump from the kitchen step, wanting simultaneously to run to the *Rainbow Series I* and to pause the Earth's spin right here, right now, and soak it in. The roses a cloud of apricot-orange-amber; the back garden burning up beneath all. This. Sunset.

"What a night!" she would say to this moment. "Minnie, what a *life*."

Yeah, and you let it all go.

I think of this, and I invite the hurt to come roaring in.

This blazing sky is the very same one she stepped into. Same city she left behind, same sun, same moon, same clouds. It's only me who's changed—who'll keep changing, moment after moment, growing and flourishing where she stopped. This is the same stupid world where suicide exists and it is seven years before you can commit a missing person to the grave.

Then again, seven years is nothing; it's the blink of an eye. And it doesn't matter how many minutes-hours-days I grow older, how much I change . . . there will still always be a little piece of Minnie buried here in the past. I know this now: I will spend my life peering over my shoulder, jumping when the phone rings, forever wondering if one day she will reappear and grab my hand, saying, "C'mon, Minnie—around the corner there are dinosaurs!"

This hope will last a lifetime, because that's how a fully functioning heart works.

You don't have to feel terrible the whole damn time. But a lot of the time, you won't be able to escape it. That's how it goes. And if it's only sometimes, well. That's bearable. Because it has to be.

The grass is sodden and I grab the last, lone daisy from it, start stripping it of petals. They fall from my fingers as I head along the road, past my graffiti and the Full Moon Inn.

And there on the table outside is an addition to my poem. Where I've spray-painted our names in blood orange, Felix has added, in charcoal: . . . ARE TO BE CONTINUED (MAYBE). Huh. I smile as I walk on, entering Meadow Park and climbing up the hill.

Step by step, petal by petal, Mum's heels click on the path beside me. Blond hair blows in the breeze. A Beatles song hums in the air: "She Loves You." She loves you not?

When I reach the walled garden, I pause outside, take a deep breath, prepare to conjure her one last time. This is it. On Monday I will go back to school, start completing my portfolio and my SCAD application, see the school counselor, make a doctor's appointment, perhaps bring the shoebox with me, open the lid on the truth.

But for now, I turn to her. She leans against the stone wall, smock splattered in clay. One arm is wrapped around her waist, the other holds a cigarette aloft. She looks . . . not peaceful, exactly, but quiet. Neither sunk nor starlit. Like she's finally okay.

"Ah, Min, again?" she says. "I'm on a break here."

"Kind of a forever one . . ."

Mum blows smoke, smiles in a way that crushes my bones. She drops the cigarette, stomps it beneath the toe of her pink snakeskin stiletto. "So, what do you think? Ready to let me go?"

Never. There's so much I want to talk to her about. But if this moment is all I get, there is one thing in particular nagging at me. "Did you mean what you said, on the bus? That I would only get into SCAD because you're famous?"

She comes to stand in front of me. We search each other's faces, committing them to memory. There are tiny lines around her eyes, skin starting to soften at her jaw. She's getting older. She'll never get older.

"That's not what I meant at all. Oh, my orange girl." She tucks a stray piece of my hair behind my ear, but it flies straight back. "You're my daughter, which makes you belong to me, and you're clever, and funny, and hardworking. And yes, you're a Sloe, but it has nothing at all to do with fame. It means I'm your embarrassingly proud mother. Do you understand?"

She doesn't wait for an answer. She moves past, leaving the *Rainbow Series I* and me behind, a puff of Noix de Tubéreuse against my cheek as she whispers: "She loves you. No doubt about it."

I don't know if it's her, or the breeze, but then she's gone.

The sun is rapidly sliding down the sky. Bare trees raise their skeleton branches and, spread out below, London is alive. The remains of my poem glow against the dark sidewalk. I want to eat all the colors in the city.

I step into the walled garden and sit down on a bench, not a flower bed for once, taking out my sketchbook and a pencil— all I have left to draw with. Stroke by stroke, I sketch a portrait of Mum in soft gray lines. The world is in color and her memory is monochrome, the way it should be. I'm drawing slowly and carefully, not fast and furious the way Felix does: but this is more me, more Minnie.

What works for him doesn't work for me. And another thing—I'm going to need the funeral. It's going to suck, but I want one anyway. *Rachael Sloe: The Retrospective.* I want us to choose a sequin-drizzled party dress—or better yet, a clay-covered smock—to bury in an empty coffin. We'll ask the Professor for theological advice on how to have a ceremony without a body. I want there to be a gravestone with her name on it among tall green grass. Even if she's never found, it will be a place we can point to and say: she is here.

By the time I get close to finishing the portrait, it's night. A damp scent tells me winter is on its way. But the night is not black. The shadows are too rich, too textured. Then there's that pink-silver-yellow London sky, which Emmy-Kate calls romantic and Niko calls light pollution and I call COLOR.

I decide to leave the portrait unfinished. I might find a way to make my incomplete portfolio paintings seem deliberate: Call it *Unfinished Stories*. I prop the sketch pad on top of the memorial flowers. The pile is smaller than it was; her story gradually being forgotten by everyone but us. Then I lie back on the bench, thinking about Felix Waters and that TO BE CONTINUED (MAYBE).

If I wanted him to be my boyfriend, I could invite him to climb inside one of the Crystal Palace dinosaurs. Buy him every single pastry in the Bluebird Bakery. Take him to see some knockout art. But am I ready for him? Something tells me things with Felix would go Roadrunner fast: wham, bam, kiss, love, sex, the whole kit and caboodle.

I have no idea who I am, and I think I need to get to know me for a while, alone, whoever Minnie Sloe is, whoever I am:

Ginger. A sister. A non-girlfriend. An artist? Almost eighteen. Possibly batcrap-bananas-nutso-insane.

Rachael Sloe's daughter *and* her own person.

Not so much a story with a different ending, but one that doesn't have an ending yet—

Citrine

(An Ongoing List of Every
Color I Have ~~Lost~~ Found)

*Montana Gold Acrylic Spray Paint in shade
G1040 Asia, a yellow-gold that dries drip-free
and water-resistant and doesn't fade from the
lampposts of Poets Corner for many,
many months.*

CHAPTER 33
Let's Fill This Town with Artists

Here's how you hold a funeral for someone who isn't dead. Here's how you paint it black—and every other color. The whole effing spectrum.

My sisters and I are standing on the very edge of the pool, about to jump.

The whole way here Emmy-Kate has been bombastic, claiming it won't be as cold as we think, but even she's shivering beneath the winter sun. No one else is here. It's as if all of Poets Corner instinctively understands that this isn't about Rachael Sloe, Famous Artist. This is for us. Okay, and it's freezing. Penguins would have second thoughts.

Surrounded by emptiness and damp gray concrete, she should seem more missing than ever. Yet she's here in Emmy-Kate's shocking-pink lipstick, in the decisive movement of

Niko's hands, in the three of us teetering on the brink of hysteria, double-daring each other to dive-bomb; procrastinating with endless silent talking, talking, talking. About anything but her. Yet.

"We should invite the Professor round more often," muses Niko. "I think he's lonely."

"Agreed," I sign. Since the night he came to find me in Meadow Park, I've forgiven him his bumbling. If not his cooking. "But not tonight, though."

"Of course not." Niko smiles, stretching her arms above her head, revealing more-feminist-than-you armpit fuzz. She drops them to add, "And tonight's the last time we're having pizza, okay? We're going to learn how to cook. With vegetables."

"But pizza every night is the dream life, it's Andy Warholian." Guess who.

"I wish it was pizza every night," I sign. "Emmy-Kate, your Alphabetti Spaghetti Surprise yesterday was revolting."

Niko has started divvying up the chores, relaxing her grip on the guardianship. So far I've broken the vacuum, Salvador Dalí has hidden in the shed, and Emmy-Kate has served up an almost entirely sugar-based diet. Yesterday was her first attempt at savory food.

"Shuddup." She giggles, then pouts. "Ash can cook. Remember that one time he made turmeric eggs, last year? He could teach us . . ."

Niko and I exchange uneasy glances. I haven't spoken to or seen Ash since that day at his house. Our story has ended; he's a chapter in my life, not the whole book. I don't know if Niko ever dared to ask him out. It might be enough for her that I'm no longer with him.

"Okay, enough stalling," Niko declares, changing the subject. "Ready?"

Emmy-Kate slips her hand into mine and squeezes, lets go. "Three, two, o—"

She jumps before her own signal, and Niko follows her, then in I go—one, two, three Sloe sisters; splish, splash, splosh.

The water punches me or I punch it—either way I gasp, lungs filling, a stream of bubbles emerging with my cough. I watch them bob to the surface and break. Time is on my side; gravity too, because this is all happening in slow motion: three balled-up sisters reverse-floating, landing on the bottom of the pool. My contact lenses float out, making my vision blurry, but it doesn't matter. When I look up, everything is light.

. . . . .

Afterward we walk through the park with damp hair and hot chocolate. The sun is turning the trees extra-green against the bruised sky. Everything shines and I can't stand it.

"*La Passeggiata* by Marc Chagall," announces Emmy-Kate, fingerspelling the title.

A cubist painting with a green landscape, a blue tree, and a pink house. A Professor-ish man stands beside a red picnic blanket, filled with flowers the same way the backpacks we're wearing are filled with the tiny shards of clay from the studio. And in the sky, there's a woman dressed in purple.

"You know, I don't think she fell?" signs Niko. "I think she floated."

"Yeah." Emmy-Kate, who knows by now that *missing* is more or less a euphemism, is on cloud nine with this idea. "Like a Mum-balloon."

We climb and climb and climb the hill. As we get higher, the sky opens up like the sail of a boat, billowing forward. My pockets don't have rocks in them anymore. Correction: I'm a little weighed down, but at this precise moment my sadness weighs pebbles, not continents.

Thumping our backpacks down in the walled garden, we capture the attention of stray tourists near the sign. *Go away*, I think, and magically—they do. This might also have something to do with Emmy-Kate's glare and Niko's aggressive hand jiving.

Whatever, we're alone now.

We're never alone. Memories can't be deleted, can't be scrubbed out the way graffiti can, can't be smashed to pieces like stoneware. And the permanence of Mum's presence is comforting. She's not falling from the sky over and over again anymore: Like Niko said, she's floating. She's flipping us heart-shaped pancakes every day. She'll never not be winning the Turner Prize, having three daughters, laughing at the Professor, making microwave meals, learning to sign, buying a rabbit, drinking tea, descending into a sinkhole, emerging like a supernova, working too hard; ignoring us, sometimes; dancing to the Beatles, always.

Speaking of which . . .

Emmy-Kate navigates to a YouTube video on her phone and presses PLAY, and a tinny, subtitled version of the Beatles song "In My Life" blares forth. The lyrics talk about memories, and people, and love, and thinking about the past—but ultimately, moving on. It's right. It would be better if Ash were here to play it on his guitar, but it is what it is. She props the phone up on the bench.

"Let's do it," Niko commands. And so we do.

Accompanied by John, Paul, George, and Ringo, we unzip our backpacks. Inside, we each have one third of the shattered clay pieces from the studio. Without her, this is what we have to bury. And I discover a small, secret part of me likes it this way. The not-knowing.

I go walking among the bubbles and the bare, thorny roses, tipping *The Rachael Sloe Retrospective* onto the flower bed, mulching the roots for winter. This is my idea. I haven't told Niko that the clay will probably create an impenetrable soil barrier, syphon off the rain, destroy the entire park's ecosystem, kill all the bees, and create an environmental catastrophe . . .

But isn't that art? Isn't that what life and love is all about? Taking risks. Looking death right in the face, with your heart wide open.

No joy without sorrow, remember (and vice versa).

Can't die unless you've already lived.

Love goes hand in hand with loss.

Sun streams down as dust chokes the soil. Most of it is gray. But dotted here and there are tiny scraps of sharp, shiny glaze. They catch the light, turning red-orange-yellow-green-blue-indigo-violet, becoming luminous.

Ultraviolet

(An Ongoing List of Every
Color I Have ~~Lost~~ Found)

Sometimes life is like looking directly into the sun.

THE END

Author's Note

If you're struggling with suicidal thoughts and feelings, it's important to tell someone.

There is help and support available. There are also free and confidential help lines for you to call to talk to someone about your mental health and any issues you're having. In addition to these numbers, you can ask your GP for an appointment, go to the emergency room at a local hospital, or visit the counseling center at your school or college. If you feel that you want to end your life, please seek immediate help from the emergency services on 911.

NATIONAL ALLIANCE ON MENTAL ILLNESS
Website: nami.org
Telephone: 1-800-950-NAMI. Monday–Friday,

10 am–6 pm EST
Email: info@nami.org. Monday–Friday, 10 am–6 pm EST

NATIONAL CRISIS TEXT LINE
Text: text HOME to 741741.

NATIONAL SUICIDE PREVENTION LIFELINE
The Lifeline provides 24/7, free and confidential support for people in distress, prevention and crisis resources for you or your loved ones, and best practices for professionals.

Website: suicidepreventionlifeline.org
Telephone: 1-800-273-8255
Telephone for the d(D)eaf and hard of hearing: 1-800-799-4889
Teléfono en Español: 1-888-628-9454

THE TREVOR PROJECT
The leading national organization providing crisis intervention and suicide prevention services to lesbian, gay, bisexual, transgender, queer, and questioning (LGBTQ) young people under 25.

Website: thetrevorproject.org—online chat available every day, 3 pm–10 pm EST/noon–7 pm PT.
Telephone: 1-866-488-7386.
Lines open 24 hours a day all year.
Text: text TREVOR to 1-202-304-1200.
Monday–Friday, 3 pm–10 pm EST/noon–7 pm PT.